THE DARK SIDE OF GIBSON ROAD

ISBN: 978-1-68313-217-2
Library of Congress Control Number: 2020934215

First Edition
Pen-L Publishing
Fayetteville, Arkansas
www.Pen-L.com

Printed and bound in the USA

Cover and interior design by Kelsey Rice
Cover photo by Benjamin Balázs on Unsplash

THE DARK SIDE
OF GIBSON ROAD

BY

JANICE GILBERTSON

P
Pen-L Publishing
Fayetteville, Arkansas
Pen-L.com

ALSO BY JANICE GILBERTSON

Summer of '58

Canyon House

ACKNOWLEDGMENTS

I began writing *The Dark Side of Gibson Road* during the fall of 2017. In the spring of 2018 I was diagnosed with lung cancer. The stress of dealing with the illness played havoc with my imagination. My writing regimen became sporadic at best. After surgery and then several clean scans, I summoned my imaginary friends and we jumped back on the wagon and told the rest of the story.

I will forever be thankful for all the love, caring and prayers from my family and friends

Thank you, Kimberly and Duke Pennell for waiting on my spirit to mend. Thank you, Ken and Betty Rogers for editing for me once again. You get me.

CHAPTER ONE

By summer, I had been looking out of the same window for over ten years. Even at that self-absorbed age of fourteen, some curious fascination for the old, ramshackle Wendell house kept me aware of the changes and goings-on which took place there. I should have known it was a place that would, one day, give rise to evilness. I should have known.

We lived in what had been the Franklin house, six miles due north of Pickering, Texas. If you turned onto Gibson Road at the Mile Market, it was a straight shot on the narrow, paved road to our house. Exactly two telephone poles farther north, and across the crumbling blacktop, was the dirt lane leading to the Wendell house. I could view it all from my upstairs bedroom window.

As the story goes, sometime in the 1890s, the two dark-eyed, handsome, Gibson brothers accumulated substantial wealth in the mining business, and bought an expanse of property outside of Pickering, a tiny coal mining town in far north Texas. They were young, educated men who made investments in the tools of the trade and came out successful. Their fraternal relationship was one that kept them close at heart and, at the same time, fiercely competitive. What one did, the other was determined to do better.

Preparing for eventual family lives, they'd each chosen a plot of land on their newly-gained property and built their houses. The homes were grand for their time. They were two-storied with high ceilings, polished wainscoting, tall windows, and boasting enough rooms for a growing family. The upstairs windows viewed the sweeping land all around them. There were stoves to keep them snug in the frigid winter months and wide porches for sitting in the summer. It wasn't by accident that the houses had the same floor design. Planning them to be built the same, down to the last board and shingle, assured Wendell and Franklin, both, that one didn't have something the other did not. As time passed and the brothers' lives took some unforeseen turns, the property was divided, and sold off for grazing cattle or growing cotton on the lower land near the river. The old houses stood on a dozen surrounding acres that had been kept with them.

Our house, Franklin's, was handed down and modernized by kin until it went on the market and my father bought it for us. It was a beautiful house with its polished oak wood banister rising with the sweeping stairs, carved wooden doors and, by that time, modern plumbing. The kitchen was large, meant for a family to use. From its back door we could step out onto a stone pathway with an ornate ivy trellis. Franklin's heirs had built a barn for hay storage and kept a few milk cows. It still stood in its aged and sagging but determined state directly across Gibson Road from our house. The Franklins had been paid a good amount from the county to allow the road to make a direct route to the river.

Because Wendell had never had his own family or a will, after his death his house was sold by the state to a Mr. Danner, who rented it out to anyone who could pay a few months' rent. Unknown to the absent Mr. Danner, who lived in south Texas, as each family came and left, the house deteriorated a little more. When we came to live across the road, the Wendell dwelling was in a shambles, and by the time I was five or six the eerie looks of the place caused me to have nightmares. I was fearful of the dark in my room at night and afraid of the house across the road.

It was almost always my father, the bravest man in the world, who came to sit next to me on the edge of my bed beside the warm yellow lamplight, and talk to me about good and beautiful night things when I called out in the dark. He knew about the stars and the planets, the universe, and he would remind me how perfect the night sky was, and how wonderful I was. That's why he named me Donna Jean when I was born. He said it meant Daddy's pretty girl, and I was his star. I believed every word. Daddy was an only child. He told me stories about his childhood and how wonderful his parents were. The best, he said, and that is how he wanted to be for me. I would wish that I had known them but they had "gone on to Heaven," as Daddy said, when he was a young man.

Mama, my beautiful mama, in her practical way, tried to assure me there was nothing there, inside or out, for me to be frightened of. She explained rationally how the Wendell house was built the same as ours, and how children had slept in a bedroom like mine, and had eaten at a table in a kitchen like ours.

When the sun rose up from the horizon behind our house and shone above the roof of a long implement shed sitting on the swell behind our home, lighting the lane and leaving no long shadows slanting darkly, it was easier to believe the things she said. But, by late afternoon and into those summer evenings that stretched on forever, those deep, dark shadows cast by the enormous oak trees clustered around the old house, and the gnarly, half-dead elms along the lane, turned it back into a place eerie and mysterious looking.

Made brave by daylight, I would pedal my bicycle to the dented mailbox sitting cock-eyed on its crooked post at the edge of Gibson Road and gaze down the lane. From that safe place I could see the front of the Wendell house and, nearby, an outbuilding squatting beneath one of the great oaks. Branches, low and heavy with foliage, brushed the shed's roof. Driven by curiosity, I would make up imaginary reasons to ride my bike to the house. Maybe I would say hi, and tell the people who lived there I was the girl from across the road. But I didn't do it. I could never work up the courage.

As the months and years passed, I continued to steer clear of the Wendell place. I played outside our house spending hours across the road in the old barn. I was comfortable inside the wooden building where the sunlight poured through the spaces between the shrunken boards, making streaked patterns in the soft, silty dirt of the floor. When the wind blew, faint moans and whistles pushed through the gaps. Owls and doves perched upon the high rafters and didn't seem to mind my intrusion. They rested above me, the owls watching in silence, tilting their heads this way and that as if trying to understand my meddling. The doves cooed and flapped in the timbers. I found a stack of old burlap gunny sacks, shook the dust from them, and spread them so I could sit on the floor. I suppose I should not have climbed into the loft because some of the boards were missing and the rusted nail heads protruded. But I loved being higher and looking at my own house from such an angle. Both ends of the barn had open hay doors beneath gabled overhangs. From the backside of the barn I could look across the pasture to the Wendell place, but the trees snugged the house, preventing much of a view.

The only time our family ventured farther to the north on Gibson Road was when we drove to the river. From the edge of town, the road began its sweeping climbs and dips as it crossed the rise and fall of grassland dotted with small copses of trees. The pavement ran out a couple miles beyond our house, and the road became one lane of gravel and dust. The Young River was nothing spectacular, a narrow blue ribbon meandering from the east and making a far bend behind the property that had, at one time, belonged to the Gibson brothers. In the hot months of summer, the stream offered a cool pool to splash and play, and shady places to have a picnic. I cherish the memories of going there, my father driving the station wagon, my brother and I riding in the back with the windows rolled down. Those were happy times.

They ended abruptly.

Four days after my twelfth birthday, a county sheriff's car pulled into our driveway. I know it was late on a Friday afternoon, springtime, 1970. I also know I wore jeans and a yellow shirt, and had a silver barrette in my straight, dark hair. From my high window I watched two deputies leave the car and walk, slow and side-by-side, to the front porch. I heard the knock on the door and my mama answer, "Coming," in her pretty singsong voice. There was the low, muted tone of male voices followed by silence, until the eerie sound my mother made flew up the stairs and shook my body. Jolted me to my bones. For what seemed like a long time, I couldn't move, I couldn't breathe. I became aware of loud footsteps pounding down the stairway and knew it was my brother, Christopher. I felt light-headed. I've no memory of descending the stairs myself, but I recall watching one of the deputies guide my mama by her thin arm to a chair. When her eyes met mine they were enormous and wild. She said, "Donna Jean, call Grandma Gabby. Tell her to come right now."

"Why, Mama?"

"Just do it, right now."

Christopher began to cry, and followed me into the kitchen. "What's wrong with Mama?" he sobbed.

"I don't know, Christopher. Be quiet while I call Grandma Gabby."

When she answered, I began to sob, too. "Come to our house right now, Grandma Gabby. Something is wrong. Hurry!" And I hung up. What a terrible thing to do to someone.

Back in the living room, the uniformed men were still there, seeming awkward, shuffling their shiny, black boots and patting their uniform ties. Mama was saying they must be wrong because he wouldn't be driving so far from home at that time of evening. They must have the wrong name, she said, and they should be more careful about delivering such horrible news to the wrong family. I heard one deputy ask for Daddy's full name. "Joseph Aaron McGuire," she said in someone else's voice. Daddy was a lawyer with a small office in Pickering, she explained, and, yes, he often worked in surrounding towns. One of the men said, with a catch in his voice, how sorry he was, but there was no mistake. He asked if someone would be coming to be with us. I answered and said my Grandma Gabby was coming.

"We'll wait," he said.

It seemed that hours of time passed before our grandmother came bursting through the door. White as paper and breathless, she looked us over one at a time and rushed straight to my mother.

"Ellen," her voice trembling, "Ellen, what happened? Are you hurt?"

A deputy spoke up again. He told her Daddy had been in a bad automobile accident, head-on, and was dead. The other man was at fault. No, maybe he didn't say it exactly that way. Maybe he said Daddy hadn't survived. That was the first time Christopher and I heard it being said outright. Christopher began to sob and wail. I sat on the edge of a chair and did nothing. I remember thinking there was too much. Too much everything: crying, sobbing, wailing, and mama yelling, "No, no, no . . ." Grandma Gabby saying, "Oh, my Lord," over and over. It was too much to hear.

I ran upstairs and threw myself on my bed and cried until my insides hurt and my pillow was wet with tears and snot. I turned it over, and fell asleep with exhaustion. When I awoke it was dark in my room, but there was a dim light from the hallway. I kept picturing Daddy in his car and the other one crashing into him. I trembled with anger. Why didn't the other man die instead of my father? If it was his fault, he should have been the one to pay. I crawled from the bed and walked on shaking legs to stand at the window. The moon-glow shone pale yellow on the lane to the Wendell house. The ground was ashy white and the trees were in silhouette.

Out where the rutted dirt lane met the crumbled edge of the paved road I noticed a dark impression of something I hadn't seen before. I rubbed at my swollen eyelids and looked again. I also saw what I recognized as the glow of a cigarette tip, brightening as a person took a long, deep pull from it. I stared for a long time, and, at last, crawled back into my bed. I never mentioned what I saw and, in fact, by the following day, I believed I might have dreamed it.

———

Grandma Gabby came to live with us. Grace Shanks (that was her real name, but we just called her Gabby) was Mama's mother. She rented out her little house in Pickering and moved in with us within a few weeks after my father's funeral. His funeral. Part of me never left the cemetery that day.

Christopher had cried and cried like Mama did, but I sat in front of the terrible, gaping hole in the ground and trembled until I nearly vomited. I shook so hard I bit my tongue through and swallowed the blood as it filled my mouth. I don't know what the preacher said. His voice was singsong. I have no memory of words, only physical sensations. The air was sweet and smothering. I pictured the ladies dabbing musky perfume behind their ears and on the pale underside of their wrists before they pulled on black clothing and slipped into black shoes. I wondered why they wore perfume to a funeral. Who cared how they smelled? The nauseating sweetness mingled with the earthy tang of damp, red dirt piled beneath a tarp, waiting to be dumped on top of Daddy's casket. I wondered if he might hear it falling on him. I hoped his soul was gone so he wouldn't know.

When we rose to leave and made our way around gravestones rising from the well-groomed lawn, my knees kept giving out as if there were no bones or muscle in my legs. The dew on the grass seeped into my good shoes and my socks felt cold and mushy. A kind hand slid beneath my arm, guiding me.

That night in the dark of my room when I wanted my Daddy, an intense ache pressed downward on my body and I wished I could disappear into a dark hole beneath my bed. I know, now, the ache was my broken heart.

Christopher and I loved Gabby with the passion only grandkids could possess for a grandparent. She was warm and funny and adored us all. She smelled of lilac talcum powder and mint toothpaste. In spite of her own sadness, she held us and hugged us, and hummed tunes from the forties. She curled her shining, silver hair on tiny pink curlers once a week, and put lipstick on every single morning. Her skin was crinkled over her cheeks and felt soft as suede. She was the epitome of kindness. I believe she saved my mother's life. Mama escaped to her bed on the evening of Daddy's funeral, and didn't get up for many days. Gabby tended to her every need, though Mama would never have said right out that she needed anything. She had never been the kind to bother anybody.

When Christopher or I went into her room, desperately seeking something she couldn't give us, we would find her pale, thin, and so quiet as to seem peculiar. She didn't feel like Mama to us. We were confused and lonesome for her loving devotion. She was the guiding light of our lives.

Gabby kept assuring us our mama would heal. She would come back to us with all the love she'd given us before Daddy died. While we waited, Gabby took perfect care of us. We loved her cooking. She fed us tons of fried chicken and mashed potatoes. She made apple pies and chocolate cakes, and told us every single day how much she loved us, and how our mama was coming back.

I didn't believe her about Mama, but Christopher did.

"Don't be mad at her, Donna. You're being mean," he would say when I skipped my visits with her.

"I'm not mad. I just don't think she wants me around right now, so why bother her?" That's how I felt when I saw Mama there, in the dim light of her room. If she was lying down, she often closed her eyes or turned over and pretended to sleep, but her shallow breathing told me she wasn't. Even if she was sitting on the edge of her bed, or on her chair at the tall south-facing window, she would often fail at the attempt to offer a weak smile. I would try to come up with something to say, anything at all that would sound like conversation. She, too, seemed to struggle for appropriate words. We all learned right away to never mention Daddy. She would begin to cry at once and tell us she needed to sleep, so we would go away. Going away, for me, most often meant walking to the old barn, climbing the wooden ladder into the loft, and sitting alone.

Grandma Gabby worried over Christopher and me every minute of her day. She tried endlessly to make things better for us all.

"Donna, honey, I can only imagine what a sad time this has been for you," she'd say gently. "You've lost your daddy, and now you believe you've lost your mama, too. My prayer for you is this: If, every day, you could take only a few minutes, maybe five or ten, and tell yourself a story about how your mama is going to come back to you and love you with all her heart, you will find a deep comfort inside yourself. Before you know it, it will be truth. You can talk to her about it when you visit her in her room. She'll hear you and love your story. Please. Try it, Donna Jean."

So, for Gabby, I tried. Even when Mama turned her back to me, I would speak to her slight shape beneath the blanket about how one day she was going to give us big hugs and how she would make us laugh again, and I would ramble on until I ran out of things to say. The day she reached out for my hand was the first time I'd cried since Daddy died. When I left her room, I hurried to find Christopher.

"Go now," I urged him. "You might get a surprise." When he came out several minutes later he was red-cheeked and crying. She'd held his hand also, and said she loved us.

A few days later, in mid-afternoon, I heard Gabby's voice on the staircase. She was whispering, so I had to investigate. There they were, my Grandma Gabby and my mama, taking slow, careful steps, side by side, Mama gripping the rail and Grandma Gabby clutching her other arm. Mama was wan and weak, but she had on her pretty pink robe and her hair was pulled back and clipped at her neck. She looked like the ghost of our mother.

Our lives, Christopher's and mine, had to carry on. We had to get back to going to school until summer vacation. Gabby saw to it that we were clean, dressed, and on time to catch the school bus that came within a couple miles of our house. Sometimes Mama would be sitting in the overstuffed living room chair when we got back home in the afternoon. She looked small and fragile in the big chair. I would dread seeing her that way, but some days I worried she would not be there at all. I thought she might disappear.

The only time she left the house was when Grandma Gabby drove her to a doctor appointment. Grandma Gabby still insisted to us that one day she would be herself again. Mama saw a doctor who was "helping" her get over Daddy's death. I didn't see how it was doing any good and I would get angry when Gabby talked about it. In fact, I became aggravated at everybody. Mama wasn't trying hard enough. If I insinuated how her lack of caring affected me, tears would well in her eyes. But I didn't even suffer the least bit of guilt about hurting her feelings.

I spent time with school friends again. For a while, after the funeral, they'd remained distant. They looked at me as if waiting for me to do something rash and weird. I didn't know what. Their distant attention wasn't to do with sympathy, but more a curiosity. They were trying to figure out how I'd changed because of Daddy's passing.

I did change. I was angry. I became bolder, louder and a bit sassy. I got in trouble a few times at school for talking back. The principal was a kind man who sat me in his office and talked to me about how some people, after tragedies overtook them, had to find themselves again. He believed that was what I was doing. I was acting out my misery. He promised not to tell my mama or Grandma Gabby about my acting up, if I would try to do better. He was as good as his word.

I felt motherless, but began to grow accustomed to our new life. I worried about Christopher. He couldn't understand how I was able to distance myself from Mama's gloom. He doted on her. He did everything he could think of to put a smile on her face. He spent hours drawing funny pictures for her. He told her silly knock-knock jokes. He even read the funny papers from the Sunday newspaper to her.

"You don't have to try so hard," I told him.

"Yes, I do," he answered.

I drew pictures, too. But mine were for myself. I must have been about five, or maybe six, when I first began to draw with a desire to be good at it. Daddy had been my fan. He always took time to look at each drawing I'd considered good enough to share with him. I received a drawing pad and pencils for a birthday gift, and ever after, I sketched and drew anything and everything that came to mind. I could sit for hours at my little desk in my room and transfer the images in my head to a sheet of clean, white paper.

Of course, I knew nothing about perspective or shadows but, with practice and subtle hints from Daddy, my drawings had begun to get better and more realistic. At school, the teacher often held my artwork up in front of the class, saying what a good job I had done. I would blush and squirm with embarrassment.

For a time after Daddy died, I drew odd things having to do with him. I had pages of pictures of belongings, like his leather briefcase, or his shoes, and even one of his bottles of aftershave. I thought I would keep them forever and look at them when I was old like Grandma Gabby.

CHAPTER TWO

Two sad years after Daddy died, a new family moved into the Wendell place. They would be the fourth tenants since we had lived in our house. It was a significant occurrence when cars or pickups drove by on Gibson Road. When we heard them coming, one of us would head to the nearest door or window to see if it was someone we knew. There had been a time, before Daddy died, when we had visitors often. He and Mama had many friends, and weekends were for inviting them out for supper. Barbeques and sweet tea and games on the lawn were the usual in the summertime. Those occasions came to an end after he left us, but we still had the old habit of looking to see who might be coming. That Sunday afternoon, I was the one who went to the screen door when I heard engine noise. I watched as two rundown cars and a pickup passed by and turned to bounce down the rutted lane to the Wendell house. The pickup was loaded precariously with furniture and boxes, all tied with a tangle of ropes. It was ages old with dented, rusted fenders, and the back end sat low to the ground with the weight it lugged. The backseats of the cars were stacked with boxes, and one car had the trunk lid strapped closed over a shabby swamp cooler. I could see little blonde heads poking up in the front seats of both cars, and watched the dust rise as they bounced and teetered along the rutted lane.

"Somebody is moving in across the road," I called to Gabby. "They look close to the same as the ones who moved out." We laughed a little, but it was true. The people who came to live in the old house had all shown signs of being drifters. They didn't broach any intentions of being friendly neighbors.

Gabby had come to the door with a dishtowel in her hand and watched the procession bump along. "Mmm-mmm, looks to be quite a bunch of folks there," she said. "Wonder how long these will stay in the old house." The idea set Gabby to jabbering on about the last people who had lived there, and how they had not paid their rent for months. She knew things like that because of all the gossip in Pickering. If Grandma Gabby missed anything about living in her little house in town, it would have to be the convenience of gossip. It was her weakness. She had always been a talker, hence her nickname, and she loved to know what was going on in Pickering. She also loved sharing her new information with us as she moved around the kitchen cooking or cleaning. She jabbered during the commercials when we watched television, and kept us up on all the town's happenings whether we cared to know or not.

With Mama finally getting out of bed most days, our grandmother became free to go to town more often. She visited friends and went to the local cafe for coffee and got caught up on current rumors. She would come back home brimming with news. She could never wait until Mama was up and ready to listen, so she would tell Christopher and me the news, and then tell it all again when Mama came downstairs. She talked fast and hardly took a break until all was told. By the second telling she added more detail to her commentary. Mama, so overcome with depression and not at all herself, would sit in the big living room chair and listen without saying a word.

Grandma Gabby Gabby's prediction about Mama turned out to be right in some ways. As time passed, she began being part of our family again. She was not the same as before Daddy died. Not at all.

But she started, finally, to get up and dressed, and fussed with some chores around the house. She sat in the big living room chair through the middle of the day and watched television. She completely lost herself in the lives of soap opera characters. If any of us interrupted her concentration during Days of Our Lives or General Hospital, she shushed us. She had no desire to go out except to see a doctor, and didn't go to any trouble to fix herself up like she used to. Some days she was so quiet she was like a phantom moving about the house.

Gabby continued to take care of the household finances. She received rent payments from her own house in town, and Daddy had left some savings and a life insurance policy, yet I knew she worried about money. Some days she would walk slowly back from our mailbox after Mr. Abbot had delivered in the mornings. I would see her studying the envelopes as she came into the house. She would sit for a long time at the little desk in the small room we called the office, paying bills or making lists before she ever went shopping for anything.

On the Sunday the new neighbors showed up, Christopher and I could hardly wait for Mama to come join us so we could tell her the news. It wasn't often we had something of interest to talk to her about. When she was settled in her chair with Gabby's tea, I began the conversation and tried not to hog the story.

"Me and Christopher have some news, Mama!" She looked at me without saying anything. She waited, so I went on. "We saw a new family driving in to the Wendell house today. You should have seen all the stuff they had. And it looked like there were a lot of little kids, too. Maybe we should go over there in a few days and say hello." I'd only said it for conversation's sake.

"No way am I going over there," Christopher said. "That place is too scary for me. Besides, we never went there to meet anybody before. Why do we have to go now?"

He was right, of course. In the years we had lived there we had not, one single time, been to the house across the road. Watching the people who came and went from the place, and from what we could see of them from our windows, kept us from even attempting to walk the lane. Daddy had warned us away in his own polite manner, saying something about how maybe they would not want to be bothered. That was fine with me.

As for our news that Sunday, Mama feebly said maybe someday we would get to know who the new family was. She didn't say how it might happen, and her lack of any curiosity took the fun out of our announcement anyway. I went upstairs and stood at my window for a while, watching the movement around the Wendell house. It was evening, the shadowy time I didn't like, and I couldn't see much.

I thought about Mama sitting in her chair, looking wan and sad, and I wondered again when she was going to get better. I was getting tired of waiting for her to be herself again. I missed Daddy, too, and still cried at night sometimes. My heart ached once in a while, but I was pretty sure I was okay most of the time. I got up in the mornings and helped Grandma Gabby around the house. We joked about the silly things she said and we cooked together in what had become her kitchen. Christopher had always been a quiet kid, and he worried about Mama, but he joined in our activity when he wasn't playing outside. So, when was our mother going to get on with life? If the rest of us could move on, why couldn't she?

Nothing would ever be more unexpected to me than what happened next. Only a week or so after the new neighbors moved in and we had tried to stir Mama with the news, she made an announcement at the breakfast table. She calmly placed her fork on her plate, wiped her mouth with her napkin, and said, "I am going to get a job."

I thought the silence was going to last forever, but finally Gabby said, "Ellen?"

"I am. We need the money. I know you are struggling, Mother. These are my children, and Joseph's children, and he expects me to take care of them. He is angry with me. He comes to me at night and tells me I must get better and be a good mother. He doesn't want me to mourn my life away."

I had a mouthful of food I couldn't swallow. My mother had gone crazy. Off the deep end. When I forced myself to look at Christopher, the poor boy was pale and wide-eyed. He looked to Gabby who was batting her eyes and shaking her head. She put her hand on Mama's arm.

"Oh, sweetie. Getting a job isn't necessary right now. We're still doing okay. I can make what we have stretch a bit more."

"No. No." Mama shook her head. "School is going to start up, winter will come and we will have extra expenses. I should have done this a long time ago. Joseph is very disappointed in me."

The silence fell over us again. No one moved. We sat. I was more intrigued about her communication with Daddy than I was about her job announcement. Did she believe she was seeing him, talking with him, or was it all a figure of speech? There had been a boy at school whose mother had been sent to an insane asylum and mean kids teased him about having a crazy mother. Did I have a crazy mother?

Gabby said, "Well, honey, what would you do? For a job, I mean. You've never worked since you married Joseph. You had the one little office job at Crowley's."

Mama picked up her fork with a trembling hand and began eating again as if everything was normal. "I'll find something. I can always learn something new. I will apply to every single place in town. Eventually someone will leave, or die, and there will be an opening. Who is the lawyer on First Street? Is he still there? I learned a lot from Joseph's career, you know. We talked about everything. I knew all of his cases and how he represented people. Maybe I could work in a lawyer's office."

"Well," Gabby said and pushed her plate away.

Mama's behavior kept all of us on edge. She did what she said she would do. After spending two days dragging clothes from her closet and piling them around her room, hanging them on the curtain rods, matching and mixing, she announced she had plenty of nice outfits to get by with at her new job. On the following morning she rose early, dressed and used Grandma Gabby Gabby's car to drive into Pickering. I stood at the door as she left at a good clip. Her expression was pure determination. It was the first time she had driven herself to town in two years.

Of course, Mama taking Gabby's car left us stranded at home. The car Daddy had the accident in had never been replaced. As the hours passed, we became more anxious and snappy with each other. Gabby slammed things around in the kitchen. When I went in to get something from the refrigerator, she threw a hissy fit.

"How many times do I have to tell you to wash your hands before you rummage through my refrigerator?"

"Your refrigerator! Since when is it yours?"

"Since I came to this house to take care of this family, that's when. Who takes care of it, cleans it, puts the food in it and then takes it out and puts it on the damn table for you all to eat? WHO?"

I was stunned. Speechless. I had never heard Grandma Gabby swear, and I sure had never seen her cry, not since Daddy died, but there she was, tears rolling down her soft pink cheeks. She leaned back against the sink and put the dishtowel up to her face with both hands. She stood there for so long I grew scared. I closed the refrigerator door without making a sound.

I whispered, "Grandma Gabby, are you all right? I'm sorry I sassed you." She took in a long, loud, quivery breath, dabbed the tears away and looked right at me.

"Listen, Donna Jean, I have worried over and prayed for this family for some time now. I love each one of you, but your mother is my girl, and I would give my life for her. I don't know where this change in her came from and I don't know if it is good or bad. I don't always know the answers to things or what I am supposed to do. I've wanted to be strong for you kids because strength is what you needed, but your mother's behavior has thrown me for a loop." She stood straight, smoothed her blouse and tucked her hair back. "Now," she said, "I'll be fine. Go on. Get out of my refrigerator."

We tried to act like we weren't waiting for Mama to return home. When she came through the front door, the three of us were waiting in the living room pretending to be doing something. Grandma Gabby had a dust cloth, I was reading a book and Christopher had the TV on. Mama looked tired. She wore a grim expression as she put her purse on the little table by the door. She glanced up at us, but her expression didn't change.

"Ellen?" Gabby said.

Mama threw her arms up in the air and hollered, causing all of us to flinch. "Surprise! I got a job already! I start next week at Goldie's."

Our reaction was too slow for Mama. Our weak smiles didn't begin to match her enthusiasm. With her arms still extended, she waited for us to say something. Gabby came to the rescue.

"Oh my! That's wonderful news, honey. I didn't realize they were looking for someone at Goldie's. I guess I thought you were looking for something more like an office job."

Mama flopped deep into her big chair and kicked off her shoes, looking satisfied with herself. I hadn't seen a look like that for so long I had forgotten it. But Goldie's? My mother was going to be a waitress, or a barmaid, at the bar and café in Pickering? I had walked by it many times, but Daddy wouldn't let us go there, not even to eat in the little café. He used to say it was an adult place. If the door happened to be propped open as we passed by, I always tried to get a look inside, but it was too dim to see much. It reeked of fried food and cigarette smoke. It had a "'reputation.'"

"Mama!" I said without thinking it through, "Daddy wouldn't want you to work there."

She turned to me, eyes flashing. "Well, sweetie, Daddy isn't here. It is up to me to earn a wage to keep this family fed and clothed, and I will make good tips at Goldie's. You all should be glad." She looked like she was pouting, for goodness sakes. The mention of Daddy brought a lump to my throat. I knew I was going to cry. I had learned to control my tears, but this time I couldn't. I got up and ran up the stairs and slammed my bedroom door. I thought to myself what a stupid life we'd led since my father died, and now, my mother was going crazy.

I sat at my desk and began drawing a picture of my mother. I scribbled in her hair and made her eyes big and round with the pupils looking in different directions. It was a picture of a crazy woman. I studied it for a few moments, picked it up and tore it into tiny pieces.

I let the tears flow.

CHAPTER THREE

It was late summer and the nights were still and warm. Gabby, Christopher, and I would sit on the wide front porch of our house, or laze around on the front lawn in the late evenings. If the slightest sound drifted from the Wendell house, one of us would shush the others so we could listen. Maybe it was a malady of country people. There was something exciting about eavesdropping on other people's' lives. Especially people who, so far, appeared to be so unlike ourselves. We often heard the children; the little high-pitched voices of the older ones came through loud and clear, and the younger ones shrieked, either in delight or discontent. Gabby said they were allowed to stay up too late, and the little ones were likely tired and fussy.

For the first days and weeks the new people had company coming and going all times of the day and night. What gripped our attention and made us sit up and cock our heads to hear better was when the grown-ups' voices floated to us on the evening currents. Often, they would become boisterous and we could hear all the familiar swear words, and one or two I had only heard in school. Sometimes I was embarrassed for Grandma Gabby to hear them. But Christopher and I listened shamelessly anyway.

They sometimes fought and argued among themselves. Even without faces to match, their tones became familiar. We named the voices. There was Dumb Guy's deep, rumbling voice, and a woman, Whiney, whose voice was high and nasal. There were others, Mr. Loud and Mr. Cusses-A-Lot. Sometimes there would be several people speaking at the same time. Most evenings they cooked outside and the odor of the smoky meat would drift to us. We made a game of guessing what they were going to eat. Christopher always thought it was hotdogs, but I thought it smelled like old stinky meat and I would hold my nose. Gabby said she didn't know how they all kept from getting sick.

The first time we heard the rifle shots, it scared Christopher and me. Before dark one evening several shots rang across the field, coming close together. A barrage from a different gun came next. Christopher ran inside to get Grandma Gabby and brought her out by the hand.

"Listen! They're shooting something over there."

Gabby stood still and listened as the shooting started again. "I believe they're target shooting," she said. "Lord, I hope they are careful around those little ones. People like them shouldn't own guns. They're too irresponsible."

They would sometimes shoot until dark, and then we wouldn't hear shots again for days. Mama said it was because they had to buy the bullets and were probably out of money. That was another thing. It didn't seem like anyone there ever went to work. No one drove out or came in at regular times, but cars and pickups came and went often. I heard them revving along the road late at night.

Mama worked late but sometimes we sat on the porch and waited for her. Christopher and I would trail inside with her and settle around the kitchen table. After she kicked her shoes off and had taken her plastic container from her purse, we watched her peel the lid off and let the coins inside spread out across the table. We helped sort them into piles so she could count the money out. To us it looked like a fortune. Once in a while there would be dollar bills, and we asked about the customers who left them for her. I would wonder if she sometimes made up the answers because it was always some special couple or a nice, polite gentleman who left the biggest tips. Being old enough to have an idea of what kind of people went to Goldie's at night, I doubted there were many like she described. But we all liked the money, and her tired eyes would shine as she counted.

We told her our version of the goings-on at the neighbors and she would laugh at our stories. I mastered the whiney voice of the woman we heard loud and clear, and repeated her dialog to Mama, adding my own humor. It was wonderful to be the one to make her laugh. We tried hard. We wanted the old closeness with this new Mama. Sometimes, if only for a second, I forgot Daddy was gone and I visualized him coming through the door. But reality came back like a slap and for a while I would feel sort of scared and vulnerable, even though I didn't know what it was I was afraid of. Out of necessity, Christopher and I were learning to be more responsible for ourselves. Mama reminded us often how we were never to take advantage of Grandma Gabby Gabby's love and care for us.

Summer felt too long, and had become boring. With no other kids our ages nearby, Christopher and I began to get on each other's nerves. Sometimes we went into town with Gabby and spent a couple of hours at the public swimming pool while she went off to shop and catch up on the gossip. One afternoon when she came back to pick us up, she didn't seem her normal, cheerful self. On the drive home, I asked if she was all right. She said she might be coming down with something. Late the same night, Mama and Gabby's voices woke me. They were arguing, and I heard Mama say what she did or didn't do was nobody's business, and Grandma Gabby needed to stop listening to small town gossip. Grandma Gabby said Mama better mind her Ps and Qs because she had two children to think of. Mama said she didn't need reminding that she had two kids. Mama and Gabby acted mad for a few days.

They avoided speaking to each other, and sounded irritated when they did. I avoided them when I could and stayed in my room. Christopher played around outside and rode his bike back and forth along the road. I was lying on my bed one afternoon, reading and listening to Mama's sounds as she got ready for work, when Grandma Gabby came up the stairs. She went into Mama's room and quietly closed the door. Their voices were muffled but I could hear some of what they were saying. It was enough to cause that familiar anxiety again.

"I talked to Freda today," Gabby said, "and she told me what was going on at Goldie's. People are saying you are getting mighty friendly with a few of your men customers. Is it true, Ellen?"

Mama's anger was instant. "Freda has a big mouth. And, no, it isn't true. Mother, I am almost thirty-six years old. I am a widow. If, and I'm only saying if, I want to be friends with a gentleman, I am free to do so. Tell Freda to mind her own business."

"Well, I worry, that's all. You're so moody these days. Happy one day, mad and sad the next. I don't know how sound your decisions are."

"My decisions are fine. I need to finish here."

Grandma Gabby was dismissed. It was true what she said about Mama. She was moody. There were days when I feared her depression was returning. I could almost see the shadow engulf her. I would find myself watching her, and when she noticed, she left the room.

Three days before school was in session, Mama spiraled down the tunnel of despair again. She had come in from work a little later than usual. We had stayed up to count her tips with her. With the school year beginning, we would have normal bedtimes, so we were determined to wait up for her while we still could. She looked different to me the second she opened the door. Pale, red-eyed, emptied, and she was moving slow. She brushed us off, saying she was going to bed because she had a headache. She didn't get up the next day, or the next.

Gabby was beside herself with worry. Christopher and I got ourselves ready for the first day at school and went out the door to catch the bus. Christopher was so worried, he didn't want to leave home. As for myself, I was relieved. The brisk walk to the bus stop through the pure morning air had me breathing in long, deep mouthfuls that left me light-headed. I felt like I hadn't taken a real breath in days.

It took a week for Mama to recuperate. Like she had done before, she got up one day and went on as if nothing had happened. We were all learning to read the signs of her "'spells,'" as we came to call them.

CHAPTER FOUR

The kids from across the road didn't ride the school bus. I had assumed, by their voices and how they spoke, that one or two of them were school age. My curiosity about the family in the Wendell house had not waned and, in fact, had grown stronger than ever. I had begun to withdraw from my family again. It was easier to lose myself in some make believe world than to dwell on the realities in our house. And the neighbors were a perfect distraction for my active imagination. I continued to watch and listen from my window.

As the evenings grew cooler and our bedtimes earlier, we were inside by dusk. I scooted my small writing desk to my window so I could see the Wendell place while I did my homework, and sometimes I would draw yet another picture of the spooky old house. If I got caught with my window open, I would be in trouble. Gabby reminded me more than once what it cost to heat our home and I had to listen, again, to the subject of how heat rises and how wasteful I was being. It was all traveling right up the stairs and out my open window. I began shutting my door, but inevitably Christopher came tapping. My closed door seemed to trouble him. He had his own anxieties to deal with. I knew he didn't like being alone, whereas I relished it. I began to seek out ways to be by myself.

On a chilly Saturday in October, I bundled up and went out to the old garage and aired up my bike tires. I rode around our yard a few times, eventually pedaling out onto Gibson Road. I rode south first and felt the cold wind on my face, and huffed and puffed as I pedaled against the gusts. When I turned back, I felt like a human sail. With the wind at my back I rolled along smooth and easy with little effort. Before I knew it I'd reached the turnoff for the lane. I slowed so I could get a better look at the Wendell house. The elms had lost their leaves and the branches that had died out were covered with scabby-looking lichen. The litter and garbage along the fence line was more visible than in the summer. Old tires, engine parts, and stacks of rotten lumber lay in the high, dead weeds. Bits of paper sacks and shredded canvas hung on the barbs of the sagging fence wire. I saw bedsprings leaning against a fence brace. It was a trash disaster. I circled and stopped, and stood straddling my bike, squinting down the lane.

It was at that moment I saw something coming toward me. At first I couldn't guess at what I was seeing. But, as the image came closer, I made out two blonde heads moving along at a good pace. A boy, not much more than a toddler, really, was pushing a stroller with a baby in it as fast as he could. As they zigged and zagged, the little wheels falling into the ruts, the baby began to shriek and I didn't know if it was from joy or fear. The boy kept running as fast as his little legs could go. He barreled right out onto the pavement and stopped at my bike's front tire.

"Hi," he said, and waved a grubby little hand. "Hi."

"Hi," I said back. "What are you two doing out here?"

"I drive Leland," he pointed to the baby. "It's my brother."

They were the dirtiest kids I had ever seen. The smell of urine was strong and only bearable because the wind blew it away. They were both towheads and had masses of curls. Deep blue eyes looked up at me through blonde eyelashes.

"What's your name?" I asked the bigger boy.

"Jefferson. I three." He held up two fingers.

"That's quite a name for a little boy. Jefferson, you better turn around now and go back home, okay?"

"Why?"

"Because it isn't safe for you to be on the road."

"Why?"

This was already tiresome. "Go home," I said, "or I am going to tell your mama."

Jefferson stared at me with defiance. Leland began to cry. When I looked, I could see how his grubby bare legs and feet looked red from the cold wind.

"Go home, Jefferson. You baby brother is cold. Go on, now." I raised my voice and used my I-mean-it tone. He began to struggle with the stroller to turn it back around toward home. As he left the rough edge of the blacktop, the back wheel came off, rolled in a circle and fell over in a rut. Jefferson continued to push the stroller that would no longer roll forward. He gave up trying and looked puzzled.

Now what? I put the kickstand down on my bike and picked up the wheel. The plastic center was completely broken out. No way was it going back on. I grew nervous. I couldn't decide if I should leave them there while I hurried to get Gabby. The baby kept crying. I knew what I should do, and didn't want to do it. I forced myself to lift Leland out of the stroller and tried to hold him away from me. The putrid odor told me he was more than just wet. I drug the stroller to the fence, took Jefferson by his filthy hand.

"Come on. Let's go."

"Why?" he said.

We trudged along. My arm grew weak and I had to shift Leland tighter against my side. He immediately stopped crying as if I had performed a magic trick. His legs felt icy cold. Suddenly, a hard lump of sympathy made my throat ache. Poor little guys. What an awful way to be. I had no choice. I was forced to walk all the way to the Wendell house. Up close, I could see there was even more trash along the lane than I had realized. The wind gusts swirled garbage and dead leaves into spirals that spun dirt into my eyes.

As we neared the house, Jefferson let go of my hand and ran ahead to the porch. I was getting my first close look at the place I had spied on from a distance for years. It was even worse than I had imagined. The porch was collapsing. Someone had shored up one corner with cement blocks, but there were floorboards missing or broken. The once-yellow paint on the house was curled and peeling. A dingy curtain hung in the dirty glass pane of the front door. Jefferson stretched for the knob but could only touch it with his fingers. I took a deep breath and knocked gently on the door. We waited and I listened for sounds from the inside. Baby Leland began to cry again. I knocked louder and we waited again. Finally I heard the thump of footsteps.

The door opened with such force I stepped back. The stale odors of cooking and something sour made me take another step back. I only had a few seconds to take in the woman who stood before me before she reached out and yanked the baby from my arms.

"What are you doing with my babies?" It was Whiner's voice, plain as day. "Get in the house, Jefferson. Now." She was looking past me down the lane.

"Where'd you come from?" she asked.

"I was riding my bike and saw the kids out by the road. The stroller broke so I brought them here."

"Well, don't you be messin' with them again. I'll take care a' my own kids." And with that she slammed the door shut. Shocked, and angry at the woman's rudeness, I stepped off the porch. I took the opportunity to peer around her yard, or what once was a yard. There was trash strewn everywhere. I saw an old weathered doghouse with a rusty chain twisted in the weeds. There was a fire pit made with a circle of rocks and a greasy, black grate across them. I knew it had to be where those cookouts took place all summer. I looked over my shoulder to be sure the woman from the house wasn't watching me, and noticed the windows with their ratty curtains pulled close. Looking up, there were two windows on the top floor the same as our house. As I walked back toward the lane, I could see that the ruts continued on around the house.

To the left stood a rickety wooden outbuilding with a canvas tarp draped over one corner of the wood-shingled roof. Its door looked like an old house door, the style with a small window in it, and had been painted a garish green. There was a paned window on one side of the shed, but boards had been nailed across this way and that. I took a few steps toward the window to see if I could peek through, but I was distracted by another sight.

Back beyond the house I spotted something that made my blood run cold and took my breath away. I stood stock-still and squinted into the shady dimness. In the deepest shadows of the trees there was a body hanging from an oak limb. The sight caused me to take a step back in horror, but I couldn't tear my eyes away. The corpse swayed in the wind and spun in slow circles, one way and the other. It appeared to be the body of a man. Dirty denim overalls and faded, plaid shirtsleeves draped loose on him. His neck hung at a sharp angle inside a knotted noose, and he wore a black beanie cap on his head. My stomach heaved. I stared in spite of my revulsion. I couldn't make my feet move and my legs began to quake. My mind was trying to process the fact that I was looking at a dead man, and make some sense of it at the same time. Suddenly, I saw he had no feet or hands and for a moment my horror grew.

Then I sucked in a breath of relief as I realized it wasn't a man, but a dummy. It was misshapen, lumpy, and the denim of the overalls was full of holes. Bullet holes. When I finally could turn to leave, my spine prickled with the wild fear that someone was going to chase after me, and I cried out a hard sob. I ran as fast as I could, all the way to the paved road. I grabbed my bicycle but I was so frightened; I kept missing my pedal. After several tries I gripped the handlebars and ran beside it to my front yard where I threw it on the lawn. When I stumbled through the front door, panting for breath, I was met with another shock.

JANICE GILBERTSON

There, on the couch, sat a man I had never seen before and next to him, my mother. They both held coffee cups in one hand and stared at me open-mouthed. I stared back, gasping and wiping tears from my face.

"Lord! Are you okay? What's happened?" Mama stood and plunked her cup down on the table. "Where's your brother? Is he with you? Is he okay?" Without waiting for an answer she called up the stairs, "Christopher. Are you there?"

Grandma Gabby hurried from the kitchen. "What's happened? Did someone get hurt?"

"No, Grandma Gabby. Nobody got hurt, I got scared. I'm all right." My voice faltered. I was still out of breath. I knew I was peering at the strange man too long, but I couldn't help it. It was so odd to see him sitting beside my mother in our house.

Mama was flustered, it was plain to see, and she came to me and patted my head and shoulder.

"Donna Jean, this is my friend Harold . . . Harry. You can call him Harry." He and I looked at each other again.

He said, "Nice to meetcha," and I simply nodded.

Gabby took my arm and led me from the awkward situation into the kitchen. She sat me at the table and brought me a glass of water. She pulled out a chair and sat near me.

"Donna Jean, what in the world happened to you?" Gabby's kind and probing eyes could make me tell her anything.

So, I told her. I told her everything from beginning to end, and as I talked I felt calmer, and even a little foolish when I told her the part about the hanging dummy.

"I knew it. I knew those people weren't normal. They could be dangerous. Don't ever, ever go there alone again. Oh, those poor babies." One hand covered her heart. "Go wash up and change those clothes. I'll fix you some soup."

When I passed through the living room, no one was there. Now what was going on with Mama, I wondered? Who was that man and why was he here? I met Christopher at the top of the stairs.

"OOH. You stink!" He backed away from me and looked me up and down. "What happened to you?"

"I'll tell you later." Because I could smell the sour odor of dirty diaper and filth on myself, I couldn't wait to get my clothes off and bathe.

The four of us sat at the table and I told my story again. Christopher listened with big eyes and admiration for my bravery when I told them about taking the boys to the house. He asked half a dozen questions about the house and the hanging dummy. Gabby kept shaking her head over the neglect of the little boys. Mama was quiet. When I was finished telling all, I had to ask about the man in the living room.

"Who's Harry, Mama?"

"Well, he is a friend of mine I met at work. He stopped by to say hello and meet you all."

Well, first of all, nobody "'stopped by'" our house six miles from town on a road that only went to the river. I knew there was more, but I refused to ask. I wanted to punish her by acting like I didn't care.

Gabby wanted to call the sheriff's office and tell them about the neglected children, but Mama said she doubted my experience alone would be enough reason for them to do anything. After some thought, Grandma Gabby agreed, and the subject was dropped.

For several nights I had nightmares about hanging men, witches, and crying children. But the worst dream was the one where I came home from school to find our living room full of men. Mama sat in her big chair and the men were sitting and standing about the room. I stared at each one looking for Daddy, but I couldn't recall his face.

Raymond

Raymond Albert Himes and Twyla May Griggs grew up in a dusty, dirty, broke-down town in Oklahoma. The sign by the Esso station said Doward, Pop. 375. Neither of those things was true. The town was, and had been for decades, known as Dooley, and it would be a challenge to scrape up 250 townspeople. The Himes family controlled the town. In fact, they practically were the town. Raymond had seven siblings and two uncles with offspring adding up to eleven cousins. They were hard people, mentally and physically. Thin, boney, and callous, like cur dogs. Some of them worked in the mines out across the surrounding countryside and some drove to other towns for menial jobs. They got by.

The Himes boys drank, smoked, and fought, and a few of them got a kick out of intimidating the meeker folks in town. But their nemesis was the Griggs family, and though there were fewer of them, they were as tough and somewhat smarter. The Griggs brothers, three of them, endeavored to live calmer, more uncomplicated lives, and not get into anybody else's business. But, step on their toes and you would pay for a long time to come. The Griggs brothers were more educated than most town folks and they became the banker, the mercantile owner, and a barber. One Griggs wife was a grammar school teacher at the little two-room schoolhouse.

Dooley had one bar and café where people congregated in the evening. Most of them being beer drinkers, they passed the time playing pool and poker, plunking quarters in the jukebox, and downing a lot of tap beer. Mornings brought them into the old mercantile building where there was a woodstove that burned red-hot in the winter. In the wicked heat of summer, an enormous fan blew a rumble of air from the high ceiling. They stood in a semi-circle with coffee mugs held in hands, trembling with the misery of hangovers. Hat brims and cap bills were pulled low over bloodshot eyes. Hangovers tamed them.

People drank, danced, and fought with each other on hot summer nights. Pool cues were broken, bar stools sailed, and some of the women slapped and pulled locks of hair from one another's heads. But sometimes—not always, but sometimes—they bought each other's coffee at the mercantile the next morning.

There was one law enforcement officer available to Dooley. His name was Barry and he was lazy as a lizard on a warm rock. He lived and worked from a town so many miles away he wasn't especially helpful in an emergency. Not to say Dooley had many emergencies, and even if Barry had responded, most crimes would have been written up as misdemeanors. He reckoned it wasn't worth the gas and time to get there in a rush only to drive some no-account all the way back to the jail. If he happened to be in the area, he might drive the offenders home with a warning, and leave them there.

Raymond and Twyla attended school together until Raymond dropped out when it was time to go to high school. He had to struggle to get that far for two reasons. The main reason being he wasn't very smart, but he thought he was.

He boasted that he held no respect for anyone. That is, until he decided he wanted Twyla Griggs to be his girlfriend. He chose her for reasons other than a romantic crush. First of all, she wasn't bad looking with her crystal-blue eyes and pale golden hair. Her nose was too pugged and her teeth were slightly bucked but Raymond didn't mind because he knew he wouldn't have much competition for her attention. But, the main reason he wanted to claim her, the big motivation, was she was a Griggs. Everybody in town knew a Himes boy had no business chasing a Griggs girl. Oil and water, night and day, dumb and smart, they were a mismatch beyond belief.

Twyla, who had a good soul, tried to ignore Raymond's attention. She really did, but she was lonesome for someone to like her, and he sure acted like he did. He hung around and waited for her to get off the bus that brought her back to Dooley from high school, then walked her as far home as she dared allow him. It wasn't an easy feat for Raymond to keep his mouth shut, but he managed to stay quiet enough so as not to scare her away. He cleaned up his crude language and tried to remember some manners. Eventually, he held her small white hand in his big grimy one, and she let him. The day came when he steered her around a row of bushes and kissed her, feeling the hardness of her teeth pushing against his lips. She had never been kissed before, but she caught on fast and liked the way it made her feel.

After that, Twyla practiced kissing in the bathroom mirror. She would lock the door and practice her expressions as her lips neared the glass. At night she kissed her pillow until she fell asleep. She had fallen in love with a Himes boy.

Raymond couldn't for the life of him keep quiet about his coup. He'd won over a Griggs girl and he had to tell about it. At first no one believed him and the gossip was a joke around town. Soon, though, he began urging Twyla to accompany him in public so people could see it was true. Many of Dooley's citizens almost lost their minds over the idea of such a thing. His relationship with Twyla created a feud that would never end. People quit speaking to each other, bar fights became nastier and sometimes downright dangerous, and a few of the Himeses' even began to carry weapons, with switchblade knives being the trendy weapon of the times. Lazy Officer Barry had his work cut out for him. He had to make several arrests and pouted like a boy while he drove his detainees all the way to the county jail.

Twyla's mother cried and cried and her father threatened Raymond's life, so then Twyla cried and cried. And meanwhile Raymond and Twyla snuck off and "'went all the way.'" Raymond strutted like a peacock until the day Twyla told him she was pregnant. The Himes family remained indifferent, as this wasn't the first time one of them had got themselves in trouble. But upon hearing the news, Twyla's father threatened Raymond's life again, only this time he demanded the two get married so as not to shame his daughter.

There was a shotgun wedding that not many people bothered to attend. The couple lived in the Griggs's garage with a pullout sofa and a hotplate. Raymond stayed home at night for less than a week then began hanging out in the bar again. One Saturday night things turned wild between himself and one of his own brothers, and Raymond got cut pretty bad with a knife. He made his way back to the garage, trailing blood all the way, where Twyla waited for him. Against his orders, she rushed to get her parents to help Raymond. Her mother washed and bandaged his cuts and her father sat on an upside-down bucket and told them both in no uncertain terms that they had to go. Leave. Move. He bribed them with his old Buick and enough cash to eat and pay a month's rent somewhere—anywhere—besides Dooley. In two days they were gone.

They chose to drive south, only because Raymond had been that way once when he was a little boy. Twyla had never been out of Dooley, so direction meant nothing to her. All she understood was they would drive until they were in Texas.

They stayed in a few small towns for some days or weeks and Raymond tried to find work. Twyla looked for a job too, but all she could do was work as a motel maid. It didn't matter much because Raymond would get in a tiff with his current boss, and off down the road they would go again.

Twyla began to have morning sickness and it made Raymond mad. He had to pull over to the side of the road where Twyla would vomit until she looked like she might pass out.

"Damn, Twyla," Raymond would say, "when are you gonna quit doin' that shit?"

"I can't help it, Raymond," she would sob.

They lived like gypsies. Wade was born at a doctor's office in a tiny Texas town, and less than a year later, Melanie came along. Raymond found rundown places to rent while he worked one job after another. When he discovered they could get some assistance from the state, they lived a little better for a while.

Raymond would go on a bender, using their money for beer, pool, and poker, so when the rent came due they would have to move again.

Twyla tried. She tried so hard to take care of her kids and make a family for them. She cooked meals they could afford. She kept her ramshackle homes as clean as she could.

Wade had gone to school for a little while, but it never lasted long enough for him to get to learn much or make friends. He and Melly counted on each other for comfort and friendship and even though she was younger, she was also the bossy one. She took care of her brother.

Wade was a gentle boy and afraid of his father. Raymond put him down, calling him names and poking fun at him. He called him sissy-boy and teased him relentlessly about Melly being his boss.

Jefferson and little Leland came along close together. More kids meant a little more money from the state and somehow they managed not to starve or live on the street. In fact, Raymond got a job at a mine and worked for almost two years there. The pay was low, but he gave sobriety a real try and did pretty well for a while. He worked at night, slept during the daytime, ate the supper Twyla made for him, and went back to work again.

Twyla had her hands full with the kids. For a while she felt like things were almost normal until Leland was born. Then, with three and a new baby, she was exhausted. Sometimes she honestly hated Raymond. She dreamed of living in a nice neighborhood with a front yard and friends. She'd never had a real friend. Her sister, Rosalie, was the only person she ever kept in touch with, and even then the communication was sporadic because of changing addresses. Having a telephone was out of the question. When they tried, they could never pay the bill, so service would be turned off after the first month.

The last time Raymond fell off the wagon was the worst. He left home for several days, causing him to lose his mine job, then he raised hell with Twyla and the kids when he came back. They had to move again. Somebody told them about an old place for rent out on Gibson Road.

A couple of the men who Raymond had worked with helped move what few things they had accumulated. Twyla cried when she saw how far from town they would be living. Nothing would change. At least there was one other house not far away. It was right on Gibson Road and it was a nice two story with a pretty front porch and grassy yard. For a short time, she dreamed of making friends with someone, but that was foolishness because she knew Raymond would never let her have a real friend.

Raymond was more than pleased to live in the big old house away from town. He could do as he wished with no one watching. He could drive his old jalopy to town and back, and didn't care one bit about what Twyla or the kids were up to. They couldn't go anywhere. Raymond liked being in complete control.

CHAPTER FIVE

Mama's moods remained erratic. It was bewildering for Christopher and me, trying to outguess how she would be from day to day. Whether she was happy or depressed, we held on to the need to know she still loved us. She was ill, Gabby said, and couldn't help herself. But poor Grandma Gabby was beginning to show her weariness. She was literally slowing down. She moved about, doing chores and interacting with us, at a slower pace and even talked less than normal. Her saving grace was the friends she met with in town. They were dear to her and they could make her laugh. And she still loved gossip.

One day, she told Mama some things she had overheard in town about Harry. He had not been back to our house, and Mama had mentioned him only once or twice.

"I don't know how much you know about him," she said to Mama, "but he seems to be some kind of mystery person. Not a soul knows anything about where he comes from. He simply showed up in town. He doesn't even have a real home here. He stays at the old Pickering Inn. 'Course, you probably already know that."

"I do know it, Mother, but he is a nice man, and he seems such a gentleman, too. I've just met him. Maybe he's the private sort. People in this town can't stand it if they don't know everybody's life story."

Thanksgiving was coming. Trees were bare and the wind was cold. We had to bundle up for school. I diligently kept my eye on the Wendell house, but there was little to see. The people there were staying inside like everyone else. I thought of those little boys often and could only wonder about the other kids. I thought of them all, holed up in that stinky house with their awful mother. I couldn't imagine what the holiday would be like in such a terrible home . Then I came up with an idea.

"Grandma Gabby, I was wondering if we could bake some cupcakes for the kids over in the Wendell house. We could decorate them, and we could all drive over to deliver them. You could go with me to the door. What do you think?"

Her heart was too soft to say no. We had fun, and even Christopher helped with the decorating. We made big chocolate ones and drew on them with icing. Gabby packed them carefully in a box with tissue paper. I was giddy about going there again. I wanted Christopher and Gabby to see what I had described to them. I wondered if the dummy was still hanging from the oak limb. Grandma Gabby drove so slow I felt like we would never get to the yard. Our car bumped over the ruts and I gripped the cupcake box.

"Oh my," Gabby said, and I knew she was thinking the same way I did when I saw what a mess the place was. "Oh my." When we stopped, she sat so long I became impatient.

"Come on. I'll knock," I said

"Well, I sure ain't going," Christopher said. He leaned forward and put his chin on the back of our seat. "I'll watch from right here."

I stepped onto the porch with Gabby close behind me and knocked on the door with a strong rap. We both heaved big breaths when we heard footsteps. The door was pulled open fast and there was the same woman I saw before, only this time I couldn't hide my surprise when I saw her. One eye was black and blue and swollen to a slit. The side of her neck was mottled with purple bruises and the corner of her bottom lip jutted out.

Gabby and I stared rudely. I held the box out toward the woman. She didn't move to take it from me. She looked at it and peered at each of us. I became distracted by two children who came behind her and peeked out at us. A boy and a girl. The boy hung back, but the girl crowded around her mother's legs. The same stench I had smelled before wafted from the house. The woman stared at me through the open eye.

"You again," she said. "What do you want this time?"

I glanced at Gabby. "This is my Grandma Gabby. We brought your kids some cupcakes. With it being almost Thanksgiving and all." I thrust the box out toward her and she peered at it for a long time.

"Nice of ya all," she said. She glanced over her shoulder into the room behind her. "I'd ask ya in, but it's time to get the kids to bed."

"Who the hell's out there, Twyla? Shut the damn door. You're lettin' the heat out." She pulled the girl back behind her. "Twyla, you hear me?"

"I'll see that the kids get 'em." She took the box from my hands, stepped back and shut the door.

Gabby and I looked at each other. As soon as we were in the car, she flew into a tirade.

"That woman has been beat to a pulp. What's the matter with people like them." It was more of a statement than a question.

"She could have said thank you. Ignorant folks, they are. Those poor little kids truly break my heart. All dirty and bedraggled. Did you see the boy's shoes? His toes hanging off the sole like that."

While she was spitting and sputtering her anger, she was maneuvering the car around so we could drive back along the lane. The back tire rolled over something big enough to make the car bounce in the back.

"Grandma Gabby!" Christopher hollered. "What was that?"

When I craned my neck around to look back, I knew right away what she had run over. It was the gigantic rocks surrounding the fire pit. When she pulled forward again, we bounced harder than the first time.

"Grandma Gabby!"

"Hush, Christopher." She spun the wheel to the left and hit the accelerator a little too hard. The tires spun before they grabbed traction, and we spurted off toward the road. I began to laugh and so did Christopher, and then Gabby did too. We were wiping tears by the time we got to the paved road. My ribs ached from laughing so hard. Gabby didn't even stop at the end of the lane. It wasn't necessary because we could see both ways, but still, that wasn't how Gabby ever drove. She made the right turn and stepped on it again. The way she looked in the dash lights, giggling and eyes glistening, caused me to burst out laughing again. By the time we pulled alongside our house we were all breathless. We had to make a point of not looking at each other so we could pull ourselves together. Finally we left the car and staggered into the house.

Christopher and I fell onto the sofa in the living room and Gabby headed to the bathroom. "Can you believe Grandma Gabby?" Christopher said." I think she ran over the grill."

I held up my hand to him and shook my head. I didn't want to start in again.

When Mama announced she was inviting Harry for Thanksgiving supper, I got up from the breakfast table and stomped away. For a solid week, it had been Harry this, and Harry that. How polite he was, wasn't he a handsome man? She liked his car. She liked his sweater. For Pete's sake.

"Donna Jean. You get back in here. What is it with you?"

I turned back a few steps, but I didn't want to sit. "But, it is our Thanksgiving as a family. Why does he have to come on that day?"

"That's what Thanksgiving is about, Donna Jean. Being thankful for what we have and including others who aren't as fortunate. He has nowhere else to go. Besides, you don't get to decide who I invite into our home. I am going to ask him, and you will mind your manners."

Because I was pouty and disagreeable the rest of the day, everyone ignored me. It was cold and blustery out so I holed up in my room and watched the house across the road. Two cars came and left along the lane. I wondered what kind of people visited such an odd family. I had decided it was time to go back downstairs and wiggle my way back into the good graces of Gabby. Taking one last look out my window, I was surprised to see a county sheriff's car turn into the lane and slowly make its way to the house. When the car stopped before it reached the yard, both doors swung open and two deputies got out, both snugged their hats and approached the front door. I couldn't see much more, but I stared anyway.

I waited. One of them walked the driveway around the house, the other stayed out front. I was bursting with curiosity and wished Christopher was there with me to share in the excitement. Next thing I knew, the deputy reappeared from behind the house, guiding a man with his arms behind his back. That did it. I thundered down the stairs.

"Gabby, Christopher! Hurry! Something is happening across the road." We all three charged back up the stairs and scrambled for positions at my window. The three men were standing in a cluster, presumably talking. We strained to see clearer when one deputy climbed onto the porch and entered the house. We waited without speaking. And waited. When he came out, he said something and they let the man go. We watched as the deputy backed the car all the way to the paved road.

"They have to back out so the bad guy won't shoot 'em in the back," Christopher whispered as if they might hear us.

"Christopher!" Gabby was truly horrified. "Such talk."

"It's true, Grandma Gabby. I saw it on television. Never turn your back to the bad guy."

We were all headed for the stairs when Mama came from her room.

"What are you all up to?" she asked, looking at Gabby. It was Christopher who jumped into telling the story while adding a little extra drama.

"Why didn't anyone call me?" She sounded insulted.

It struck me then, how I had fallen into the habit of overlooking her involvement in most everything we did as a family. She was seldom available. Either she was sleeping, working, or too depressed to be bothered. She had shooed us from her room and shushed us in front of the TV set. It had come naturally for Christopher and me to turn to Grandma Gabby with our family conversations.

I felt guilty and ashamed and must have looked it. I slunk downstairs and went to the kitchen.

Gabby came behind me and gave me a pat of understanding on my shoulder.

"Don't suffer over it so, Donna. You can't blame yourself for how Ellen is acting."

"It's true, though, what she said. I do forget sometimes that she's still my family. Sometimes I feel like I don't have a mother. We don't talk about anything, like school or television shows or anything we used to talk about. Remember how she used to be so funny and make us all laugh and Daddy would say . . . ?" The tears flooded my face and I lost the rest of my words. I let out a shaky breath. "I'm going outside for a little while."

Gabby looked so sad when I left the kitchen.

I walked along Gibson Road in the opposite direction of the lane. I pulled the collar of my warm, blue-plaid coat over my numb ears, and stuffed my hands deep into my pockets. My insides felt tight and uncomfortable and gloomy. Or, maybe I was more angry than sad. I'd recognized such feelings more and more often. Angry about things I couldn't fix or change. I even got mad at Daddy sometimes. Why did he have to get in that stupid accident? Couldn't he have turned the wheel or stopped faster or something? And why couldn't my mother act like one? And why did she have to let Harry into our lives? I was even mad at those people across the road. Stupid, ignorant people who couldn't even take care of their own kids.

The angrier I felt, the faster I walked. I became absorbed in imagining myself telling them all what I thought. I had visions of telling each person my opinion of them and their behavior. I liked it! I felt better. I breathed freer, deeper, and my stomach relaxed.

I thought I heard a car coming from behind me and I realized how far I had walked, spewing my wrath out across the silent fields. At least two miles, maybe more. I turned to head back home and kept up a good pace. I didn't want to worry Grandma Gabby. I watched a car come toward me. It was the old brown clunker from the Wendell house. I made up my mind before it reached me that I wouldn't look at it as it passed me, and turned my head away. From the corner of my eye I could see how the car slowed and slowed until the tires were hardly rolling at all, and stopped as it came even with me. The driver rolled the window down, letting a cloud of cigarette smoke billow out.

"You that neighbor gal?" he rasped. The man was grizzled looking. Long, limp, gray-streaked hair hung from beneath a Dodgers baseball cap. He had a dirty-looking, untrimmed mustache that covered his mouth, and his beard was stained a yellow-brown around his chin. I stopped walking and faced him. A sense of righteous braveness seemed to prop me up like a steel rod.

"What do you want?" I asked in an even tone.

"I want you to stay away from my place over there." He jerked his head over his shoulder. "We don't like people comin' 'round uninvited."

"I've been over there two times, and both times I was doing something nice for your kids. You could at least say thank you."

"I'll thank you to mind your own damn business. And you need yer sassy mouth washed out."

I turned away and began walking toward home again. He put the car in reverse and began backing the car, staying beside me.

"What's your mama's name? Ellen, is it? I'd like to have a talk with yer ma."

"None of your business. Leave me alone." I walked faster.

"She's a looker, your mama. You tell her I said howdy." He giggled, showing a dark, ugly maw, teeth stained or missing.

"How old are you? You sixteen yet?" He puffed on his cigarette again and blew the smoke toward me. "Ain't safe to be walkin' out here all by yerself. Some ol' man might come by and steal you." He cackled at what he had said. He didn't say any more, but he kept right on rolling silently beside me. His stare burned my face and neck.

I refused to look his direction, but it wasn't until we had gone a ways that he drove away and I began to tremble. My whole body shook. I ran the rest of the way home.

That evening I drew his likeness, giving him stringy hair and a cap with Dodgers embroidered on it, and his nasty beard hanging long. I erased and redrew until I began to see wickedness on the page. I closed it and put it away.

CHAPTER SIX

Harry was a no-show on Thanksgiving Day.

Mama, Gabby and I had spent the morning in the kitchen. Mama was quiet, but pleasant, and Grandma Gabby lived up to her Thanksgiving meal reputation. The aroma in our kitchen was exactly what it should have been. The one we anticipated. Roast turkey with cornbread stuffing, yams, and pumpkin pie. Christopher was in charge of the mashed potatoes and, feeling important, he announced every step as he carried out his responsibility. I believe, for that one morning, we were all enjoying ourselves. I had decided I would try to be decent about Harry coming for dinner. Maybe Thanksgiving Day had me wanting to turn over a new leaf.

Mama excused herself and said she needed to run and change and "'at least'" put some lipstick on. She acted as if Harry's arrival wasn't that big a deal. She looked beautiful when she came back to the kitchen. I saw her glance at the wall clock a couple of times. Apparently Gabby did too.

"What time did you tell him to come, Ellen?"

"He should be here anytime now." She peered through the window above the kitchen sink.

It wasn't long until everything was ready and Gabby was putting some things on the table. Five place settings of good china were enough to cause me to glimpse the image of my father sitting in his chair. He was there and gone in a flash of time and memory.

We waited. And waited. It was Christopher who finally spoke.

"Can we eat now? I'm starving."

"He's right," Gabby said. "We should go ahead or it will all be cold. Maybe Harry will let us fix him a plate when he gets here."

And so we ate. The meal was delicious, but the mood was strained. We struggled for conversation until we all gave up and ate in silence. I knew what was coming before Mama said anything, and I lost my appetite to the clenching in my stomach.

"I'm sorry." She put her fork on her plate, wiped her mouth with the good cloth napkin. "I'm not feeling well. I am going to go rest a bit. I'll help clean up in a while." She trudged up the stairs.

Harry didn't come. The phone didn't ring. Mama didn't come back. Not that evening and not for the next two days. Gabby called Goldie's and told Mama's boss how ill Mama was feeling. I could tell by Gabby's end of the conversation he was unhappy to hear she wasn't coming in. Later I heard Grandma Gabby tell my mother what her boss had said.

"He wasn't happy about you missing work. In fact, what he said was, if you don't get yourself together soon, he was going to have to let you go and get someone else. I didn't know what to tell him, Ellen. Why don't you go back to the therapist? "

"I don't need a therapist, Mother. I just don't feel well."

"It's about Harry, isn't it? Why waste your time on a man who doesn't show up and doesn't even call?"

"You don't know. Maybe something happened to him. Look what happened to . . ." She couldn't even say Daddy's name.

Her boss let her return one more time. Christopher and I went back to school for that period I'd always thought of as "'the waiting days,'" those days between Thanksgiving and the December break from school. The mood of the house was dreary. Even the thought of the holiday didn't cheer me up at all. Christmas was for little kids. I wondered what kind of day the kids across the road would have.

I spent a lot of time at my bedroom window. The winds came, and the copse of oaks flailed their heavy limbs around the house. The elms along the lane stood stiff and brittle, but I could see the trash, caught up in the fence, flapping madly as if it wanted to escape and rush off across the land.

I began noticing car lights bouncing along the lane to Gibson Road most nights. They flashed across our yard and front porch as the car left the lane, bumped onto the pavement, and headed toward town. I imagined the same grubby man who had stopped me on the road was behind the wheel and wondered where he would be going at that time of night.

One Friday night, we had stayed up waiting for Mama to come home. Christopher wanted to help count her tips and begged me to wait with him. When she came into the house and went to the table with us tagging along, I could tell she was changed by the way she carried herself. Her step was quicker, her head a little higher. As she scattered her coins across the table she said, "Well, you will never guess who came into Goldie's tonight." Of course, it must have been Harry. That was why she was happy. I refused to bite, and Christopher was oblivious.

"Well, it was our neighbor, from across the road." What she'd said didn't sink in for a minute. Who was she talking about?

"His name is Raymond. He said he knew me, or, at least he knew I lived across the road from him. He was nice enough. In fact, he said if there was anything needed doing over here we couldn't handle, he would be glad to help us out."

I couldn't believe what I was hearing. I stared at her face, struggling to read if she was being serious.

"Mama! That man is a creep. He beats his wife, for Pete's sake. He's grubby and he smells bad. He even stopped me on the road one day and told me to stay away from his family."

That stopped her. "Well, you never told me about that." She didn't sound worried about me; she was offended because she was left out of some news again.

"If you ever paid attention to any of us, we would tell you things." I was so irritated at her for her selfishness.

"Don't be smart, Donna Jean. I work, you know. I have a job to go to. Besides, what were you even thinking, talking to a stranger out on the road?"

It was no use. I had to give it up. I didn't have the urge to cry like I usually did when we quarreled. I didn't feel much of anything except tired.

"Never mind," I said. "I'm going to bed."

As I left the kitchen, I heard her say to Christopher, "Guess who else showed up tonight. Harry!"

Bingo. That was what the happy face was all about.

On a mid-December night, while Gabby and Christopher and I were hanging out in the living room in front of the television, there came a soft knock on the door. It was so soft we didn't recognize it as a knock at first. When it came again, Gabby went to the door. She opened it enough to peer out with one eye. When she swung the door wide with an exclamation, Christopher and I flew to our feet.

Two children stood on the porch. The boy, skinny and long-limbed with a mound of blonde, curly hair, began to talk to Gabby. He spoke fast, looking here and there as if anxiously searching for the words to explain why they were at our door. The girl, shorter and square-shaped and wearing a dress much too big for her, kept interrupting the boy to add her comments. Both of them shook with the cold, but, at the same time, didn't seem to be aware of their own discomfort. Grandma Gabby took the girl's arm to guide her through the door, but she balked and pulled back.

"You kids get in here. It's too cold out there. Come on." She reached for the boy and he came willingly. Christopher looked at me, and I shrugged my shoulders.

"Has there been an accident? Did someone get hurt?" Gabby asked. The boy nodded, but it was the girl who piped up.

"Our mom," she said. She was animated and motioned with her arms and hands as she talked. "She had an accident. She fell on the floor in the kitchen, and she has blood by her, and we couldn't get her to wake up. Wade said we should come and tell you."

They were finally far enough inside the entry for Gabby to close the door behind them. The boy looked all around the room. I could smell him. I knew who he was.

"I bet you live across the road," I said. He nodded. "Are your little brothers at home? Is your father there?"

First he nodded yes, but then he shook his head no. The little girl answered for him.

"Jeff and Leland are upstairs, and Daddy left in his car. I think he is getting someone to help our mom." Her wide-eyed innocence was so sincere.

"Did he tell you to come here?" Gabby asked.

"No," the boy said, "but a long time ago Mom said to come here if we needed to use the phone or if we needed any help or anything." It was understandable he had never thought about what kind of help they might ever need. The girl was vigorously nodding her head in agreement.

We all fell quiet. The children stood, looking awkward, not knowing what else to say. Gabby guided them to the couch and sat them side-by-side. She pulled an afghan around them. I saw they were shivering harder. Gabby told Christopher to go in the kitchen and make some cocoa.

"So you are Wade, right? And what is your name?" I asked the girl.

"My name is Melly." Now she was looking all around the room. "You have television."

"We do. Do you have television, Melly?"

"No."

Grandma Gabby was getting impatient with the small talk. She sat on the edge of the coffee table in front of the kids. She began asking some serious questions and made the kids answer one at a time so she could get the facts. They didn't know exactly what happened to their mother. They didn't know where their father was going to get help. They were pretty sure their baby brothers were okay as long as Leland didn't fall down the stairs like he had once before. Grandma Gabby rolled her eyes at the answers. Wade said he was sure Jeffy would help him, but Melly shook her head emphatically and said, no, Jeffy wouldn't help because he was too little.

Christopher came with the warm chocolate and Grandma Gabby said she was going to call the sheriff's department and went to the kitchen. She talked for several minutes before she came back to sit by us.

"The sheriff deputy is coming," she said. "He's going to help you, okay?"

"Daddy says we aren't supposed to call them," Melly said.

"But, I'm sure they will help you," Gabby assured her.

I caught Grandma Gabby's eye and wrinkled my nose indicating the potent odor radiating from the children as they sipped the chocolate and their bodies warmed beneath the afghan. Wade wore the same shoes he'd had on the night we'd gone to their door with cupcakes. This time he wore no socks so his dirty toes pushed over the soles. Melly had on a pair of filthy white sandals and she had a scraped knee with dirt and grit caught in the scab. Who knew the last time they had ever bathed or even washed their hands and faces? I felt sick to my stomach for a few minutes and needed to move away from them.

Christopher followed me into the kitchen. I washed my hands with soap, holding them under the hot water tap until they reddened. Christopher pulled a chair away from the table and sat. When we finally spoke, it was at the same time. I motioned for him to go first.

"What do you think happened to their mom?"

"I don't know, but I wish someone would get there in a hurry. She could be dying, you know." Christopher paled as if it had not occurred to him at all. "Wade said there was blood."

We heard the car pull into the driveway and both of us headed for the front door. A deputy came to the porch and asked if someone had called about a couple of kids. I said my Grandma Gabby had and motioned him inside. Another patrol car drove past on Gibson Road and turned into the lane.

The deputy wasted no time. He told us his name was Wilkes. Gabby told him the names of the boy and girl sitting silently on our couch. Wade looked frightened. Melly looked curious. Deputy Wilkes asked what happened. Of course it was Melly who answered.

"Our mom got hurt so we came to tell somebody." She told him the same things she had told us, and also that her little brothers were upstairs in their room. He looked surprised, and asked a chain of questions. Melly's answers were vague. He told them someone was already helping their mom, and would see to the brothers. Wade stood quickly, pushing the afghan from him and moving around the coffee table. He said they had to get back to their house. I knew he wanted to be sure his mom was all right.

The deputy said he would be back in a minute and went back outside.

Wade paced our living room and looked at all our things. He stared at our family photos.

"Wade, do you go to school?" I asked.

"I went to first grade." His little voice sounded so happy in telling me, I could tell he was proud.

"What about this year? Are you going this year?"

Melly was there behind us. "We don't go to school. We have a special excuse," she said.

"Really? What is that?"

"Because our mom is sick. So we don't have to go."

"Oh, I see." But, I didn't.

Deputy Wilkes came back inside. He told us Mrs. Himes, the kids' mother, was going to be okay but she needed to be examined by a doctor. He was sure she would be back at home in an hour or so. Mr. Himes, or Raymond, had not been located yet. Another deputy would be transporting Mrs. Himes to town and would give her a ride back home if a doctor released her. They had someone from the office to stay with the little kids. He asked if Wade and Melly could stay at our house until their mother returned. Of course, Grandma Gabby said yes.

Gabby's goal became scrubbing and feeding Wade and Melly before they were taken home. She sent Christopher and me into the kitchen to heat canned soup and make cheese sandwiches, and she herded the bewildered kids into the bathroom. When they came out nearly a half hour later, their faces were shiny and their blonde hair was already spiraling back into damp curls. Having nothing else to wear, they had to put their dirty clothes back on, but they smelled better. They sat at the table and slurped the tomato soup and gobbled the sandwiches. Melly ate every crumb and Wade left all of the bread crust. They ate fast and sat back in their chairs when they were finished.

First, Wade began to yawn wide and deep, and his sister followed suit. Little bluish circles formed beneath their eyes. Back in the living room, they fell asleep leaning into each other on the couch.

When another deputy came to the door to take the kids home, he said their mother was waiting in his car and she was going to be all right. She had a nasty cut above her temple which required stitches, and was insisting she'd slipped and fallen, banging her head against the counter. Wade and Melly stumbled out our door half asleep. We stood in the dark and watched them crawl onto the back seat of the patrol car where their mother sat. Christopher and I went in to get out of the cold, but Grandma Gabby stood on the porch until she saw the car pull into the long lane.

CHAPTER SEVEN

Christmas Day arrived, and so did Harry.

Mama didn't tell us he was coming until the afternoon of Christmas Eve, and for good reason. It allowed less time for us to fuss and mope about sharing our day with him. Christopher and I didn't say anything, but my first thought was maybe he wouldn't show up, which would be fine with me.

We opened our gifts without the excitement we'd had when we were younger and Daddy was with us. Christopher and I got clothes. Mama was bright-eyed and acted like the dime store bracelet I'd given her had real diamonds in it. She oohed and aahed over the book Christopher gave her, saying she would get to reading it that night. Gabby accepted her own bracelet and book with sweet eagerness. Christopher and I hadn't been wholehearted shoppers.

We had finished cleaning up the ribbons and paper in the living room when there came a knock on the door. Mama rushed to answer it, and opened it wide to Harry. He came in with a cheery looking Christmas bag in his arms and handed it over to Mama.

"Merry Christmas, everyone," he said, looking at all of us. "I brought a few things. They aren't much, but I wanted to add a little Christmas cheer."

I don't believe I had ever felt as awkward as I did in that moment. Accepting a gift from someone I was determined to hate left me anxious and confused. And maybe a little guilty. Christopher and I sat beside each other and carefully removed the bright paper from our gifts while Harry stood, seeming relaxed with his hands in his pockets, and watched.

I'm sure I gasped when I removed the lid from the small white box. Inside was the most beautiful watch. Everything about it sparkled. It lay on the cotton, a band made like a bracelet, and a clasp with a dainty safety chain. There were tiny red gems all around the face. I know I stared at it for too long.

Christopher let out a "Wow!" when he saw he had a watch also. It was handsome with a big face and a leather band. He put his on immediately.

"Oh, my gosh, Harry! You did way too much. Those are beautiful gifts." Mama was honestly surprised.

"That's okay. I wanted to do it. Open yours. And yours, too, Mrs. Shanks." His voice was deep and charming.

Mama's gift was a beautiful cobalt blue bottle of French perfume. She sniffed it and batted her eyes at Harry like a movie star. I physically cringed when she put her arms around his neck and kissed him on his lips. Christopher, so enamored with his watch, didn't notice. Grandma Gabby held up the most beautiful necklace I had ever seen. A string of small black and turquoise stones held a tiny silver pendent shaped like a butterfly.

Gabby's eyes twinkled, but she spoke right up. "Harry, this is absolutely beautiful, but honestly, it is too much. This must have cost a small fortune."

"It wasn't that much and when I saw it, I knew it was meant for you." Harry's smile was kind. "Please," he said, "enjoy it."

Grandma Gabby thanked him again, and she and I moved to the kitchen to prepare the holiday meal. The ham was baking in the oven, the kitchen was warm and smelled like Christmas Day should. We talked about my watch and her pretty necklace. She said she hoped I could accept that Harry might be coming around more and maybe I could learn to like him.

"I'll try. But there is something about him." I couldn't even say what it was, but something.

Supper went all right. Christopher gabbed his head off, and I knew he wanted Harry's attention. Mama had to tell him to hush and eat his food. I suppose it was nice for him to have a man around for a change. The poor kid had us females surrounding him all the time. Harry told us he liked geology and had studied it in school. He asked Christopher if he was interested in rocks and gems. Of course, Christopher said yes, though I couldn't recall him ever showing any curiosity about those sorts of things. Harry said one day maybe we could all go to the river and see if we could find anything special.

Mama laughed and said she loved gems, too, and gave a big wink. She looked young and happy, and pretty. She looked like Mama before Daddy died.

That evening, I sat at my desk, and for the first time since I had drawn the picture of a crazy woman, I attempted to draw a sketch of my mother. I drew slow and careful, and remembered to use the right pencil leads in the right places. I lined with light strokes, and put in shadows. I under-shaded the planes of her cheeks and added the tiny creases in her bottom lip. Her eyes came alive when I erased specks of gray to highlight her irises. I shaded her temples and softened her hair around her face. When I felt I was finished, I propped the drawing pad up on the desk and stepped back. I stared for a long time. There she was. My mother, pretty as ever.

I seldom showed my drawings to anyone. They felt private to me and I thought they weren't good enough to share. Long before that Christmas evening, I had read every book in both the Pickering and the school libraries that had anything to do with drawing. By the time I drew Mama's portrait that night, a stack of sketchpads filled with pictures had accumulated. It was easy to see the gradual improvement from the first to the most recent. I'd placed a sheet of tissue paper from old shoeboxes between a few of the pages to protect some of my favorites from smearing.

I took the top pad from the pile and opened it randomly. There, looking back into my eyes, was the scraggly-looking man in his old car. Raymond. I had caught the evilness in his expression. Leaving the irises of his eyes nearly unshaded and penciling in his low, heavy eyebrows gave him the same sinister look I had seen. I turned back to gaze out my window at the Wendell house. I wondered if those little children over there had any Christmas at all. I felt so sad for them that tears welled in my eyes. There we were in our nice warm home, eating the best food and receiving expensive gifts, and those poor little kids right there, so near us, most likely had nothing. Maybe they went to bed dirty and hungry like any other night.

It was right at that moment I made a vow to myself to help them. I wasn't sure what that meant, but I knew it was the right thing to do. I would talk to Grandma Gabby the next day.

———

"I'm not sure," Gabby said. "Maybe we could go by the sheriff's department and ask them what we can do. This county has a welfare office. Donna Jean, I don't know that people can be ordered to take care of their children. Raymond and Twyla are either ignorant or lazy, or both. If this is going to be something you honestly want to pursue, it could end with those kids being taken away and put in foster homes. Because there are four of them, they would most likely be separated."

"Would they get to see each other?"

"I don't know. Sometimes people get their kids back if they change their lifestyle. That would be the ideal situation. Mull it over until Monday. You have another week out of school."

Grandma Gabby gave me the tightest, longest hug and told me I had a good heart. She helped me realize I could be brave and purposeful.

When we entered the sheriff's office late Monday morning, it was dim and quiet. A large silver-haired lady looked up from her work at her desk and asked if she could help us.

"Maybe so," Gabby said, and introduced herself and me to the woman. "We have some concerns about some children who live near us, and we wanted to talk with someone about their circumstances. Their last name is Himes. Raymond and Twyla Himes?"

The silver-haired lady stood from her desk. "Oh, yes. I know the name. Out on Gibson Road, right? Our deputies have been out there a couple of times. Oh, my name is Alice, by the way." She held out a large, flat hand to us both. She was as chatty as Gabby. "I can't recall now what it was about. Something to do with Mr. Himes. I believe someone called in a complaint about him raising heck somewhere. Oh, wait. I remember, it was an anonymous caller. Said Mrs. Himes was in bad shape because Raymond had beat up on her. Thing is, you know, they go all the way out there and then Twyla won't sign a complaint so there is really nothing they can do. They gave him a talking to and a warning about not doing that anymore or he really would go to jail for it whether Twyla wanted him to or not."

"What about the kids?" I asked. I was thinking of the night we watched the deputies go to the Wendell house.

"The kids? I don't know, hon. Unless the deputies make a welfare report, I wouldn't hear about any kids."

"There are four of them and they aren't taken good care of. I know because they came to our house and they were cold and hungry. Deputy Wilkes came out, and some others. "

"The thing is, we are very concerned about the children's welfare," Grandma Gabby said. "Is there a child welfare department we can get in touch with?"

"Let me see . . ." Alice lumbered to a file cabinet across the room and began shuffling through its drawers. "Here's a number you can call, but if you would like to speak to Deputy Wilkes, he will be in at one o'clock."

Grandma Gabby said we would be back and thanked the woman for her time. Once outside, we shared our frustration at how little help we'd received. We would go back and talk with Deputy Wilkes at one.

We had an early lunch at a place called The Coffee Cup. It was good to spend time with Gabby without Christopher and Mama there. We settled into a vinyl booth and Gabby gave me a quarter to put in the jukebox player. I flipped through and made my choices. Bad Moon Rising played first and Gabby rolled her eyes. The waitress knew Gabby as a regular customer and chatted when she came to take our order. They exchanged a short conversation about some things going on in town, and then the waitress, Annie, was her name, asked about Mama.

"How's Ellen doin' these days? We haven't seen her for a while. I heard Harry spent Christmas Day with y'all."

"He did. How was your Christmas, Annie?"

"Good. It was good. So, I guess Ellen and Harry are a thing now, huh?"

"Well, I can't really say. He seems like a nice enough fellow."

"Nobody knows much about him around here. Seems he sure likes Ellen, though. Rumor is he's the jealous type. He don't much like those other men hangin' around her at Goldie's."

Grandma Gabby picked up her menu and said, "I think we are ready to order, Annie."

Annie took the hint. Gabby wasn't sharing any information about Mama and Harry. I watched Annie hurry off to turn our order in. I wondered why Mama's life seemed so interesting.

Back at the sheriff's office, Alice showed us along the short hall and into a small office where Deputy Wilkes sat at a table sipping a cup of coffee. He stood as soon as we entered. "Sit, sit." He dragged two more chairs around his own. "Can I get you some coffee or anything?"

Gabby said no thank you, we'd had lunch. She explained briefly why we were there, our serious concern about the Himes children.

"I understand your feelings," he said. "Myself and another deputy talked to Welfare about the kids, but you have to understand how hard it is to remove kids from their biological parents' home. If there is food, and clothing, and shelter, it makes it difficult to get children out of those kinds of environments. All of those things were present when we looked at their home on the night the two oldest were at your house. "

"That's ridiculous!" Gabby said. "Those kids walked alone, at night, to our house in the freezing weather without proper clothing. I fed and bathed them. They were starving and filthy. How can such things be allowed by people who are supposed to help them?"

Deputy Wilkes held a hand up as if to calm Grandma Gabby. "I know, I know. And I agree, but until Welfare says they must be removed, there isn't much we can do."

"What if we called Child Welfare? Would it help?" I asked.

"If you had new complaints to file, it would help. Sometimes these cases can be challenged with an accumulation of information. You know, over a period of time."

"And meanwhile, little kids suffer." I said it with the anger brewing inside me.

The deputy looked directly at me. "You know, Donna Jean, taking little children from their homes isn't always the best answer. They end up being separated and going to different foster homes. There are many stories about kids living in several homes until they become adults and then they seek out their brothers and sisters. It can be hard on them."

I looked at Gabby, remembering she had said the same thing. I felt defeated. I wished I was an adult. I knew exactly what I would do. I would march over there and tell Raymond and his sorry wife how they had better straighten up and take care of their kids like they should be, like they were supposed to. I wanted to yell at them, tell them how awful they were.

I swear, Grandma Gabby was reading my mind. She reached for my hand. "Come on sweetie," she said. "Let's go on home. We'll keep mulling it over."

We stood to leave. Deputy Wilkes stood with us and let out a huge sigh. "Listen, call me anytime. If you think you know about something or see something having to do with those kids, call me. I'll do whatever I can to help."

CHAPTER EIGHT

I guess you could say I became a bit obsessed about helping those kids. For a few days, I spent even more time watching the Wendell house from my window, but when I didn't observe anything out of the ordinary I began going for walks again. I walked north on Gibson Road. I felt it was safer since I would be close to home if I encountered Raymond again. If I walked farther, beyond the lane, I could look upon the old place from a different viewpoint. Seeing the elm trees along the lane, and a glimpse of the oak-guarded house from the north changed the picture, but not the mood.

Mama still worked late hours and was sleeping until afternoon, but if we had early supper, she joined us before she left for her work. Harry came for supper a number of times, and I didn't get mad and Christopher was thrilled to have him come. After the meal, Mama and Harry would go out and sit on the porch so he could have a smoke. Christopher would wait at the door for them to come back inside. I worried about him liking Harry too much.

"Be careful, Christopher. I don't want you to get your feelings hurt if he quits coming around."

"Just because you don't like him, Donna Jean, doesn't mean I can't."

I knew he had a point. But honestly, there was something about Harry I couldn't get comfortable with. Something in his manner made him seem . . . I don't know what. Dishonest maybe. He never talked about his own life. He didn't speak of friends or other places he went. I knew Mama didn't see him for days at a time, but yet, when he came to our house he acted as if he was part of our family. And, there was something about the way he watched Mama; his eyes constantly followed every move she made.

Days would go by when I would forget to think of Daddy. I would be shaken when I realized I had done such a thing. I wondered if he knew, and I'd be swallowed by guilt. I often talked to him when I lay sleepless in my bed. The dark made it easy to look up and imagine him in Heaven, listening. I would apologize for leaving him out of my life and promise I would never consider anyone else as my father. I honestly thought he would want to hear me say so.

Mama still had bouts of depression, but they didn't linger as long as in the past. She would grow quiet and withdrawn, but she managed to go to work, keeping her job at Goldie's. If Gabby was hearing any more unkind gossip about her, she didn't bring it up. We seemed to be learning how to live around one another. If we let each other be, we got on fine.

When I headed out for walks, or wandered over to the barn on weekends, I was supposed to tell Grandma Gabby first, but I didn't always. She drove to town on Saturdays as regular as the day came. She shopped and visited with her friends, spending most of the afternoon there. Christopher went with her most Saturdays and hung out with his pals. It was a treat for him to go to town and do things the town kids did. He didn't like hanging out with an older sister anymore. He had friends and relationships of his own. Sometimes he loaded his bike in Gabby's car and spent the night with a friend in town.

Walking back toward home on a clear but cold day, I saw Raymond's old brown car bump along the lane beneath the ragged elms and stop at the pavement. I kept walking on the opposite side of the road. Being so close to home kept me from feeling too anxious about meeting up with Raymond. I watched as his car door opened and he hauled himself from behind the wheel as if he must weigh a ton.

"Hey," he hollered. "Hey, Donnaaa." He stretched my name out as if to make fun of it. His taunting made the hair on my neck bristle. With a false braveness spurred by my anger, I stopped and faced him across Gibson Road. I saw little Wade's blonde head above the dash of the car.

"My boy here wanted to say hello. He said you was his friend." I saw Wade's small hand reach high and wave at me. I waved back and called out hello.

Raymond pushed himself away from the car with effort and came around the open door. One foot crossed over the other and he caught himself on the fender to keep from falling. He was drunk.

"Come 'ere," he said, waving his hand. "Come 'ere, and say hi to ol' Raymond."

Seeing him filthy and swaying on his feet made my stomach churn, so I turned to walk on toward my house.

"Got somethin' 'ere ta show ya." In spite of myself I looked again. He giggled drunkenly, pointed at his crotch, and fumbled to unzip his pants. He made a gesture with his hand, an unmistakable one even to a fourteen-year-old. Next, he held a grimy finger against his hairy mouth and made a sshhh sound, and spittle flew in the sunlight. He pointed toward Wade and gestured again, as if he didn't want the boy to know what he was insinuating. How I loathed him in that moment. Hot tears of embarrassment sprang to my eyes.

For the hundredth time I wished I still had my father. He would take care of this horrible man that was for sure. I wondered why Raymond couldn't have died instead of Daddy.

"You're sick!" I yelled out and ran to my house. I slammed the door behind me and turned the lock. I felt ashamed as if I was the one who had done something disgusting. My stomach turned and I hurried to the kitchen sink for water. I sat at the table for a long time before my emotions began to calm. I started with a jerk when Mama came through the door.

"You're not sleeping," I said stupidly.

"What's wrong? Are you sick?" She studied me.

"Not feeling too good," I murmured.

"Come on. Get your coat off and let's go watch television until Grandma Gabby gets home."

And that is what I did. I never said one single word about what had happened out on the road. I don't know how. Every time the picture of Raymond, pointing down at himself, crossed my mind, I felt a wave of shame and sickness again. He was nasty. I was embarrassed and didn't understand why. I hadn't done anything wrong. Even later, sitting there with Mama watching some TV program, I couldn't come up with a way to tell her what happened or how I felt. Had I told her right then, everything might have ended differently.

Grandma Gabby caught cold. We all did, but hers grew serious. I couldn't recall ever knowing her to be sick enough to stay in bed most of the day. "Oh, I'll be fine, it's just a nasty cold," she would say when we expressed worry or fussed over her. She became weak and shaky and the slightest physical effort made her cough. When she finally relented to visit a doctor, Mama drove her to town early one afternoon. He gave her medicine to help clear her lungs and ease the terrible coughing spells. It was strong stuff and had Codeine in it that, Mama explained, would help Grandma Gabby rest better. For a few days she slept for long periods of time and her cough did lessen for a while, but soon it all came back with a vengeance.

Back to the doctor they went. When they didn't come home after several hours, I became anxious with worry. When at last we heard

Mama's car pull up, Christopher and I ran to the front door. Grandma Gabby wasn't with her.

"I took her to the hospital over in Newell. She has pneumonia and needs to be there where they can watch over her." She looked drained, Mama did. She was pale and fragile appearing, like a flower past its prime. She told us if Gabby had to stay more than a couple of days she would take us to visit her.

Mama couldn't miss work no matter how tired she was. While we ate bowls of vegetable soup at the table, she stood in our warm kitchen and laid down the law. We were not to go outside after she left for work. Under no circumstances were we to let anyone in the door. In fact, she said, we shouldn't even open the door. Stay inside, clean the kitchen, watch TV, and go to bed at the regular time. Call her at work if we had an emergency. We were old enough to learn to be alone for a while. She peered intently at us, searching our faces to be sure we were listening.

It shouldn't have been such a big deal to leave us home alone. I knew plenty of kids my age who stayed home by themselves all the time. I was fine, and liked the independence of it right away, but Christopher, ever the worrier, wasn't happy about it at all.

"So, what kind of emergency would we call her for?" Christopher asked after she'd left.

Exasperated, I said "I don't know, Christopher. Maybe if I cut my finger off or one of us broke a leg. You know, something serious."

"You don't have to get smart, Donna Jean. I just wondered."

I felt bad for talking to him that way, so I got us both some Neapolitan ice cream from the freezer. That night he sat in my room while I watched out my window.

"Why do you look over there all the time?"

At first I didn't know how to answer. Why did I?

"I don't know, Christopher. It's such an odd place, you know? It's the kind of place where odd stuff happens."

"Like bad stuff?"

"Maybe. Maybe like bad stuff."

On Saturday, Mama drove us to be with Grandma Gabby in the hospital. The town of Newell was fifty miles away, and it was on that part of the highway where Daddy had been killed. I didn't know where the accident had happened. As we drove along I would think, maybe here, or here, or here. I didn't dare ask Mama if she knew.

I was stunned when I saw Gabby lying in the big, cold-looking bed. I looked to Mama, whose face was stony. It was difficult to believe the person I was seeing was our Grandma Gabby. I wondered how she became so frail looking so quickly. She was slight, and her skin was the color of mourning dove feathers. Without her short, silver hair waved into soft curls, it laid against her skull making her head appear too small. There was plastic sheeting draped high over the head of her bed. Mama said it was an oxygen tent. The nurses closed it, and blew oxygen from a machine into it when Grandma Gabby's breathing became labored.

"Mother." Mama bent close and spoke to her. "The kids and I came to visit you. Are you awake?" I stared. I couldn't tear my eyes away from her. Christopher began to cry a soft sob.

"Is she dead?" he asked in a hoarse whisper.

"No, Christopher," Mama said. "Of course not. She's only sleeping. Here, come hold her hand." She guided his hand to Gabby's and he held it as if it might fall apart.

Grandma Gabby opened her eyes, closed them, and opened them again. She tried to find us without moving her head. Her blue eyes rolled around, looking far too huge for her face. Her mouth moved as if to speak but no sound came. I moved around the bed and took her other hand. I felt her cool, dry fingers close softly on mine.

"Grandma Gabby. We came to see you," I said. "We miss you at home. You have to hurry and get well."

The slightest smile turned up the corners of her mouth. Someone else might not have even noticed it, but I did.

"Love you all." She whispered it so quietly it was more the shape of the words than the sound of them. We sat for a while. A nurse came into the room and tried to be cheerful which I thought bad-mannered.

"How is Mrs. Shanks doing this afternoon?" she tittered. Her voice rang through our silence.

Hearing Grandma Gabby's other name spoken—Mrs. Shanks—sounded strange to me. I had not heard her last name in I didn't know how long. That moment was the first time in ages I'd thought of Gabby as her own person. It came to mind how I'd hardly thought of her as anyone but my grandmother. I had forgotten she was Grace Shanks.

We arrived back at the hospital the next day only to find Gabby looking the same. There was a glass of juice and a dish of tapioca pudding, missing only a bite or two, on her table. She was awake, but she still couldn't talk to us. When her doctor came into her room he greeted us with a stiff glance and asked to speak with Mama in the hallway. When Mama finally came back into the room, she was dabbing tears from her eyes. She gave us a smile that wasn't real, and hovered close to Grandma Gabby with us.

"Hi, Mother, we're back." She touched Grandma Gabby's face so gently with trembling fingers, and kept up a chat about the tapioca pudding and how she needed to try to eat something so she could get strong and come home. Christopher and I held tight, maybe too tight, to her hands. I wanted to lie next to her on the bed and hug her. I wanted to so badly my arms ached.

After a few minutes Mama said we should go so she could rest. Leaving her there alone was torture for Christopher and me. I was furious at Mama for making us leave. None of us spoke all the way back home. I sat at my window every night and looked over at the Wendell house. I wondered if children who were mistreated loved their families anyway. I thought of the night Wade and Melly had come, desperately looking for help for their mother, and concluded that, yes, they did love their families.

Gabby had been in the hospital for eight days. We tried to go to school but after a few days it became useless. Of course, Mama visited

Gabby every day. She brought back reports to share each afternoon, but there wasn't much to tell us. On a midweek evening she told us she had something to talk to us about. The doctor had told poor Mama that Gabby wasn't getting better and if she grew much weaker she wouldn't live. The news sucked the breath right out of me. How in the world could it be possible for Grandma Gabby to die? I refused to believe it.

"Well, the doctor is wrong," I said. "Gabby isn't going to die. We'll go tomorrow, Christopher, and talk to her."

Christopher stood and kicked the chair as hard as he could. It careened across the room, hitting the far wall and crashing to the floor. He whirled and stared at Mama and me as if daring us to say anything. He pounded upstairs and slammed his bedroom door. I had never before seen him show such anger. His actions sort of frightened me. It must have showed.

"It'll be okay, Donna. It's normal to be angry when we don't know what else to do. He'll get over it in a while."

He didn't, though. He was still angry and sullen when we drove to the hospital the next morning. There had been no question about us missing school. All the way there I silently practiced what I wanted to say to Grandma Gabby. I didn't want to cry and make her feel worse. When we entered her room and took our places, I reached to hold her hand. For the first time, her cool fingers clutched mine first. I felt them give the faintest squeeze. I looked quickly across the bed at Christopher. His eyes met mine. I saw her fingers entwined with his.

"Gabby," I said in as normal a voice as I could muster. "I have been thinking about this sickness, and I believe it is time you got back to being your old self. We need you to come home, Grandma Gabby. We can't do things right without you there. You should see the refrigerator! It is a mess." Mama let out a soft laugh behind me.

"Come home, Grandma Gabby and let us take care of you. You can watch As the World Turns and give us orders," Christopher said.

There it was. That tiny curve of her poor chapped lips. This time, we all saw it. Her eyelids twitched, fluttered a couple of times, and opened wide. Her mouth began to move as she formed words.

"Ellen," she rasped. "Are you taking care of these kids?"

The tears ran down Mama's cheeks. "I'm trying, Mother, but I really need your help. Donna is right. It's time for you to come home."

"I will," Gabby whispered and went back to sleep.

Raymond

That neighbor kid, Donna was her name, was really getting on his nerves. Every time he turned around, there she was, sticking her nose in his business. She was a pretty little thing, that was for sure, but she was getting in his way. The day he spotted her walking along Gibson Road by herself gave him the opportunity he needed.

He put his old car in reverse, and rolled along beside the girl as she hurried along. He was surprised, though, when she suddenly stopped and faced him. The kid had grit.

When she asked what he wanted, he decided he needed to spook her a little to get her to pay attention to what he was going to tell her. Her sassy attitude didn't sit well with him, so he flat out told her he wanted her to stay the hell away from his place and his family. Leave his kids alone. She sassed back some stuff about taking gifts to his kids and being nice to them or some such baloney. He felt his anger building like it did when anyone crossed him. She was a troublemaker, that one. He couldn't let it go. And he couldn't help but bring up the girl's mother. He definitely had a thing for that woman. When he asked about her, the kid wouldn't talk. Ellen. That was her name, Ellen.

By the time he had shifted gears and pulled away, the kid was scared to death and running for home. He laughed aloud through rotten teeth and headed on down the road. As he bumped along the road, he forgot about Donna and instead thought about her mother. He knew where Ellen worked. If he could get a few bucks from Twyla, he'd go have a couple of drinks there and maybe strike up a conversation.

Hell, she was a widow woman. That guy, Harvey or Harry or whatever his name was, came around to see her, but there was something fishy about the guy. He'd hang around Ellen like a hound dog for a week or so and then disappear. At first Raymond thought the little romance was over, but then here he'd come again and Ellen would act like a teenager cuz he showed up.

The night he went into the bar, he even combed his hair and pulled it back into a smooth braid and wore a clean shirt. He would be on his best behavior and have a conversation with Ellen. Maybe flirt a little. That would be easy. He'd imagined flirting with her a lot of times. In his imagination, she liked it and flirted back, smiling at him and touching his arm.

If his thoughts kept on coming, uninterrupted, he would get all hot and bothered and would really get going. There was a time or two when he couldn't control himself and imagined it all.

He'd sat at the bar and watched Ellen work. He liked seeing her smile and he could hear her voice when she spoke to the other customers. He finally caught her eye and motioned her over to him. He introduced himself. "I'm your neighbor across the road," he said. Oh yes. She'd seen him drive by many times.

"Well, I wanted to let you know if you ever need help, you know, like, a man to help do something, why, I'd be glad to come on over and help you out." He looked her straight in the eye when he said the last part. She looked right back, which got his attention and made him sit up straight.

"Why, thank you, Raymond," she said coyly. "That is really nice of you. I sure will remember that." But she had to get to work and that was the end of the conversation.

Raymond was pleased. If he could get a few extra bucks from Twyla, he sure enough would go back again. He could tell Ellen liked him.

When Raymond told Twyla he needed some money, she said they wouldn't have enough to get by as it was. Sometimes, if he spent too much, she couldn't stretch out their check from the state to buy food and a few things the kids might need. It made Raymond spitting mad. Them kids ate, didn't they? They had a roof over their heads. If other people wouldn't mind his business, they'd get along fine. It was always either the sheriffs or them people from CPS who come nosing around. They all made their big threats about taking the kids away. Sometimes Raymond thought that might be a good idea. But then they wouldn't get those checks anymore.

So, when Twyla said she couldn't give Raymond any money, he flew into an angry fit. He called Twyla all kinds of names and told her how worthless she was. When he saw tears shine in her eyes, he puffed up like a peacock. He liked it when he had the power. He'd teach her to never tell him no.

Twyla tried one more time to explain to him about feeding the kids, and that did it. He shoved her clear across the kitchen floor. Her feet tangled and down she fell, hitting her head with a thump on the edge of the counter. Raymond looked close at her lying there on the floor and thought he saw a little blood. He said her name, and then said it again, louder that time. She groaned and became silent. Raymond took off, planning not to come back home for a while.

He'd told his kids, and Twyla, too, never to call the sheriff's for anything. All it would do was cause trouble for them. He'd worked at convincing the two older kids that the law wasn't any good. Other people would make them think they were helping them, and then they would take them away and give them to someone else. He'd also told them to keep away from the neighbors over on Gibson Road. He said he didn't like that girl, Donna, coming around either. Later, when he found out they'd gone straight over there and blabbed his personal business, he was hotter than a firecracker. It turned out Twyla wasn't hurt bad after all. A few stitches and she was fine as could be. Raymond began hating nosy people more and more.

He went on a bender. He drank anything he could get his hands on and stayed drunk for a week. For some reason, he drug little Wade around with him everywhere he went.

"Get in the car, Wade. We'll go get the mail. Check should be here." And Wade did what he was told.

That's when he saw Donna on the road and as luck would have it she was right there by the mailbox. She'd crossed the road to the far side when she saw the old car coming up the lane, and kept walking toward home. At first she looked away but Raymond called out to her. He waited for her to finally look and then he drug himself from the car and leaned against the hood. He hollered over to her, said her friend Wade was in the car.

Later, when he remembered what he'd done, he was mad at himself. Not for doing those things, though. No, he was mad because he might have ruined any chance he had to get next to Donna's mother. It was Ellen he wanted to expose himself to.

CHAPTER NINE

Each time I saw Raymond Himes's old car go by our house I felt the same sick feeling that had taken me over on the day I saw him and little Wade out on Gibson Road. He always gawked at our house as he drove slowly by, not speeding up until he was well past our driveway. I hadn't been outdoors much since Grandma Gabby had been sick, so I hadn't come face-to-face with Raymond or any of the kids. I still couldn't get over the nasty, nauseating image I had of him imprinted on my mind.

Wind and rainstorms were lined up, coming one after another. In fact, it was raining cats and dogs the day Grandma Gabby came home. Weak as a cat and pale as its cream, she had insisted on getting dressed in nice clothes and "'proper'" shoes to come home in. In spite of her resilient spirit, she gave in and sank into her own cozy chair in the living room and heaved a deep sigh of contentment. She remained unusually quiet. She looked around the room as if she was inspecting it.

We were quiet, too. We had worked hard to be sure things were orderly, and the kitchen spotless for her homecoming. I guess we were waiting for her approval. Mama brought her tea and I tucked a warm, soft afghan across her lap. When she smiled at us and said thank you, my heart swelled in my chest. I believe we were all so relieved we felt practically giddy with the joy of having her back home. Christopher had made her a welcome home card that said "We have mist you so much," and it made her laugh. He blushed over his silly mistake and she assured him it was the best card she'd ever received.

We waited on her, scrambling to meet her needs, for several days. Mama napped when Grandma Gabby did, and Christopher and I had to get back to school. In the evenings we fell back into the routine of early suppers so Mama could go to work. Gabby turned in early while Christopher and I cleaned the kitchen.

Mama was tired. On stormy mornings she got up to take us to the school bus, took care of Grandma Gabby's needs and napped until time to make supper. We helped with all we could. By that time, I could make a pretty good meal by myself because Grandma Gabby had taught me a lot about cooking. Mama shopped on Saturdays while Christopher or I stayed home. Our routine worked well and Grandma Gabby was finally getting stronger. I saw a twinkle in her eyes again.

We began to have power outages when the wind furiously blew across the wide-open land around us. I would watch the slack wires whipping back and forth between the power poles. Phone service came and went. I worried about the kids in the Wendell house. I wondered if they were cold and afraid of the dark. I doubted they would be prepared for either. I pictured poor little Jefferson, and baby Leland in wet, stinking diapers, in some dark, upstairs room. What if they cried because the wind frightened them, and it was so dark, and no one came to comfort them?

Some of the weakened elms along the puddled lane uprooted from the saturated ground and fell into the field. Trash and pieces of broken plastic toys were carried away. I worried about the old barn, my decrepit old refuge. Every morning as soon as I arose, I checked the Wendell house and eyed the barn carefully to be sure it was all intact.

Raymond still rumbled by in his beat-up car. I wondered if he knew I was watching, and slowed to mock me. Sometimes I was sure he looked upward, directly at my window, as if he knew which room was mine.

On a Friday night when Mama got home from work, she told us Raymond had stopped by Goldie's again. He hadn't said much but she had been busy and didn't have time to stop and chat. He'd had a few beers at the bar and left. It was barely after midnight, after counting Mama's tips, and we were all getting ready for bed when a car drove by. Of course we looked to see who in the world it would be at that time of night. Mama said it was probably kids, up to no good, but we saw it was a sheriff's car and it turned into the lane. Up the stairs we clamored like a bunch of Nosy-Rosies. There wasn't much to observe through the dark, but the sheriff's car stayed for a long time.

When we told Grandma Gabby the next morning, I plainly saw her old determination.

"I believe it is time for another trip to the sheriff's office. What do you think, Donna Jean?"

"Yes, ma'am," Deputy Wilkes said. "We went out to the Himes's place to do a welfare check on the kids. Children's Services had asked us to go there after they received a call from a concerned friend." He shuffled around for a report and opened the file folder. "Says right here, the kids were all in beds and sleeping when the deputies entered the house." He read to himself for a moment. "Says, the house was cluttered and the bedroom where the children were had a strong stench of urine . . ." He paused and read again. The subject changed. "Says the mother, Twyla, was quiet and cooperative, but Raymond was defiant and argued over letting the deputies have access to the upstairs floor where the children were. When he was told he would be arrested if he didn't comply, he gave in."

"This deputy's personal note here says he himself is the father of small children, and in his view, the Himes's children, even in their sleepy stage, did not look healthy or well taken care of."

"So, what does it all mean?" Gabby asked. "What happens next?"

"I don't know. This is a report that goes over to Children's Services. If they decide to take kids from their homes, they call us to assist. I am sorry I don't know any more to tell you. Do you have anything to report?"

I knew this was my opportunity to tell about the day Raymond talked to me from his car as I walked along Gibson Road, and more recently, those nasty things he said and did when I saw him at the lane, and with little Wade sitting right there in the car. By the time we left the office that day, I hated myself for not speaking up.

After we got home, Grandma Gabby perched on a stool by the wall phone in the kitchen and called Children's Services. She had a notepad and pencil at hand. I sat at the kitchen table, waiting. When she was finally speaking with someone who was in contact with the Pickering Sheriff's Office, the conversation was short. They had nothing helpful to tell her. They would be happy to take any information about children who might be in harm's way, but they would not give out any reports because it was a privacy matter. Again, guilt burned inside me.

"Don't fret, Donna. We will keep our eyes and ears open. If we are meant to help those kids over there, we will get our chance."

Harry had been absent for a while. Mama mentioned him from time to time, always singing his praises and explaining why he hadn't come around. He was doing what salesmen do. He traveled around the county and, in fact, any northern part of the state where there was mining going on, selling the tools of the trade.

I didn't hate Harry, but I couldn't decide if I liked him or not. He had definitely won Christopher over. Gabby told me more than once that Christopher needed a man in his life, but I still worried about their relationship. When Harry started coming around again, I noticed his attempts to befriend me. He asked me questions about school and books and friends. Because the subject had become household conversation, we even talked a little about the Himes family and the kids. It became harder and harder not to like him.

He had supper with us often and left when Mama had to go to work. Sometimes I was embarrassed because of the way she flirted with him. They held hands a lot and it made me squirm. I figured they probably kissed like the people on television, but I didn't want to see it. High school girls did those things with their boyfriends, but not moms.

On a chilly but sunny day, Harry came and Gabby packed a lunch and we all drove to the river for the afternoon. We walked the rocky banks and dug around in the sand to see who could find the prettiest or most unusual looking stones. That was the first time since Daddy had died more than two years before that my family had fun together doing something outdoors.

When we got back home and pulled up to our house, Raymond came driving by in his noisy jalopy. I saw Harry turn to watch him as he slow-poked past us. Raymond made no bones about staring directly back at him. I knew they looked eye-to-eye, and Harry's expression turned to a serious frown. Raymond drove so slow his car barely crept along. He was taunting Harry. Once inside our house, Harry asked questions about Raymond.

"What do y'all know about that guy? Does he drive around all day?"

"Not much. Other than he is creepy and dirty." Gabby's ire was raised quickly. Her words came clipped and angry. "Has a wife and four kids over there. I don't know what they live on. I'm darn sure he doesn't hold a job.'"

Harry looked at Mama and Gabby. "I don't much like the way he acts when he comes by here. With y'all out here by yourselves. I could talk to him if you want me to."

77

"I don't want you to get involved with him, Harry," Mama said. "Besides, I doubt he's dangerous."

Oh, how I wanted to say something. Anything. But I sat in silence, keeping all my thoughts to myself. What could I say? How I thought Raymond was more than creepy? That I felt threatened by him? How could I explain all of it? With Harry there, I would die before I told them how something dirty and disgusting had passed between Raymond and me.

"They must live on some sort of county assistance if they aren't working," Harry said.

"It could be that somebody helps them out," Gabby said. "Children's Services said they have reports from a 'friend' about the welfare of those kids. Maybe it's a relative of Twyla's, since someone also called the sheriff's to report her getting beat up. Somebody knows things about them."

"Taking children from their mothers is one of the hardest things to do. The court is always on the mother's side. The kids never get to have a say until it's too late." He seemed to care about Raymond and Twyla's kids. I wondered what he meant by "'too late.'"

Harry frowned. "I'd sure like to have a talk with old Raymond. I sense he's trouble."

Something about the fact that Harry understood how Raymond might be a genuinely dangerous person made me feel better, safer maybe. I don't know.

Raymond

Raymond was good at collecting people like himself. Who knows where he met them. Maybe a bar or a gas station. Some pit hole. His kind seemed so easily drawn to one another. They were rough and irresponsible, like him. They liked going to the old house out on Gibson

Road. They could do whatever they wanted out there and nobody bothered 'em about it. They cooked slabs of greasy meat on a makeshift grill, and target practiced with various rifles and pistols, most stolen at some point. They made targets and blasted away until their ammo was used up. They whooped and hollered until they eventually passed out or drove home.

Twyla would be frantic as she tried to keep the kids away from Raymond and his foul friends. If one of them kids even came outdoors, he would rave at 'em, belittle 'em, and send 'em back in the house. Twyla would pay later for not controlling her kids.

Raymond didn't keep his friends for long. He was still the same bully he always was. Maybe even worse. He seemed to enjoy nothing more than making fun of someone or even threatening them with some sort of harm. He wasn't cruel to Twyla and his kids. They just needed to learn how to act.

He drank every day until the money ran out and then he would rage against his family because they'd wasted his liquor money.

"It's your fault we have all these damn kids," he would holler at Twyla. "I didn't want them little moochers in the first place. What are you all gonna do if I up and leave you out here in this Godforsaken place? You're so dumb you'd all starve to death."

And Twyla would hunker over and cry her heart out because she believed him. He was right. What would she do? She would have no money and nowhere to go and no way to get anywhere. One night after a nasty fight, Twyla took Wade and Melly outside and whispered to them furtively that if she ever got hurt or wasn't able to protect them, they should run fast over to the house on Gibson Road and ask for help.

"Papa told us never to go there," Wade said in a worried voice.

"Well, this time you have to listen to me, Wade. Promise?" The most she could get back was a tiny nod.

CHAPTER TEN

It was at least a week later that I saw the kids. It was sunny out and warmer than it had been in several days. I had started out to walk across the road to the barn and as I stepped out onto the front porch, I saw them come from the lane and walk side by side along the edge of the road. They looked little and bedraggled. I crossed the pavement and walked to meet them.

"What are you two doing way out here?" I asked.

Wade and Melly looked to each other and Melly answered.

"Our mama is sick today." Wade nodded in agreement.

"Does she need help?" I asked.

"I think so," Melly said and Wade nodded again. "Can you come to our house?" She fidgeted a little, shuffling her sandals in the gravel.

"I don't know, Melly. Maybe I should go call someone to help. Do you know someone who would come and help? Is your father gone?"

"He left," Wade spoke up. "He left yesterday."

"Where did he go?"

Wade shrugged, but Melly said, "He went to Oklahoma. He told Mama he ain't coming back."

"You really heard him say that? Did he take anything with him like clothes and things?"

They both shook their heads no. So, there I was again. In a position I didn't know what to do about. Grandma Gabby and Christopher had gone into town and Mama was sleeping.

"How about you two come to my house first and I'll try to help you, okay?"

They both nodded and we turned back, walking together on the gravel shoulder. I already knew I was going to call the sheriff's office. When we entered the house, they went right over and sat on our couch where they had the first time they came. They never said a word.

From the kitchen stool, I called the number on the list. I expected Alice to answer, but it was Deputy Wilkes. I told him who I was.

"Hey, Donna Jean. Everything okay out there?"

"The kids are here again. They said their mom is sick and their father went to Oklahoma."

"Oh boy. I'll be there as soon as I can. Are you home alone?"

I explained that Gabby was in town and Mama was sleeping, and I wasn't supposed to wake her unless it was an emergency because she had to go to work later. I heard him huff into the phone. My reasoning must have sounded ridiculous to him.

I returned to the living room with cookies, and turned the TV on and the volume low. The kids' eyes got big as they watched a cartoon brighten the screen. They were awed. I watched them silently until Deputy Wilkes came. I noticed Wade had on a different pair of shoes. They were worn but they were in one piece and the laces were tied. The skinned place on Melly's knee was pink and smooth with the scab gone. Their hair was tangled and wild but didn't appear as dirty as it had last time I saw them.

When I heard the sheriff's car pull into the driveway, I hurried to meet Deputy Wilkes at the door. He motioned me to step out on the porch and pulled the door closed behind me.

"I've called Children's Services. They weren't happy to get my call on a Saturday, but someone is on their way here this time. It will be an hour or so before they can get here. If the kids can stay with you for now, I will head over to the house and find out what's going on with Twyla." He stepped off the porch, stopped, and turned to me. I'll never forget how he said so kindly, "You did the right thing, Donna."

The kids ate cookies and watched television. They didn't even ask any questions about what might happen. I felt nervous for them. I had wanted them taken from their parents, but I wondered if it was for their own sake, or because I thought their awful mother and father should be punished for not taking better care of them. I could hardly look at them there across the room with their little pale faces and dark places below those clear blue eyes. They were so innocent.

Deputy Wilkes, along with a man and woman from Children's Services, came to the door. The lady spoke quietly. She said they would be taking the children, all four, with them. Their mother was sick and their father was away from home and the kids needed help and care. As I turned to go back inside to get Wade and Melly, Grandma Gabby drove up and hurried across the lawn to the porch. When I looked at her and she looked back with question in her eyes, I began to cry.

The kids came out to see what was going on. The man and woman took them aside and talked with them for a time. I saw that Melly did the talking and Wade did the nodding. Deputy Wilkes was explaining everything to Gabby. I sat in a porch chair and felt sick.

When they had all driven away to the Wendell house, Gabby took my hand and led me into the kitchen where she set a glass of milk in front of me and gave me tissues for my tears and runny nose.

"Remember, we told you it might happen like this," she said. "The kids will go to a foster home, or homes, for now. The deputy said Twyla is pretty ill. May be only the flu, but she can't take care of the kids and doesn't know where Raymond is or when he'll return. The babies were wet and hungry and there is very little food in the house." She stood to peer out the kitchen window. "They are going there to gather them up now."

Mama came into the kitchen. One look at Gabby and me was all it took to know something upsetting had happened. I told her about finding the kids walking along the road and that's where Gabby took over and told the rest.

CHAPTER ELEVEN

I sat out on the front porch until I saw them drive by. Blonde curls bobbed in the back seat and one small hand reached to wave to me. I struggled to yank my hand from my pocket to wave back, but it wouldn't come fast enough. I was sure the wave I saw was from Wade, and now he would leave thinking I didn't wave back. As I watched the car disappear down the road, a huge sob broke from my chest.

I sat for a while, thinking how scared and confused they must be. Guilt was overwhelming and made my insides churn. I wondered if I would ever see them again. And Twyla. I pictured her over in that dirty old house, sick and miserable. I knew she had no phone to call for help and most likely no food either.

Our own supper was dismal. I finally excused myself and went to my room. I sat at the window and stared over at the Wendell house. As dark fell, there were no window lights to be seen. I imagined Twyla lying in a rumpled bed, probably wishing she could die of whatever malady she had.

As I crawled into my own warm, clean bed that night, I reminded myself of the kind words Deputy Wilkes had said to me. I had to believe he was right.

When I awoke Sunday morning, all the events of Saturday came flooding back, drowning me in guilt and causing my heart to weigh heavy. Already, I was wondering what I could do to make things better. I knew there must be something. Twyla was the only one left to be helped. Maybe she was feeling better and needed food. Maybe she was worse and needed a doctor. By the time I hurried down the stairs and into the kitchen, I had a plan. Other than a few fibs and a couple of lies-by-omission to keep myself out of trouble, I had never intentionally lied to Grandma Gabby or Mama. By morning, I was prepared.

After quickly wrapping up two biscuits and grabbing an orange from the refrigerator, I stuffed them in my coat pockets and called over my shoulder that I was going to the barn. I didn't wait for an answer. Across the road I entered the big barn door and made my way through the dust motes and sun shafts to the back corner where there was a man-door. The rickety door hung crooked from its rusty hinges, a corner dragging the ground. I lifted and pushed my shoulder against it until I could squeeze through. I made my way to the end of the high outside wall. As I stood there, measuring the distance to the shed next to the Wendell house, I saw something that puzzled me. On the ground was a mound of cigarette butts that had been snuffed with someone's boot. They had no filters and had been crushed with treaded soles. It was obvious some had been rain-soaked. There were dozens. My first reaction had been anger, because it would be so easy for a careless smoker to burn the old barn to the ground, and besides, whoever left them was definitely trespassing. But, I was curious. Why would they be there at all?

I put the find out of my mind for the time being to get on with my plan. I knew I would be visible from areas in our house, so I had to take a chance. I ran like a deer, straight toward the shed. The ground was bumpy, rutted, and I almost fell several times. As soon as I reached the big oak beside the shed, I leaned against the trunk and caught my breath. I stared over at the front porch of the house for a moment, took in a big gulp of air, and went to the door. I knocked. It was quiet and still out there on the porch. I knocked again and waited. Finally, I heard a sound. I knew Twyla must have still been sick and she had a grating cough. I knocked one more time.

"Who is it?" Her voice was hoarse.

"It's me, Twyla, Donna Jean from across the road."

"Go away. I'm sick"

"I know. That's why I came. I brought you something." There was a long pause.

"Trouble? That what you brought?" She was closer to the door.

"No. I brought . . ."

The door swung open and there was poor Twyla. She wore a dirty blue robe, and filthy, sloppy slippers. Her hair hung in oily strands and she was pale as a ghost. She hacked up the rattle in her throat. I tugged the biscuits and the orange from my pockets.

"Here," I offered. "I brought you these. Have you eaten?"

She took them from my hands, and this time she looked me in the eye. I knew she was hungry.

"I had soup yesterday. Or maybe it was the day before." Tears welled in her eyes. "They took my kids. People shouldn't be able to come and take my kids," she wept.

"Maybe when you get well they can come back," I said.

Twyla stepped back and said, "You may as well come in. I don't much care if you do or don't."

I should have been prepared, but I was far from it. Everything was a shambles. The linoleum was worn and covered with filth. Cupboard doors were missing and the ones remaining were greasy and black around the knobs. The sink and drain board had dirty dishes crusted with dried food and stacked high. A garbage can overflowed and the stench from it was almost unbearable. I swallowed quickly so as not to gag. I didn't even try to stop my next words.

"Oh, Twyla. How can you live like this?"

She didn't show any offense at all. She looked around as if seeing what I was seeing. Finally she shrugged.

"I don't know. I didn't always. When Wade and Melly were little I kept things nice. By the time Jeffy came along Raymond was turning mean as a snake and I cared less and less about things. We have moved so many times." She sighed and shook her head. "Something happened to me. I don't know what. My sister tried to get me some help, mentally that is, but Raymond wouldn't let her." She pulled out a kitchen chair and dropped onto it. "I'm too weak to stand."

"Did you tell the people from Children's Services this?"

"They don't give a hoot. Alls they care about is how it looks now." Tears wet her cheeks. "I love them kids with all my heart, but maybe I ain't supposed to be their mother."

"Is Raymond coming back? What if you got better and cleaned all this up?" I looked around and wondered what the rest of the house looked like.

"He's always come back before. I don't much care. With my kids gone, I got nothin' to live for."

I struggled to come up with something nice or helpful to say. I was wishing I had Grandma Gabby Gabby's advice. She always knew the right thing to say or do. I must have been quiet too long.

"Don't fret. Ain't nothin' you can do. I know you people mean well, but all y'all do is aggravate Raymond. He don't want nobody in our business. I can't even see my own sister anymore. Last time she came, Raymond beat me pretty bad before she left. Any little thing he don't like, he takes it out on me."

"I'm real sorry, Twyla. I wish I could help. I'll try to bring more food over for you. Maybe you should eat and rest." I left her sitting in her chair while I let myself out. I gulped the fresh air as I stood for a moment and looked around the place. I guess I was too young to realize what it would take to put the house in decent order. I merely wanted it to happen.

I headed back to the barn, but this time I didn't feel it necessary to rush. Maybe because I knew I would have to tell Mama and Gabby the situation, and it meant admitting to being at Twyla's. I stopped and looked again at the pile of cigarette butts. I squeezed back through the door and climbed to the loft. It was a place where I did my best reasoning. I sat on a burlap sack and looked through the hay door at my own house. There it was, so neat and tidy, and I knew how clean it was inside. I thought how the Himes kids should have a home like ours. Maybe I didn't have a father anymore, but I had a good place to live and people who loved me.

I dreaded having to tell on myself. If I came right out and told it all, Mama and Gabby would have to know that sneaking food was part of the plan to go to the Wendell house. I sat there in the barn and worried over the words I might use to explain it all.

There I sat, at the kitchen table. The place where the truths came out and the important discussions took place. Gabby's hands cupped her warm mug, and I nervously swung one foot back and forth. Christopher had sat with us, and even though I knew he was only being nosy, it was good to have him there.

"Whatever are we going to do with you, Donna Jean? You go off and do these things on your own, and anything could happen. I don't care a whit about the food. What if Raymond had been there, or what if Twyla had passed?" Gabby had listened to me tell what had happened without any interruption. Now it was her turn.

I had to be careful of sounding sassy, but I would never have entered her house if Twyla hadn't come to the door. I wouldn't have been the one to find her lifeless. At least, I couldn't imagine I would have. I couldn't visualize the horror of finding a dead person. Seeing the hanging dummy that day had been enough to terrify me.

"You're fourteen years old, Donna. You might be too young to know the consequences of your actions, but you are old enough to stop and think about what you do. And I trust you know right from wrong. You'll have to tell your mother, you know."

I did know, but disappointing Gabby made me sorrier than anything. Christopher had sat through the entire conversation without saying a word, which was extraordinary for him.

"Maybe Mama won't be mad," he said. "She'll know you were trying to help Twyla. Anyway, don't feel bad about being nice, Donna."

Gabby let out a big sigh and smiled at Christopher. "He's right, of course. Your kindness is a good quality, Donna. It's your safety I worry about." She rose from the table. "Now, let's get a package fixed up to take to Twyla. I have medicine left from when I had pneumonia and some cough syrup. We have aspirin. Let me see what I can put together for her to eat. We can't leave her to starve over there."

I stood and hugged Gabby as tight as I could. She was the kindest, smartest woman I knew.

CHAPTER TWELVE

Mama wanted to go along when we took the supplies over to Twyla. I wanted to keep it all between Gabby and me, but I knew it would hurt Mama to know that. Thing was, I thought she was being more nosey than caring. Little by little, Mama had developed an aloofness about a lot of things after Daddy died. Except for the girlish affections she sometimes showed for Harry, her emotions remained flat and worn-out around us kids.

My nerves were buzzing when we stood at Twyla's front door. I knocked. The three of us stood in an awkward row on the collapsing porch and waited. I couldn't imagine that Twyla would invite all three of us into the house. Gabby slipped an arm around my shoulders and gave a little squeeze. Mama had an ear cocked, waiting to hear footsteps. Finally, Twyla came, not coughing this time, but looking the same.

"Can we come in, Twyla? We brought you some things we thought you would need," I said.

She didn't speak but turned away, leaving the door wide open. We followed single file into the kitchen. I avoided looking at Gabby and Mama. I didn't want to read their reactions to the mess and stench surrounding us. We set the things we had brought with us on the dirty, stained tabletop. A plate of biscuits, a cube of oleo, some canned soup and saltine crackers. Oranges, apples and the grape juice Christopher had so generously given up.

"We can't leave you over here to starve," Gabby said. "This will get you by for a while. If it's all right, we will check in on you from time to time. There's some medicine here. Follow the directions. Can't hurt you any."

Twyla finally spoke. "I wouldn't ask if it wasn't plumb necessary. I was wondering if you could call my sister and tell her I need her to come. I don't know what else to do." She pulled a smudged and tattered envelope from her robe pocket. It had the name Rosalie, and a phone number scrawled on the back. "Be sure to tell her Raymond ain't here. She won't come if she reckons he is." I couldn't help but wonder why she carried her sister's number in her pocket. She had no phone.

Mama had stood away, arms crossed tight across her thin ribcage. She glanced toward the door several times. I could read her thoughts by her expression. She wanted to bolt outside without touching anything.

Gabby asked if there was anything else we could bring over and Twyla shook her head. "Just call Rosalie for me," she said.

When we all climbed back in the car, Christopher pinched his nose. "You guys smell," he said.

"Lord. I'm sure we do," Mama said. "It smells like a garbage pit in there. I can't believe she lives in such a mess."

"Well, what would you have her do?" Gabby sounded miffed.

"I don't know, Mother, but I'm sure I would just die."

"My guess is she thought she might die in there. Alone. That's why she had her sister's phone number right there in her pocket. It was there so somebody would call her if they found Twyla dead. The woman is living a nightmare."

Christopher lowered his window. I wished the bad smell and the sick feeling in my stomach would blow away.

Grandma Gabby sat on the stool by the phone. She talked to a long distance operator and the call was put through.

"May I speak with Rosalie? Yes, I'll wait."

"Rosalie? This is Grace Shanks. I live across the road from your sister, Twyla."

"Yes. That's right. We've come from your sister's house. She asked us to call you and say she needs you to come here, to her place, that is."

"No. She's not good. The kids were taken from her by Children's Services. Raymond is gone. He left a few days ago. She says he is in Oklahoma and said he wasn't coming back."

"I don't know about that. Twyla is awfully sick. We took her some food and medicine, but she should be seeing a doctor."

"That would be good. We'll let her know you're coming. I know it will help her. She's in a real bad way, Rosalie."

"Okay. Thank you. Good bye."

CHAPTER THIRTEEN

We all pitched in, except Mama. We lugged Gabby's Electrolux, brooms, mops, rags, and enough Lysol to kill every germ in the Wendell house, up the rickety porch steps. Rosalie and her husband Herb were robust folks, determined, and they both worked tirelessly. The upstairs rooms were dark and dirty, and the smell made my eyes water. Curtains were opened or taken away, and windows were raised to let in light and fresh air. The kids' beds were dreadful enough to make me weep for each of them. No wonder. No wonder those kids were taken away. The guilt I'd felt for being a part of the reason they'd been taken away began to lessen. They deserved better.

It took all five of us two long days to put the house in decent order. It was in need of many repairs and new, clean paint. I wished we could do it all. Gabby took loads of filthy sheets, towels and children's clothes to our house and washed them in our automatic washer with Borax and bleach.

After the previous short discussion with Rosalie, we had all agreed getting Twyla's kids back home was the goal, and exhausted as I was, my heart was singing at the end of the second day of cleaning. Rosalie and Herman went shopping for Twyla, stocking a clean refrigerator and kitchen cupboards. Twyla was still weak with illness, but she did what she could and more than a few times I saw tears in her eyes.

"How could I have let this happen?" I heard her say to Rosalie. "Our mama would die of shame if she'd seen how I've been living."

"You know Raymond will be back, Twyla. He is no good for you or the kids. You have to decide what you are going to do about him."

"I have no money, Rosie. I'll get assistance from the county for the kids when they come home, but there ain't any extra."

"We'll get you a phone installed before we leave here and pay the rent through next month. But, Twyla, you know you have to decide what you are going to do whether you get those kids back or not. We're not rich either, honey. You might have to move somewhere and get a job. You have to get yourself strong again. Like you used to be."

"I know," Twyla said. But she put her head on her arms and cried. Grandma Gabby and I looked away from her sadness.

After Twyla's phone was installed, we didn't go back to the Wendell house for several days. We were all so wrung out. Christopher and I had to go to school and Mama, of course, had to work. We needed a break from all the emotion that had taken us over. In the evenings I continued to watch diligently from my post upstairs. I saw a car leave Twyla's one day. A nice, late-model car. I thought sure it was someone from Children's Services. I ran downstairs to tell Grandma Gabby.

"Maybe so," she said. "We'll have to wait and see if Twyla tells us. Just because you help someone out, doesn't mean they owe it to you to tell you what goes on in their life."

I couldn't stand not knowing what was going on at the Wendell house. By the time Saturday rolled around, I had talked Gabby into letting me go check on Twyla. When I headed there, I had a sack full of food and a pretty flannel nightgown to take for Twyla. After she let me in, I handed her the sack, and when she saw what was in it, she put her hand over her mouth and gawked at me. You would have thought we gave her a million bucks.

"I don't know why you folks are so good to me. I don't deserve all this," Twyla said.

"Sure you do. Everybody has to eat. Besides, it's my Grandma Gabby who thinks to do this kind of stuff. I guess I'm learning from her. It makes me feel good when I help somebody out. Doesn't it you?" I asked.

"I reckon it would if I was ever in the position to do so. Maybe I will be someday." Twyla gazed off as if looking far ahead in time.

"You will. And you'll like it, too."

We sat at the kitchen table with its red-checkered tablecloth and I looked around, happy to see everything still looked neat and clean. I said what I was thinking to Twyla.

"Well, it's easy with me bein' here by myself."

"Have you heard anything about the kids? Do you think they'll be coming home anytime soon?" I had to ask.

"The people from Children's Services were here a few days ago. They were real surprised when they saw the place. They said they'd be back in a couple of weeks to check on me again and then we could talk about my kids' future. They said they're doin' fine. That was about all I could get out of 'em."

"I bet they'll be back soon. I know they are missing you, Twyla." I shouldn't have said it, because tears streamed again.

After a few minutes, she took a great big breath and said, "You people will think I'm crazy, but once in a while I wish Raymond would come back home. I know it sounds awful, and I know I said I feared him comin' back, but I have been with him since I was a kid myself, and it seems like he should be here. I want him here, but I want him different, know what I mean?" She paused, looking away again. "I'm sorry. I shouldn't bother you with that kind of stuff."

I saw a flash of Raymond, weaving drunkenly, standing against his old car and reaching for his zipper. I saw the spittle fly from his dirty mouth. I felt my stomach turn. I wanted to beg Twyla to never take him back.

"I don't think it would be a good thing for you to take him back, Twyla. He isn't a good person in a lot of ways." That was the closest I could get to telling on him.

"He's always had a mean streak. Even when we were kids. He bullied people to get his way. I wasn't a smart girl like you, Donna. I didn't know he was gonna treat me the same way he treated all them others."

I couldn't come up with anything helpful to say so I changed the subject. "Have you used your new phone, Twyla?" I asked.

I got a weak smile. "Rosalie called. Scared the wits out of me when the phone rang. We never had a telephone but once a long time ago. They're coming back to help me clean up the outside. I'll be able to do more this time since I ain't so sick now. "

I told Twyla I had to get back home and to be sure to call us if she needed something before Rosalie and Herb came. She thanked me all the way out the door. I wondered if her life would ever really be better.

Harry came that day. Mama arose early. We sat around the table eating lunch and talked about Twyla's situation. Harry shared strong opinions about Raymond and how worthless he was, and how he harmed his children by being so. He talked a lot about how kids learned about life from watching how the grown-ups around them behaved. I listened and wondered how he knew so much about kids. While he expressed his ideas in that deep voice of his, little instances from my own past flared clearly in my mind. Daddy came into my thoughts in flashes of sweet memories.

"Those kids need someone they can admire for good reasons, not bad ones," Harry said. "They are too little to know the difference. Little Wade, he's a sensitive boy who needs a strong man around. Melly might be okay. She's the tough one."

Gabby agreed. "Melly will be nobody's fool. Kids like her muddle through somehow. They seem to be born with a sense of what is right."

"What about the babies?" I asked. "I worry about Jeffy. He's already taking care of his baby brother. He's barely four and if it weren't for him, what would happen to Leland?"

Gabby shook her head. "Maybe Twyla will get some kind of counseling about that sort of thing. She's let those kids take care of themselves for too long."

Mama had been nibbling her lunch and listening quietly. She put her unfinished sandwich on her plate and looked at us all. I heard an edge in her voice when she spoke.

"I'm a bit weary of everybody feeling so sorry for Twyla. Far as I am concerned, she's about the same as Raymond. She should have been taking care of her own kids like a mother instead of living under Raymond's thumb. She has some kind of mental issues."

"Like you did." I said it too loud and I heard my own sarcasm. I froze. Right then and there. I desperately wished I could take those words back. My face and neck burned and I couldn't raise my eyes to meet anyone's. I knew Mama was looking at me, though, because I could sense it. I was sorry, but more for the probable consequences than for the words I'd spoken. The silence was long.

"Go to your room, Donna Jean. Now. I'll be there in a minute." Mama's tone was flat and hard.

"Ellen . . ." Harry started to speak, but Mama gave him a look that shushed him. Mama could shush the whole world with her look.

I pushed my chair back and stood. Suddenly, I was so angry I couldn't control myself. I began to tremble all over. I felt a hate so strong it caused a physical pain in my chest.

"I don't care what you do to me. It's true. Since the day Daddy died, you've had mental issues yourself. You quit being our mom that day and you never came back. If we didn't have Grandma Gabby to love us and care for us, we would have been no different than Twyla's kids. You sure don't care anymore." I heard myself practically hollering. "It's true, Mama, and you know it. You went away from us when we needed you most." I had to stop because I ran out of breath.

Gabby stood and took me by the arm in a firm grip. "Donna! Stop. Don't speak to your mother that way. You're being disrespectful."

"I don't care," I declared. "I don't care anymore what she thinks." And I fled upstairs. I didn't care. Not a single bit, and on top of that, I was mad at Gabby for taking Mama's side. I sat at my desk and opened my drawing pad. I drew fast in big hard lines. Thick and dark. I flipped to the next page and the next. They were all terrible drawings, but each one looked like who it portrayed. Gabby with a frown, lips drooped at the corners, eyes sad, and brows low. Harry, square-jawed, dark-haired, peering straight off the page. And Mama, with no face at all.

I lay my head on my arms and closed my eyes. I knew someone would be thumping up the stairs soon. Mama, I guessed, but maybe Gabby. I didn't cry, which surprised even myself. In fact, I felt weightless in a way. All that dire emotion had vaporized into midair. My insides were still, quiet, and it felt good.

I heard the front door close and I looked out my window to see if Harry was leaving. I would not have blamed him. When I looked over the sill I saw he and Mama were walking side by side out into the yard.

Mama's arms were crossed tight and Harry's hands were deep in his pockets. I wanted badly to raise my window so I could catch some of their words, but I was afraid they would hear it slide in its frame. I had to be satisfied with watching their body language. It was easy to read. Mama was angry. When the two of them stopped and faced each other, she looked into his face. She was talking fast and at one point she flung her arm out, pointing back toward the house. She shook her head a lot. Harry straightened his back and crossed his arms, too. Next it was him talking and shaking his head. Mama stepped back and put her hands on her hips. While she was carrying on, Harry fumbled around and lit a cigarette. He looked up, and right into my window. I didn't try to hide. I knew they were fighting over me, or at least, what I had said. It seemed like he was sticking up for me.

Next thing I knew, Mama was leaving him to stand in the yard as she turned back to the house. Harry walked to his car with his long stride, threw his cigarette on the ground and slid into the seat, pulled the door closed and drove away. I heard Mama close the front door with a slam and call for Gabby. I stood at the open door to my room and listened to their voices come up the stairs.

"What in the world, Ellen?"

"He has no right to butt into my business with my kids. How dare he cast an opinion about how I'm raising them up," Mama huffed.

"Oh, Ellen. He was upset as the rest of us about what Donna said. You can't blame him for that, can you? Donna Jean's behavior was wrong, but she is only a girl and she is having a hard time. It's her age, Ellen. Her emotions run away with her."

"There you go, sticking up for her, too."

"Can't you, for one minute, put yourself in her place? She lost her daddy for Heaven's sake. She longed for you to comfort her. Not me, Ellen. You. Please don't tell me again how bad it was for you. I know that. I do. Please try to consider Donna."

There they came, the loud steps on the stairs. I hurried back to my desk chair and waited. I heard Mama's door close, and then nothing.

CHAPTER FOURTEEN

Christopher tapped on my door. I knew how uneasy he was the moment I saw him. He was pale and wide-eyed. With his hands still in his pockets, he slumped on the edge of the bed and looked at me.

"I know," I said. "I've done it again. I couldn't help it, Christopher. It all came out. I guess I've wanted to say it for two years."

"Maybe you could say you're sorry. It's going to be miserable around here again."

"It wouldn't be true. I'm not sorry. We're different, Christopher. You have always had a special relationship with Mama and you can forgive her anything. If she would change back to how she was, maybe I could feel more like you. She doesn't even try."

Poor Christopher. He hung his head and looked at the floor.

He was right, of course. From that day on, the mood in the house felt like a cold, overcast day. Mama completely ignored me. She could enter a room where I was and not even bother to look at me. She quit eating supper with us and left early for work. Gabby was so unnaturally quiet the house felt dismal. How I missed her cheerful chatter. She went about her day as usual, cleaning, cooking, and watching her soap operas. She was the same kind-hearted Gabby. In fact, though she was quieter, she was particularly nice to Christopher and me. I suppose, as a way to pay her back, I hurried to do my chores without being told, and took extra care to do helpful things.

I spent as much time as I could over at the barn. I would sit in the loft and gaze across at the Wendell house and wonder how Twyla was doing. It was getting close to time for Children's Services to come back and check on her. Grandma Gabby had said we needed to "'stay out of her business'" for a while. She could call us if she needed us.

On a Saturday, as I sat in the sunbeams in the loft, I caught a glimpse of movement when I gazed south toward town. I noticed a dark speck on the horizon far away. It could have been anything, a calf or a loose horse. Because it kept moving, and appearing to come closer, I continued to watch. Suddenly, I realized it was a person. Whoever it was walked fast, almost trotting across the rough ground. As I stared, my heart caught in my throat. It was a man and he was coming right toward the barn. His image was too familiar. He looked different in some way, but still, the same as Raymond. My mind went into denial. It couldn't be. Why would he be out in the field on foot? It was a crazy notion. But the man kept coming.

I crouched low and waited. I would hide until he came and left. It didn't occur to me how long that might be. I heard the old, mulish back door scrape open and knew Raymond was there, inside. I smelled cigarette smoke, and heard the stream splatter as he relieved himself against the barn wall. I thought of running home as fast as I could, but then he would be aware that I knew he was back, and something told me that wasn't a good idea. So, I sat without moving a muscle for what seemed like an hour. He lit another cigarette. In my head I whispered over and over, "please go, please go", and finally felt he was gone. There was no smoke and no sound. I waited anyway. When I stood, my knees were weak either from squatting or fear, or both. When I tiptoed to a gap between boards and peeked out, I saw Raymond slip behind the oak tree next to the shed. I bolted for home.

"It's Raymond!" I said breathlessly to Gabby. "He stopped at the barn and now he's at Twyla's! What are we going to do?"

Grandma Gabby didn't take time to ask any questions. She hurried to the phone and called Twyla's number.

"Twyla, listen to me. Raymond is there now. If he isn't in the house with you, he is right outside somewhere."

"Yes! I am serious. Donna saw him over at the barn. I think you should call the sheriff's office right now."

"Okay, then I'll call . . . Twyla! Listen to yourself. You're headed right back where you were."

"Oh, Lord, Twyla. Don't do that."

Gabby hung the receiver back in its cradle. I could tell she was contemplating what to do, so I kept quiet.

Finally she sat at the kitchen table. "If the kids were there I would call the sheriff myself, but I guess this is up to Twyla."

I told Gabby what Twyla had said about wanting Raymond back. She shook her head sadly.

"She'll never get those kids back." After a pause and a deep sigh, she said, "Maybe she isn't supposed to."

I climbed the stairs and sat by my window. There was no movement around the Wendell house, but I didn't expect there to be. Raymond was probably inside with Twyla. I wondered why he didn't have his old car. Why would he be afoot? He must have come all the way from the highway that ran through town. I pictured him in the field, coming closer and closer to the barn. Of course! His ratty beard was gone, or at least it was much shorter. I wondered about the kids again. Did they miss their father? On one hand, I thought they must. I knew how I felt about my own daddy. But, on the other hand, I couldn't recall seeing, even one time, any warmth between Raymond and any of his children. Maybe he was happy when he found out they were gone.

I stayed in my room until Mama slammed out the front door and I heard her car drive away. The phone rang as I went back downstairs. Grandma Gabby held the receiver to her ear for a time without speaking. I could hear a voice sounding like a little gnat whining over the line. Finally, Gabby spoke and her tone wasn't one bit nice.

"I am going to tell you something right now and you listen. From this time on, I will no longer care one bit what happens to you over there. But those kids are a different story, Twyla. If they get to come back and I hear, see or smell anything rotten going on again, I am calling the sheriff's. Don't tell me I can't."

The little voice whined again. Grandma Gabby looked at me while she listened. Her eyes sparked and her knuckles were white where she gripped the phone.

"Why in Lord's name would you even believe that?" Pure disgust crossed Gabby's face.

"Well, good luck to you." She placed the phone back in its cradle and stood stock still looking at it.

Of course I was practically doing a dance there beside her, waiting to hear what Twyla had said. Gabby sat heavily in a kitchen chair and breathed out a big, gusty breath. She told me what Twyla had said on the phone, while shaking her gray head and rubbing her hands over her face. She said Raymond had got himself in some kind of trouble while he was gone and had been arrested. He was out on bail while he awaited his court date. He'd run off and spent some time tramping around the country, but, as he'd told Twyla, he missed her so much he had to take the chance of sneaking back home. Even I knew that was a lie. He was back because he was hungry, cold, and broke, and needed a place to stay.

Gabby stood abruptly and went back to the phone.

"Oh, hi, Alice. This is Grace Shanks. Is Deputy Wilkes in? Thank you."

She told him the whole story, beginning from when I had spotted Raymond crossing the field, to the phone conversation with Twyla.

"I hope that was the right thing to do," she said when she hung up.

"Is he coming out?" I asked.

"Says he will after he makes some calls."

Deputy Wilkes stopped at our house first, which was a mistake in hindsight. He came towering into the living room, greeted us kindly and began asking a lot of questions. I told him about hiding in the barn while Raymond was there and how I didn't think he had his beard anymore. Gabby repeated the conversation with Twyla.

"What did he do to get arrested?" I had to ask.

"He is charged with robbery of a liquor store. The clerk said it looked like he had a gun in his coat pocket and he threatened her, so they have added that he might be armed. Whatever you do, do not let him in this house, or Twyla either, for that matter. I know you folks have done a lot for her and those kids, but you need to steer clear now." He actually shook his finger at us. "I'll stop by on my way out, with him or without him."

Once again we flew upstairs to my window, Christopher, Gabby and me, all straining to watch the Wendell house. It was dusky out, but we could see Wilkes leave his car and approach the house. Before he got to the porch, a shaft of light appeared from the opened door. He stepped inside and the door closed again. We waited an eternity.

He came back out closing the door behind him. He stood still for several moments and looked all around him. When he slid back into his car, we all ran downstairs again and waited for him on the porch. When I saw he was alone, I thought for sure Raymond had spotted him at our house earlier and hid or took off.

"She said she made him leave after she talked to you," he told Gabby. "She doesn't know where he is. He wouldn't tell her his plans. She didn't see a gun. She gave him some food and he took off. She looked real bad. Been crying."

"Well, I believe he's deranged," Gabby said, and my mind flashed back to the times he acted so disgusting. I agreed. Even after so much time had passed, I still felt my face grow warm and my insides churn when I thought about the things I'd seen Raymond do. And yet, I didn't say a word about it. I couldn't help it. I was too ashamed.

The deputy warned us again about locking up tight and being careful.

Grandma Gabby had told me she was going to wait up for Mama. She wanted to tell her about what had happened so she would know Raymond might still be around. I went to bed, but I tossed around for what seemed like hours. I turned my light on, found my drawing pad and pencils and propped myself up in my bed. I drew a sequence of sketches showing Raymond coming into view from across the field. In the last one, the one he where he was closest to the barn, I drew him without a beard. My hand didn't hesitate to draw a wide, scruffy chin. He wore a dark gray jacket and his hair was collar length. I was positive it was the way I'd seen him.

I heard Mama drive in and I waited to hear what Gabby would tell her. I sat in my doorway so I could hear them. Gabby told her what had taken place and how Wilkes had warned all of us about being careful in case Raymond was still around.

"Well, that's just great," Mama said. "The creep needs to be in jail. They'll never get him if ignorant Twyla keeps covering for him. She doesn't have any guts. If she really wanted her kids back, she'd have called the sheriff herself."

"That's enough, Ellen. I only wanted to tell you to be careful."

"Fine. Does Christopher know?"

"Yes, he knows. He misses you, Ellen. Boys aren't good at expressing some things, but I know he worries a lot. He asked me if Harry was going to come back. He likes him, you know."

"I don't know what Harry will do. He comes and goes like the weather. Then he has the nerve to warn me about seeing anyone else. Ha!"

"Well, for myself, I wish he was around a little more often. I suppose I feel safer when there's a man around. Now, with that lunatic Raymond slinking around, well, I don't like it."

Mama's voice softened some and she said, "Mother, I wish he was around more often, too. There is something he's keeping secret about. I don't know what, and he won't say."

"Guard your heart, Ellen, guard your heart," Grandma Gabby said kindly.

That was the first time in many days I heard Mama and Gabby have a meaningful exchange. Mama wasn't snide and Grandma Gabby sounded like her old self.

CHAPTER FIFTEEN

Two days passed by without a call from Twyla, or even a conversation among ourselves about her or the kids. The days were sunny but the breeze was icy cold and the nights were still frozen. The moon was waxing and the frost on the fields sparkled like jewels. My sleep was restless. Even after hearing Mama and Gabby speaking kindly to each other, life was out of kilter. Christopher was quiet and distant, causing me to worry about him. He had become more and more closed off from the rest of us. I wanted to tell Mama my worries about him. I sat in wait on the porch so I could catch her on her way out.

"Mama, I'm worried about Christopher," I said when she came through the door.

"Why so?" She had paused on the porch step. She wore her red lipstick and I could smell her perfume. She had her white coat on, her purse strap over her arm, and she wore an impatient expression. Nevertheless, she looked beautiful to me.

"Well," I struggled to explain. "He is so distant these days. He hardly talks anymore. He used to talk Gabby's ear off but he barely says anything now. He never comes to visit with me in my room either."

"Maybe he's being a teenage boy. Has he said anything to you about school? I hope he isn't having trouble there. That's all I need."

Anger flooded through me. There she goes again, I thought, making it about her instead of Christopher.

"I know he wishes Harry would come out to visit more," I ventured. "He really seems to like him. They can always talk about rocks and things."

"I'll be sure to tell Harry when I see him." She turned to go to the car, stopped, and faced me.

"You know, Donna, I really do wish things could be different around here. But, we can't go back, you know. Time changes things, and it changes people. We don't always get what we want, but you know that by now. I am doing the best I can even if it isn't good enough."

That was all. She got in the car and drove away. What she had said sure wasn't very helpful, but I felt better inside simply because she had shared herself with me.

I had a recurring dream that night. It hadn't come to haunt me for some time. I'd dreamed it several times in the months after Daddy died. It was the one in which I looked out my bedroom window and saw the tiny red glow of a burning cigarette. It appeared to be across the road near the lane to the Wendell house. The dream was brief, and I always awoke right after the glow faded away. I hated it because it brought back the pain of the horrible night I'd lain in my bed crushed with heartbreak.

It seemed to me any time there was even a tiny bit of peace or normality in our house, something had to happen to ruin it. This time it was a call from Twyla. She wanted to know if we had called the sheriff's office again. Grandma Gabby told her we hadn't and didn't intend to. Twyla was sobbing. She said Children's Services had called her and said they weren't giving her kids back at this time. There had been reports to the sheriff saying she was still not responsible enough to care for her children. They wouldn't say who called.

"Well, it wasn't any of us," Gabby told her. "Maybe it was your sister."

Twyla cried harder and hung up the phone only to call right back. She asked if someone could get some things she needed in town. She had no food again and Rosalie wouldn't be back for days. Gabby couldn't say no.

"Who lets a person go hungry?" she said to me after she hung up. "I know she can't pay for it, but what else can I do?"

The next afternoon I went with Gabby to deliver groceries to Twyla. She came to the door immediately after I knocked. Before she even said hello, she snatched the bag from my arms. She peered into it greedily. She truly was hungry.

"Has Raymond been back?" I asked.

She looked up quickly. "No. Why?"

"I just wondered." It had crossed my mind that maybe Raymond made her call us for food. He could have come back again. He would need food, too. I couldn't put anything past him.

"Thank y'all for these groceries. I'll pay you when Rosalie gets back here." She closed the door, and that was that.

Back in the car, Gabby said, "Something's got to give. How can she keep living like this? Kids or no kids. She can't expect her sister to support her for the rest of her life, for Pete's sake."

I hadn't been to the barn since the day Raymond showed up. I begged Gabby to let me go for a little while. First she said no, but she gave in, saying to be back in exactly a half hour and not a second longer. I grabbed my coat and drawing pad and rushed out. The sun was in the perfect position to lay sharp-edged beams across the loft floor. Dust motes rose from beneath my feet as I picked my way carefully to the door facing my own house. I sat on the old gunnysack and put the pad on my knees. I drew my house. In the frame of my own window I drew in a young girl with long, straight hair like my own. She was looking back at me, straight into my eyes. Her eyes were big and round. Her lips made an O. She looked surprised . . . or frightened. Below, at the bottom corner of the page, I drew an old jalopy. I shaded in the rusty dents and sketched the vague image of a bearded man in the driver's window. I stared at the picture for long minutes as if someone else had drawn it.

Suddenly I was so angry I ached to do something rash. Break something. Throw something. I ripped the page off the drawing pad and tore it to shreds. I flung the pieces around me in the loft and out of the hay door and watched them flutter to the ground. I was breathing hard and frightened myself a bit.

Raymond had left the essence of his nasty self in my beloved barn. I could still smell the stench of his cigarette and his sweat, and hear him pee against the wall by the wooden door. I took in a great gulp of air, and held my breath like I had that day he'd come. I could visualize him there below me the same as if he was actually there again. I hated him so much I began to tremble.

When I looked at my pretty watch Harry had given me for Christopher, I knew it was well past time for me to be home. Gabby would worry, maybe come looking for me. I scrambled down the ladder and headed for the wide barn door, and when I could see across the road, there was Gabby standing on the porch looking over at me. I ran across the road, flew onto the porch and threw my arms around her and cried like a little baby.

She hugged me tight and let me cry for a few minutes. When I began to gulp for breath, she held me away and brushed my hair back with her fingers.

"What has happened, Donna?"

"I don't know." I sniffed. "I got upset." How could I explain what I didn't understand? "Raymond stole my barn."

Herman and Rosalie were back. They stopped at our place before they went to the Wendell house. Gabby told them things had been quiet across the road, but Twyla had called for some help because she was out of food. Poor Rosalie squirmed in her seat. She told Grandma Gabby all Twyla had to do was call her and she would have come or sent her some money. But without a car, what could Twyla do for herself?

Gabby, not thinking she was speaking out of turn, brought up the subject of Raymond having been back. The stunned look on Rosalie's face caught Gabby off guard.

"What? When? He was here?"

"Oh my! You didn't know? Twyla didn't tell you?" Gabby looked mortified, covering her mouth with her hand. Rosalie continued on, asking a dozen questions, but we didn't have answers for her. We didn't know where he had been before or where he had gone. We assumed he was still hiding out or Deputy Wilkes would have let us know he'd been nabbed again.

Herman was red-faced with anger. "That man is a dangerous, worthless bastard. He's mean as a snake and is going to really hurt somebody one of these days. He manages to squeak out of every stinkin' situation he gets into. I wish he was in prison." He looked at Rosalie. "I know she's your sister and all, but I've about had it with her, too."

I felt sorry for Rosalie. She watched Herman walk away and tears pooled in her eyes.

"I know he's right. Sometimes I feel the same, but what can I do?"

"She needs a car and a job. Until she takes a step to help herself, she will always depend on someone else to take care of her. It isn't my business, but if I were you, I would find a cheap place for her to live in town and get her out of that house over there." Gabby stopped and patted Rosalie's arm. "Forgive me if I am out of line, but all of this affects this family too. We don't need Twyla's worries either, but like you, we can't ignore her needs."

"I know. Herman and I will talk to her again. Maybe I will have to tell her we can't help her anymore. None of us."

We all said goodbye and Herman backed their car out and slowly drove toward the lane. Gabby put her arm around my shoulders and we set out at a shuffling walk along the road. She didn't speak for several minutes, but when she did, she had a lot to say.

"My dear, sweet Donna Jean," she said and tugged me closer. "A child your age should never have worries such as we have had over that family. You are too young for this lesson in life. There are folks everywhere who live the kind of life Raymond and Twyla live. Sometimes they manage to get through it and better themselves, and sometimes they don't. I don't know how theirs will go, how it will end for them and their kids, and as much as I've wanted to help them, it isn't up to me how it all turns out. Now, you listen. It isn't up to you either." We kicked along in the gravel alongside the pavement. Gabby looked into my eyes.

"It is time to let all this go. I'll tell Rosalie when she comes back that we're all through."

"But, what about the kids? If they ever come back, we can't ignore them." I was thinking of those little blonde heads bobbing around in that big car on the day they had been taken away. I remembered Wade's wave. It seemed so long ago and it had only been weeks.

"All I can tell you is we need to hope and pray for the best for them, whether that be with their parents or not. We have no control over it, Donna." Gabby turned us back toward our house and took my hand. It was in the next stride that I noticed them.

On the ground, smashed into the gravel, lay three cigarette butts. Filterless and smoked short, they had been ground with a twist of a shoe. I stared at them and raised my eyes to my room's window. A sharp breath escaped my throat and I looked at Gabby.

"What, Donna Jean? What is it?"

CHAPTER SIXTEEN

We sat on the front porch letting the sun warm us, and I told Gabby about my dream. I explained it all, from the first one on the night of Daddy's death until only a few nights before when I thought I had experienced the dream again.

"Do you think you got up and walked to your window because doing so was part of a dream?" Grandma Gabby asked. "Like sleepwalking?"

"I don't know. Maybe I thought so. But now that we saw the cigarette butts, I'm sure it was real. I really did see someone smoking." We sat in silence, looking up Gibson Road.

"Come on, Grandma Gabby. I need to show you something." This time I took her hand and led her across the road to the barn. We didn't enter the wide front door, but walked along the outside toward the back corner.

"Look," I said and pointed to the pile of yellowed, crushed cigarette butts on the ground. "I found these a while back. I couldn't figure it out, but now I think I know. It's Raymond."

"Raymond!" Gabby looked quickly across the field to the Wendell house. "Raymond has been watching our house? All this time?"

"Who else could it be?"

"But, why, Donna? Lord! Maybe he wanted to rob us."

"He could have done that any time we were gone somewhere. He didn't have to watch our house at night to rob us," I said.

Gabby was staring at those disgusting looking butts. She bent to get a closer look, stood, and stirred them with the toe of her shoe.

"What brand are these? Oh, see here? They're Camels."

"Same kind Harry smokes," I said. Harry didn't ever smoke in our house, but when he wore his white shirts, the pack showed in the pocket. I could plainly see the brown and gold camel through the material.

"Oh, my!" Gabby said. "Raymond! But you had the first dream the night Joseph died. Surely Raymond wasn't prowling around here back then!"

"I don't know. I don't know what to think, Grandma Gabby."

After that day, a day of discovering something both Gabby and I thought important but unexplainable, I was puzzled and uneasy. Of course Raymond was the person who I believed must be the culprit. Who else could it be? But every time I mulled over the discovery of the cigarette butts there beside Gibson Road, crushed into the gravel with the twist of a shoe, Harry's face would flicker in the back of my mind like an old movie reel. I would block the image, and never spoke of it.

Grandma Gabby had called Deputy Wilkes who came right out. The three of us walked to the barn first to show him the pile of cigarettes there. He didn't hesitate to crouch low where he could study them and poke them around with his finger. Next we showed him the ones beside Gibson Road. He stood for a long, quiet time. He looked all around, at the barn, our house and up at my window. He took a small writing pad from his pocket, touched the point of his stubby pencil to his tongue and wrote something I couldn't see.

As we walked back to where his car was parked in our driveway, he told us he would be making some surprise visits to Twyla. He asked that we not mention anything about the cigarette butts or his upcoming visits if we spoke to her.

I was disappointed. I stood and watched him drive away toward town, thinking how we didn't know a single thing more than we did before he came. I don't know what I expected. I felt sad and didn't know why. Sad and even tired.

By the next day, I was sick. I woke feeling terrible. My stomach hurt and my head ached. I stayed in bed all morning. I slept restlessly and had nightmares like never before. Mama came to check on me and put her cool hand on my forehead. I was too miserable to appreciate her attention to me.

"Oh, Donna! You're running a fever, honey. Let's check that." I heard her going down the stairs and the next thing I knew I was waking up again. I'd had another bad dream and had only slept ten minutes or so. Mama came back shaking the mercury down in the thermometer and poked it under my tongue. It smelled and tasted of rubbing alcohol.

"A hundred and three," she said. "Must be the flu. I'll get you a cool cloth."

"I don't want to sleep anymore," I said.

"You need to rest, Donna. I might run you a cool bath."

"But I have awful dreams. Nightmares! I don't want to sleep. Can I go stay on the sofa?"

Gabby was the one who brought the cold, damp towel and laid it on my forehead. She sat next to me on the cushion. I stared at the TV, and fought the drowsiness that kept taking me over. I remember she gave me some pills and made me swallow an entire glass of water. When I slept and woke again, my nightmare stayed with me as though it was real. In the dimness of my dream world, Raymond, with his scraggly beard and frightening face, was trying to get inside our house. No matter which room I ran to, he was there at a window or door. When I was upstairs in my own room, in that weird dreamtime, he was at my window! I was frantic with the fear and frustration at how that could be possible. The last time I saw his face through the pane, it wasn't Raymond. It was Harry. My heart pounded so hard I could feel it thumping in my head. I woke myself crying out.

Gabby held me to her and I told her, in words muffled against her shoulder, all about the dream. She hushed me and whispered not to be afraid. She said it was the fever that caused the bad dreams and as soon as it lowered some I wouldn't have them anymore.

I was better by the next day, although tired and weepy. I stayed home and slept the day away. Two days later, when I should have gone to school, I told Gabby I was still too sick, and managed to do the same the next day. I was tired, but not from being sick. There was little sleep to be had during the night. I'd left my lamp on because I was afraid. I was afraid of my nightmares, and I was afraid of the dark like I had been when I was younger. Like then, I wanted my daddy. I knew if he was still living, Raymond wouldn't be anywhere near our house, and Harry wouldn't be in our lives at all. I wanted him back so much I could barely breathe when I thought about how he used to comfort me. My heart ached with loneliness for my father.

Gabby's sympathy ran out over the weekend and on Monday she made me get up and go to school.

"You are going to get so far behind, you'll never catch up," she scolded.

"What's going on, Donna?" Christopher asked on our walk to the bus. "We can see your light on under your door at night."

"I have bad dreams sometimes, that's all. Don't tell Mama." I didn't want her asking questions. I had long before quit talking to her about missing Daddy.

I got in some trouble at school that day. The teacher said I sassed her back, but I was only explaining why some of my work didn't get done. I got in trouble again the next day for not answering her at all when she spoke to me, so she sent a note home with me. I hid it away and never mentioned it.

Soon after that my grades began failing miserably. I didn't tell Mama or Gabby, somehow convincing myself they didn't have to know. The kids who had been my friends began to get on my nerves. I avoided them and quickly became a loner.

I closed myself off from any of my feelings of friendship, and I couldn't seem to care about doing anything for fun. I went to school and I came home. The only place I wanted to be was across the road in the solitude of the old barn. It was my place and I needed to claim it back from the intrusion of Raymond. I crossed the road when Gabby allowed. She stood guard when I was over there. I could look across and see her standing in the door with a dishtowel in hand, or sitting out on her porch chair. I knew it was because she worried about me, but I resented being watched.

I took my drawing pad with me and stayed every minute I could. I drew pictures from my nightmares. I gazed across the fields and imagined Raymond coming toward the barn. I visualized in my mind how I would hit him with rocks and boards until he fell to the ground. My heart would race when I imagined him begging me to stop . . . and I wouldn't.

I was too young to realize something had gone haywire in my head and heart. I thought I was angry, but not crazy. At home, I was quiet because it made life easier. I heard Mama telling Gabby that my behavior was simply part being a teenager. Most of my time was spent in my room obsessively watched out my window. I don't know what I was looking for exactly. Twyla stayed holed up in her house, and Rosalie hadn't shown up for a while. The Wendell place was so desolate and still, it was as if no one lived there anymore.

But, true to his word, I saw Deputy Wilkes drive along the lane and go to Twyla's front door. I saw her step out onto the porch and they talked for a time. Wilkes didn't go inside that time. The very next day, he was there again. This time, after they spoke for a few moments, he stepped inside. My curiosity went wild. It seemed he was in the house for a long time. I tried to imagine what was taking place. Was he sitting at the kitchen table? Maybe he was prowling through the house looking for . . . for what?

When he came out onto the porch, he hitched up his belt and walked over to the old shed. He passed out of view as he continued on toward the back of the house. I was practically holding my breath. He came back, got into his car and bumped along the lane. I flew down the stairs when he pulled into our driveway. Christopher opened the door and we tumbled out onto the porch, Grandma Gabby following in our wake.

"Howdy all," he said. "Everything alright here?"

"I think so. Haven't had anybody nosing around here lately," Grandma Gabby said.

"Good. Just wanted to be sure. Found a couple of things at the place over there that have me wondering if Raymond might be back. There's some boot tracks behind the shed there, but they could have been there for a while, what with no rain. I also saw some of those smokes behind the house. The place looks like a garbage dump back there so it's hard to tell how long they might've lain there."

"How's Twyla doing?" Gabby asked.

"Same as ever, I'd say. She ain't keeping herself up, but she never did much. Place still looks okay inside. She said her sister's coming back day after tomorrow."

"Well, that's good. Any word on her kids?"

"Well, I know the two oldest are in a foster home, but at least they are together. The little ones are still with Children's Services. Poor little things." He shook his head with sadness.

Tears come to my eyes and tried to blink them away. For a moment sorrow overwhelmed me.

"Jeffy and Leland must be so confused. Melanie and Wade took care of them more than Twyla did." I felt a sob coming on and put my hand over my mouth. Christopher rested his hand on my shoulder.

"If it helps you feel better you should know Twyla says she's seriously thinking of moving to town," Wilkes said. "I think she might be coming around a little. She doesn't have any money except what her sister helps her with. She's pretty stuck right now." "If Raymond would leave her alone, she'd maybe make herself a better life."

After the deputy drove away, I asked Gabby if I could go to visit Twyla when her sister came. She said maybe, and that was that.

———

Rosalie and Herman stopped at our house on their way to Twyla's. They came inside and we all sat around the kitchen table. Gabby put on a pot of coffee making it obvious there was conversation to be had.

"This is it," Rosalie said. "We can't do this anymore. This will be our last trip until she says she will move. If we are going to have to pay her rent, she will have to move where we say. I don't think Raymond will be back here again and that's all she's waiting for."

"We can't afford it anymore," Herman said.

"I'll keep my eyes and ears open for something to rent in town," Gabby said. "She'll need enough room for the kids. She'll have to be settled in and have a job before they can go back to her."

"I have a feeling this is going to take a while," Herman said. "She has to get Raymond out of her head before she does much changing."

Rosalie looked perturbed. "Well, he is the kids' father. It would be hard for her to forget that, Herman."

He ignored Rosalie's comment, giving a little snort through his nostrils. I knew he had had it with Twyla and all the drama.

Herman shook his head. "Has anybody ever looked inside the old shed there? I was thinking I'd take a look when we get over there. I'll have to break the lock off it." "I s'pose I'll find more junk we'll have to do something with if Twyla moves."

"We'll all help out when it comes time," Gabby told him. "We'll need a pickup to haul stuff to the dump. Be plenty of that, I reckon."

———

I'd listened to them talk without joining in. My ears had perked up when Herman said he was going to check out the shed. I had been curious about it since my first trip to the Wendell house. I never knew if Raymond put the lock on it or if the owners of the place kept things in storage there.

"I'll come over and help you all today," I blurted.

"Oh, hon, you don't have to do that," Rosalie said.

"I want to. Really, I do," I insisted.

Herman said we'd better get busy and rose to leave. Nobody said I couldn't go, so I moseyed out to Herman's car and got in. I waved to Gabby.

When we got to the house, Rosalie went to the door, gave a sharp rap, and let herself inside. Hanging back with Herman and I followed him over to the shed. He inspected the lock on the door and decided he would pry the hasp off so he wouldn't have to find the tools to cut the lock.

"Let's go look for something to use as a pry bar," he said and we headed to the backyard.

CHAPTER SEVENTEEN

When the lock finally fell away and the old green door creaked open, disappointment swept over me. I don't know what I expected to see, maybe something spooky like a skeleton. Whatever it was, it didn't appear. Old scarred and broken furniture took up most of the floor space, and dozens of rusty tools and ancient horse tack made of dried-up leather hung from hooks and rusty nail heads around the room's walls. Cobwebs draped from the rafters and clung to most everything below. Along the right-hand wall was one of those Army cots made of wood and canvas. Piled on top, a gray wool blanket and a pillow covered in blue ticking partially covered some tattered, mouse-eaten magazines. A thick layer of dust covered every surface. There were a few wooden crates stacked in one corner and a tall, wide cabinet in another. It was clear by the droppings that rats and mice had lived in the shed for a long time. The vermin smell was powerful.

When Herman saw the look on my face, he let out a laugh. "Don't worry," he said, "this stuff has been here for decades. If Twyla ever leaves this place, I don't think it'll be our responsibility to clean this up. It sure ain't hers."

It was a relief to hear him say it, but I was curious about what might be in the boxes and cabinet, and the drawers of the other furniture. I stepped up into the shed, raising a dust cloud into the air. Motes floated in the light causing me to sneeze hard several times. My shoes clomped on the hollow-sounding floor beneath my feet and some of the planks creaked and gave a bit as I moved around the room. I wiped a squiggly line on the old desktop with my finger and was amazed at how much dirt I moved.

"I feel sorry for whoever does have to clean this place."

"I agree, kid. Can't imagine where all this might end up. Maybe the landlord will want it, but I doubt it since he hasn't claimed it by now. Probably go to the dump. Look around if you want. I'm going to go on inside and check on Rosie. Her and Twyla might be at each other by now."

It felt eerie, being alone in the shed full of old, abandoned things. It was easy for me to picture someone sitting at the desk in another time, maybe writing a letter. There were several kerosene lamps on the desk and on a nearby wall shelf. It was easy to imagine books stacked on the mostly empty ledges. I tried to peer through the wooden slats of the crates in a corner of the room, but the light was dim and the slats too close together to even give me an idea of what was stored inside. I pulled some drawers open by their wobbly knobs and found nothing but mouse droppings and shredded papers. The tall bookshelf in the corner was massive and I thought about what a trial it must have been getting it through the shed door. It had two deep, wide drawers at the bottom with ornate bronze pulls. I bent and tugged at the top drawer. It inched out slowly with persistent yanks. I saw no sign of mice in this one, but it smelled like old, musty paper.

There were several stacks of yellowed envelopes tied into bundles with string, and piles of loose sheets of paper beneath them. When I moved them they crackled with age. Over to one side I saw a brown leather journal, and when I carefully lifted it enough to peek beneath it, there was a dark blue leather binder with gold embossed lettering. When I slid it out it felt weighty in my hands. I slanted it toward the light from the door and read the words:

THE DARK SIDE OF GIBSON ROAD

I.W. Davis and G.B. Ewing
Attorneys at Law
San Antonio, Texas

The stiff blue cover wrapped around the side and was held in place with a tarnished gold snap. I pried it gently with my thumb and it opened easily. By glancing at the first few sentences it was easy to see it was written in legal jargon and would be difficult for me to understand. What I saw as I flipped through the pages held my interest, though. The Gibson brothers' names were written repeatedly and some of the pages had to do with land deeds. I wished I could show it to Daddy. He would have been interested and known what it all meant.

Stepping back outside into the fresh air made me realize how close and smelly it had been inside. Deciding to go over to the house, I wiped my filthy hands on my pants and crossed the driveway to the front porch. As I took the rickety steps, I heard voices from inside. The tone of them stopped me and I stood and listened.

"Twyla, we have tried and tried to tell you we are through. Herman and I have done about all we can do." Rosalie was nearly hollering but there was a tremor in her voice.

"I told you, Rosie, she don't care. She wants somebody to take care of her, that's all." Herman was fed up.

"But, my kids," Twyla whined, "what about my kids? What'll happen to them?"

"You should have thought about that a long damn time ago, Twyla. You and Raymond never did make a real family for them. You're as bad as him. What kind of mother lets her kids live like this?"

"Herman! Stop it now," Rosalie pleaded. "You're only making things worse."

"Worse? Rosie, how much worse can it get? Her old man is gone, her kids are gone. Something has to change."

Turning away, I quietly left the porch. I walked out and sat on one of the big rocks circling the fire pit. The ones Grandma Gabby had backed over in her car. That night seemed like it had happened such a long time ago. I thought about what a mess the place was: inside, outside, and the people who had lived in it.

I wanted to walk back home, but I couldn't do that without telling Herman and Rosalie, and I didn't want to go inside. So, I sat and looked toward my own house. I could see the roofline and the upper story window. I squinched my eyes and assured myself no one could look into my window from the Wendell house. I stood and walked a big circle around the driveway, peering down the lane and out across the field to the barn. I thought about how nice the place must have been all those years ago when it was taken care of and the fields grew tall hay. I thought about how the poor Gibson brothers must be extremely unhappy with this place.

Finally, I worked up the nerve to go to the door again. This time I didn't hesitate. I rapped on the door and pushed it open a few inches.

"Rosalie" I called, "I'm going to go ahead and walk back home, okay?"

"Sure, hon, we'll see you all later."

It was with relief that I walked to Gibson Road along the lane. I felt only a tiny bit guilty because I hadn't done a single thing to help out, but my desire to get away from the place hurried me along at a good pace. I crossed the pavement and trotted along. I was thinking about the shed and about telling Gabby and Christopher what it was like inside. The toe of my shoe kicked away a chunk of broken asphalt, and there they were . . . two cigarette butts, crushed into the gravel. Again.

I clambered up the front steps hollering for Grandma Gabby. We met in the kitchen door.

"Good grief, Donna. You scared the breath out of me. Now what?"

"There's more!" I said.

"What are you talking about? More what?"

"Cigarettes! Along the road to the lane!" I was puffing to catch my breath.

Gabby, Christopher and I sat in the kitchen and I told them about everything. I described the shed and how awful it was inside. I told them Herman and Rosalie and Twyla sounded like they were arguing when I'd left, and I described the cigarettes I had seen on the side of the road.

"Oh, mercy," Gabby said and rubbed her hands down her face. "More. I guess I should tell Deputy Wilkes, although I don't know that it matters."

"Why is there a bed in the shed over there?" Christopher was still interested in the old shed.

"It isn't really a bed. Not like ours. It's one of those old fold-up beds. Nobody could sleep on it. It's too dirty." I shuddered to think of it.

"Well, somebody probably did a long time ago. Maybe a kid." I could tell Christopher's imagination was getting wound up.

"We should get you one," I teased. "We'll put it in the shed out back and send you there when you are being bratty." He made a face at me.

Gabby said, "Some of the furniture could be worth something if it goes way back to when Wendell Gibson lived there. My goodness! Antiques are often worth a lot of money."

"Maybe you'll get to see it, too!" I said.

I told them about the filth and trash while they both made faces that matched my descriptions. But when I told about the blue leather binder of legal papers, Gabby sat up with interest. I told her how I had wished Daddy was here to read them. She nodded in agreement.

"Do you know what all was in there?" she asked.

"I didn't understand it. I saw the Gibson name a bunch of times and I know it was partly about their land, but that's about all."

"I hope someone takes the time to look into it. Could be interesting."

Later in the day, I attempted to share the afternoon's events with Mama but she was in a rush to go because, she said, Harry was waiting for her.

"Oh, he's back?"

"He is." She gave us a big smile and off she went.

Raymond

Raymond was bursting with self-pity. Life had turned to crap, and it was Twyla's fault. Her and those damn people over across the road. Why did they have to end up being his neighbors? When he was comin' out and watchin' that Ellen, he was wishin' she was his neighbor. Now they were all a bunch of trouble. He thought he had finally found the perfect place to live out on Gibson Road. He could come and go as he pleased with nobody to bother him. He might work an odd job here and there for cash, and collect welfare money for Twyla and the kids. Somebody owed him for them kids, for damn sure. Who in the world wanted four kids to take care of? Not him, that was for damn certain. Yeah, things were lookin' good, and then those people had to stick their noses in his business. His and Twyla's.

Do-gooders. They were always lookin' at other people's' ways. They thought they were better. Smarter. It was the old woman, Granny or Gabby or whatever they called her, causing the trouble, he was sure about that. She would be the one to call the sheriff's on him if she took a notion. But Ellen! Man, now she was a looker. Hell, it was hard to go back and look at Twyla after watching that woman for a while. And she was a widow. The big-shot guy in the fancy car, he wasn't around enough to be takin' care of Miss Ellen like she deserved.

The one that worried him, though, was the kid. Donna. That gal was smarter than she should be. If he wasn't careful he could get himself in trouble with her. Those young gals like her made him act like a teenager hisself. He'd like to spend a couple hours with her over at the barn. He'd have to watch out or he'd be in jail for messin' with a teenager.

He didn't try to rob that little gal at the store, either. He didn't have no gun in his pocket. Alls he did was ask for a little cash to get him by for a few days. He'd needed some cigarettes and a little somethin' to drink. Now, he was going to have to hide out for a while, until the sheriff's figured out what to charge him with and if they could make it stick. They didn't even keep him in a cell that night. They said he needed to stay around for a few days. Well, he wasn't stupid. He was gone by the next morning. Ditched his car on a guy's farm, and had to bum a ride back to town like an old no-account. He was gettin' tired of sneakin' around. Sure would be good to go see Twyla again. See if she still had somethin' to eat in the house. She'd wash up his dirty clothes and feed him and be darn glad to do it. Yeah, ol' Twyla. She was always happy to have her man back, no matter what he'd done.

Maybe one of them men he'd worked with would loan him a car for a couple of days. That's all, just a couple. Long as there were no charges from the misunderstanding at the liquor store, he'd be okay at the old house. He sure wished he knew if the cops was still lookin' for him. Damn cops.

There was the one guy that felt sorry for him when he told him the bullshit story about how his wife up and left him and took his little kids. Bet he'd loan him his car.

CHAPTER EIGHTEEN

Not only was Harry back again, he was at our house all the time. He was eating supper with us several nights a week. He'd show up in the later afternoon, hang around with Mama and stay until she left for work. Christopher was thrilled, of course. He tagged around behind him, asking a zillion questions. I have to admit he was extremely patient with Christopher. They talked about everything under the sun: sports, fishing, mining, and Christopher's school subjects. In fact, when Christopher had to write an essay for school, Harry told him he would help him if he wanted to write about mining. They earned an A on that report.

The thing I noticed, the odd thing, was Mama seemed envious of the time Harry spent with Christopher. She'd become quiet and sit up next to Harry real close with a hand on his thigh and listen in to their conversations as if she really cared. I felt uncomfortable when she acted that way. It was easier for me to leave and go find Gabby, or set off to the barn.

It was calming to sit and draw my pictures in my familiar space. I'd piled up the gunny sacks where I could lean back against a broad upright, and hold the sketchpad against my knees. I was getting to be skillful at drawing and I enjoyed trying different ideas to make my pictures better. Drawing made me more aware of all the things around me that I hadn't paid close attention to before. The natural things.

I drew bugs and spiders and the owl that lived in the barn. I drew the boards of the barn with wood grain and knotholes. I drew the landscape all around.

There was a little ranch on Gibson Road near where Christopher and I caught the school bus. The people there were friendly, always waving and calling howdy to us. Their pasture fence ran along the road, and if their horses were turned out, they trotted to the fence to meet us. There had been a time when I begged Daddy for a horse, but he'd always said no. Wouldn't even discuss the idea. I think he was a bit afraid of them. He'd never been around horses and he would say they might hurt me. Christopher didn't seem to care much about them. He wanted bicycles and things with motors. In a way, I fell in love with those horses down the road.

I began taking my drawing pad and waiting for them by the fence after we got off the school bus. Sometimes they would come at a trot and hang their big heads over for me to pet. The one I liked the best would push the others around so he could get closer for better ear-scratching. I drew him the most and I got to be quite good at it. When the owners saw what I was doing, the man, Mr. Langley, came and asked me if I would like to ride one of them sometime. I was nearly speechless with excitement, but I managed to answer that I would have to ask at home.

That day I ran all the way home. Gabby saw me coming and later said I scared her to death because she thought something bad had happened when I bound through the door. By that time, life had been in such turmoil for all of us it caused her to feel fearful and nervous about us kids. When I told her what Mr. Langley had said she put her hand up over her heart and I knew what was coming.

"Oh mercy, Donna. You are wearing me out. First of all, you'll have to ask your mama, but I'll tell you right now she's going to say no. She's scared to death of horses. She never even had a dog when she was a girl. Her father didn't believe in having dogs unless they were for hunting, and horses were only used for work. Ellen's never had an animal."

I knew it wouldn't do any good to argue, so I kept doing my drawings, and petting, and talking to those horses. I decided right then, though, that when I grew up, I would have my own horse. Maybe even more than one, like the Langley's did.

One night shortly after that, I brought up the subject of horses at suppertime. I'll admit now, I did it on purpose to see what got stirred up. Was I ever surprised when Harry joined right in talking about horses. He liked them a lot. He said he'd ridden all his life. In fact, his family had horses when he was a boy and used them to gather and work cows. Mama even showed a bit of curiosity and asked him questions about them. He told us stories about his childhood horse he called Blue, and it was easy to imagine how much Harry had loved him. But at the end of all the talk, Mama pointedly said there was no use in me ever asking her for a horse because I wouldn't be getting one. I knew it, but it still hurt my feelings when she said it that way.

Trouble was my middle name. That's what Gabby said when I got in an argument with a girl at school and was sent to the principal's office. I guess by that time I had too many offenses because he gave me a week's detention. I had to go home and tell Mama and Gabby immediately because what it meant was, I wouldn't be able to ride the bus home. I would have to stay after school an hour every day.

We were all at the kitchen table when I told on myself. Harry was there, too. Mama wanted to know what was so important to get into an argument about. Four pairs of eyes peered at me, waiting for the answer.

"Well . . ." I cleared my throat, thinking fast. "Well, Marla came up to me with two other girls and asked me about something and I told her it was none of her business and they all started saying stuff to me that made me mad."

"What did she ask you?" I swear they all leaned in to hear my answer. Mama's eyes were cold.

"It was something about us, our family." I stared at the tabletop.

"Just tell us, Donna Jean."

"Okay, but you're not going to like it." After a pause, I blurted it out. "She asked me if you were a whore. She said everybody said so. She said her mother said you would go with anybody, even if he was married . . . and a bunch of other stuff."

I swear, I thought I was dying. There seemed to be no air in the room and I couldn't get a breath. And the quiet! I wondered if I had been struck deaf. I know it was only a minute or two but it seemed to last an eternity. Mama sat back in her chair hard. Gabby threw her hands up over her face. Harry and Christopher shifted their eyes from person to person.

"And what did you say, Donna Jean?"

"I called her a goddamn liar. I said her mother was jealous because she was so ugly. Other stuff."

"Like what?"

"I think I said I was going to beat her to a pulp. Something like that."

Mama crossed her arms around her middle and in a quiet voice, said, "Go on upstairs now. I'll talk with you later." When I glanced at Harry, I saw his face was pale and stiff as a board.

I went on up and sat at my desk. With trembling hands I drew a picture of Marla, making her as ugly as I could. I kept her bangs and her squinty eyes so it would still look like her. I listened to the voices drifting up the stairs. I heard Harry say kids were cruel. Especially teenage girls. I wasn't sure if he meant Marla or me.

"It's only natural for Donna to defend you, Ellen. Seems a shame she should get in trouble for doing it," Harry said.

"Oh, great!" Mama said. "So it's my fault she got in trouble? I don't know what to do with her anymore."

"You should be nicer to her, Mama," Christopher said. "She wants you to like her again."

"Watch out, buddy. Next I'll be sending you to your room. What is wrong with you kids, anyway? You used to be such good kids."

And to my astonishment, Christopher said, "And you used to be a good mother."

Gabby's gasp flew up the stairs loud and clear. "Christopher!" she nearly shouted. Of all of us, Gabby was the one I felt most sorry for. I sat there at my desk and felt my heart pound in my chest. I wanted to run. Run down the stairs, out of that house and along the road until I couldn't run anymore. We were all going crazy. Not only Mama, all of us. I laid my forehead on the picture of ugly Marla.

I took a chance. I quietly walked downstairs, through the living room, and out the front door. I didn't look into the kitchen as I passed the door. No one stopped me, so I went in search of Christopher. I found him behind the old implement shed. He was sitting in the dirt about half way up the small hill. He ignored me. I climbed up and sat beside him.

We sat side by side for a long, quiet time. Somewhere toward the river a cow bawled and we both gazed that way as if we might see her. Christopher said, "I wish there was someplace else to go."

"You mean like town?" I said.

"I mean like to live. If Gabby wasn't here, I would run away." His lower jaw jutted in defiance. I couldn't say much because I had thought the same thing many times. The difference was I knew it would never happen. We didn't have family to run to. No other grandparents or cousins. Nobody. The sheriff would bring us home again. Besides, I'd always felt selfish when thinking about running off from Grandma Gabby. She was so good to Christopher and me. She loved us.

"I know I'm usually to blame for starting our problems. I'm sorry, Christopher. I'll try not to cause us trouble anymore. We can get mad at Mama, but we have to remember Gabby's feelings. Think how things would be if she up and moved back to town. She has her house, you know. She could leave any time she wanted to and not have so many headaches with this family. Between us and the crazy people across the road, I couldn't blame her for going." I scooted over in the dirt and put my arm across Christopher's shoulders. He was growing up. Not a little boy anymore, and I would have to remember that.

"I've always stuck up for her," Christopher said. "I thought she would be her old self someday. I guess she's never going to be."

Me giving up on her was one thing. Christopher's giving up broke my heart.

We stood together, dusted off the backs of our jeans, and walked back down the hill and around the end of the shed toward the house. Both of us, no doubt, thinking we may as well get this over with. As we rounded the front of the house, Harry was stepping off the porch. He took a pack of cigarettes from his pocket and shook one out, lit it with his shiny Zippo. When he saw us, he stopped and turned toward us.

"I'm glad you came back before I left," he said. He still looked pale. "Your Grandma Gabby is awfully upset."

"We'll go talk to her," I answered.

"I'll be away for a few days, so I won't be seeing you kids. I hope you can make up with your mother."

"Where do you go?" I blurted.

"Go?"

"Yeah. You're always leaving. Then you show up again. Nobody ever says where you went."

Harry said nothing for a long moment. He puffed on his cigarette and gazed across the road as if he was thinking about what to say.

"I go a lot of places, for work, you know. I'm a traveling salesman."

"Do you have a house?" Christopher asked.

"I do," Harry answered.

"Where is it?" Christopher clearly doubted the truth of Harry's answer.

Harry hesitated, rubbed at the back of his neck. "I really have to go, kids. You mind yourselves, okay?" He turned and got into his car. As if on second thought, he rolled his window down, propped his elbow on the sill and gazed at us.

"Your mama has some decisions to make about some things. Life has been difficult for her."

"You don't even know Mama," I sassed. "How she really is when she's normal. She used to be happy, and she loved us. Not anymore." I was instantly angry with myself for sharing too much with Harry.

"I'm sorry," he said, and backed out of the driveway.

CHAPTER NINETEEN

Mama and Gabby were arguing fiercely when Christopher and I entered the front door, each of them shouting over the other. They were standing in the kitchen and didn't even realize we'd come in. We waited and listened, both of us holding to the kitchen doorframe.

"This entire family is going crazy . . ." Gabby flung her arms to include the whole house. Her face was red as her apron.

"I am not crazy, I'm tired. I go off to work every day and nobody, nobody, gives a damn about how I feel." I think Mama actually had a few tears on her cheeks.

"Would you like for me to leave, Ellen? I can do that. I don't want to because of the kids, but I will if it will make you happy."

Christopher and I quickly looked at each other. Open-mouthed, he appeared as stunned as I felt.

"Is that a threat? Are you saying you would up and leave us alone out here in the boondocks? I'll go to work every night and the kids will be here alone? You would really do such a thing?" Mama sounded incredulous.

"Why can't you see what you are doing, Ellen? There's a dark pall over this house and it's smothering us all. Lord only knows why you have changed so much. Christopher was right in what he said. They want you to like them again, to be involved in their lives. You come and go like a mean old aunt."

Mama was livid. She was quivering with anger. Her eyes were glassy in her flushed face. One white-knuckled fist clutched a chair back. The fingers of her other hand dug in her hair.

"Maybe I will leave. Would that be better? I'll move into town. I'll give you this house. Hell, I'll even give you my kids. They love you more than they ever loved me anyway."

"And why might that be? Ellen, please. Please help us all get back to being a family again." Gabby's face was wet with tears and she had quit trying to wipe them away.

"Stop it!" My words came with a sob. Christopher grabbed my hand and I yanked it away. "Stop yelling!"

"Go outside. Now." Mama didn't even look at us.

Without a word, we did what she said. I felt stiff and breathless. Christopher followed me out and fell into a porch chair. I crossed the road to the barn and with shaking knees climbed immediately to the loft. The day was fairly warm but I was chilled and shivery. I sat on my burlap sacks and pulled two of them around me and leaned back against the upright. I stared up through the gaps in the roof and squinted against the light of the sunrays. I could hear my mother's voice saying, Hell, I'll even give you my kids.

I don't know how long I was there, but I do remember thinking how I never wanted to go back to the house across the road. I shoved the burlap sacks around with the heels of my feet and let my body sink low upon them. I closed my eyes and the self-pity poured through me. My misery left me feeling even colder. I turned on my side and curved myself into a circle like a puppy trying to keep warm. Later, I think much later, I heard a voice calling my name. For a long moment I thought I was dreaming.

"Donna. Hey, are you up there?" A man's voice. I untangled from the gunnysacks and edged closer to the hay door. When I peered down, there was Deputy Wilkes looking up at me. "Come on down here."

He stood waiting for me out by the edge of Gibson Road. I glanced across toward our porch but no one was there. I wondered if I was in trouble for something I'd done at school. Maybe Marla's mother called the sheriff's office.

When I approached him the deputy laid his big, warm hand on my shoulder. That small act calmed me, and the weight of his hand was familiar. An image of Daddy flickered through my mind. I had missed that strong, fatherly connection, but I hadn't forgotten what it felt like.

"Come on. Let's go to the house. I want to ask you a few things about the Himes."

I didn't want to go back inside our house so when he held the door open for me to go in, I hesitated to step over the sill. The living room was empty, but through the kitchen door I could see that everyone was seated at the table. They watched us walk in and I slipped onto the chair nearest Christopher. The deputy stayed standing, strong arms crossed against his broad chest. Mama's and Gabby's faces were rigid and they both sat iron-straight, their hands clasped tightly in front of them. I wondered if they had still been arguing when Deputy Wilkes arrived. Christopher examined a small cut on his finger, never looking up at anyone.

"Twyla's sister, Rosalie, called us and asked us to come out and check on Twyla. She said she'd called her several times and got no answer. Of course, I asked if she had called you folks but she said she didn't want to bother you with their troubles anymore."

I glanced at Gabby who shook her head sadly. I knew she was feeling guilty for not checking on Twyla.

"We went to the house," Wilkes continued, "found it unlocked and checked inside. Twyla wasn't there. We've checked outside and took a look inside the shed there. The lock's been broken, but she wasn't there."

"Herman broke the lock last time they were here," I said. "I was there when he did it."

"Well, that explains it. So, I have to ask you all again if you have seen anybody around. When is the last time you talked to Twyla?"

"Not since Herman and Rosalie was here. I think they put their foot down about how much more they were willing to help her out. They want to move her to town," Gabby explained.

"When Herman broke the lock, did you all go in the shed?" Wilkes asked.

"I did. Just me and him. We looked around at the things there, but none of it was Raymond's and Twyla's. Herman said it had been there a long time." I didn't tell him I had looked in the drawers or about the blue folder I found. I wasn't being secretive. I didn't think it was important.

"So, here's what we're doing. We have some folks on their way out to do some searching. They may want access to your property here, and will cover from the Langley place to the river if necessary. Keep your eyes and ears open." He looked from Mama to Gabby and back again. "Everything okay here?" he asked. Mama still sat stiff and the two of them hadn't looked at each other. It wasn't hard to see something was wrong between them.

"We're fine. And of course we will call right away if we know anything. Poor Twyla." Gabby put her palms to her eyes.

When he left the house, I went up to my room and closed the door. I took out my drawing pad and pencils and pulled my desk closer to the window. I painstakingly drew a picture of the back of a girl's head and neck, long straight hair to the bottom of the page, and a man's big hand lying on her shoulder. I penciled in a faint design and some folds and wrinkles on the material of the blouse she wore, and I put a wide wedding band on the hand, exactly like Deputy Wilkes's. To this day, I think it was one of the best pictures I have ever drawn. Each time I looked at it, I could feel the warm, friendly weight of that hand. Through my window I saw a few sheriffs' cars come and go until it grew dark. Gabby came upstairs to say there was soup if we wanted it. I told her what I had been seeing at the Wendell house. She hugged me tight and said to try not to worry. Surely someone would find poor Twyla.

People came, some in uniforms and some not, in cars and pickups that turned and bounced along the lane to the Wendell house. As the yard filled, they began to park beneath the elms. Eventually the searchers stood in the morning sun, clustered in front of the porch for a few long minutes, and finally began to move away, singly and in pairs. I watched all morning as they came and left. My mind wandered and I imagined someone leading Twyla back across the field that stretched beyond the house. In my made-up story, she would be safe.

I drew more pictures, some of the house, some of the far fields that eventually met the river. I watched searchers become tiny disappearing specks, and specks turn back into people. I imagined someone searching along the banks of the river, peering into the water. I had questions. Why would Twyla go to the river? Why would she up and leave? Maybe someone came and drove her away in their car. Maybe she had a friend we didn't know about who came to help her. There were too many whys and maybes.

After Lunch, Deputy Wilkes stopped by. Mama was sleeping and Christopher was in his room. He'd refused to come down all morning. Grandma Gabby and I stood on the porch to talk to the deputy. He had little to report. Not a thing had been found. The weeds had grown up through the litter and trash in the backyard of the old place. It would be impossible to find footprints back there. He asked Gabby if there had been anything at all of value in the house when we all did the cleaning for Twyla.

"Oh dear, no. Nothing any of us came across."

"No firearms? No jewelry?" Gabby shook her head.

"Does anyone know where Raymond is?" Gabby asked.

"Not yet. We'll find him. He isn't going to go too far. I doubt he has any place to go."

Deputy Wilkes told us there were two volunteers coming over from the next county. They were bringing hounds trained for searching. Maybe they could pick up a trail. I stayed at my window all afternoon. I tried to make sense of Twyla walking away from the Wendell house. Did she know where she was going? I envisioned her stumbling across the rough fields through the sticker weeds. I pictured her in one of her old dresses with the little blue flowers on it, hanging crookedly to her calves. I'd only ever seen her short, wide feet in her old sandals and I wondered if she had any shoes. Would she have food? Would she be cold? Poor Twyla.

Late in the afternoon, I watched two men in bright yellow jackets leave the yard of the Wendell house. They each held onto a hound's long leash. The dogs, noses to the ground, tugged their men along. They sniffed their way along the lane and into the yard. They reappeared beside the shed, paused there, and then moved out into the field. They hurried behind the barn, and on toward the southwest. I slid my window up and listened to the baying howls disappear.

Raymond

He was right about Leon. Ol' Leon would give a guy his last dime if he thought he'd have himself a friend for it. Raymond knew a long time ago how to get what he wanted from somebody. All you had to do was find somebody that wanted to be liked. Those kinds would do most anything for you. This time, a pat on the back and a half-assed handshake got Raymond a car. Nice car, too. Better than any he'd ever had of his own, that's for sure. Leon could find himself a ride to work for a week or so. No problem.

It was nice to drive along with the radio up loud and the air blowin' through the window. With his beard gone, and a haircut, even the cops wouldn't think of Raymond being in this nice car. Neither would those damn people on Gibson Road. They could gawk out their damn window all they wanted and still wouldn't know it was him who was drivin' by. It wasn't none of their business anyway. He was really starting to hate them people. Wished they'd up and move away so he wouldn't have to worry about 'em anymore. They were always in his business and he'd had it with that nosey crap. Maybe a good scare would do the trick. Be easy to scare off a house full of women and one useless boy. He had him a half-baked plan about how he could scare the bejesus out of them. Raymond sure liked that Ellen, but she was kinda snobbish. He'd have to think about which one of them women he ought to put a scare into.

For now, though, what Raymond really needed was some food and rest. He was about outta money, but maybe he could get him a sandwich and a nap in the Chevy's backseat. That would get him the rest of the way to Gibson Road.

He woke up feeling mean as a rattler. Maybe it was what he dreamed. When he had those dreams about when he was a boy, they hung with him all damn day. Sometimes longer. Raymond grew up hating his old man. He was cruel. Treated Raymond like a stray dog even when he was still a little boy. Once he locked him in a little shed and left him for three days. Gave him a bucket of trough water. Treated him like an animal. Left him wonderin' what it was about himself that his own father hated so much.

When those dreams came it was hard to tell what was real and what was crap. Sometimes, when he remembered the time in the shed, Raymond was scared of the dark again. Nobody knew it. Not even Twyla. He'd die before he let anybody know something like that.

All day he thought about that dark place out on Gibson Road. He'd been there once.

CHAPTER TWENTY

Poor Rosalie. The tears poured from her tired, red-lidded eyes. She and Gabby sat close, clutching red-knuckled hands for comfort. Rosalie's handkerchief hung limp with dampness. In spite of the nervousness and dread over Twyla's disappearance, the day was shiny bright, the weather perfect for porch sitting. We'd all congregated there, even Mama. I knew how Mama felt about Twyla and the entire Himes matter, but at least she was cordial to Rosalie. She'd given her a stiff-armed hug and told her how sorry she was for her worries, sounding nearly sincere. Herman couldn't sit still. He paced the yard with a determined stride that seemed more angry than sympathetic. I watched him march across the road to the barn as if it was an important destination. I could see him over there, peering into the dark opening of the big door. I selfishly hoped he wouldn't have a desire to climb up to the loft. My loft.

We had discussed the situation until, finally, we sat in silence. We'd talked about Twyla's state of mind and none of it sounded good to me. Gabby said she wouldn't be surprised at anything a mother who'd lost her kids might do. Mothers had been known to lose their minds over the loss of a single child. Imagine suffering the loss of four, she'd said. Herman had stopped pacing long enough to add that he thought Twyla had gone off her rocker. She might have taken off, not even knowing where she was going. Rosalie said she thought Twyla, mentally stable or not, went looking for her kids.

But we all agreed, the other theory was that Raymond had taken her. Somehow, someway he had found a way to take her away. All the people looking for her had come up with nothing. Even the hounds gave up the trail after a couple of miles across the land lying south. Deputy Wilkes said he'd put out a bulletin for her and all law enforcement would be on alert.

I could only think about the kids. No doubt little Wade was somewhere with strangers, grieving for his mother. And Melly. I hoped Melly could stay strong and brave. "What if they never find her?" I asked Gabby. "What about the kids?"

Gabby gave my hand a squeeze. "They'll find her, Donna. She has to turn up someplace. If she is trying to get to Newell to see her babies, she is out there somewhere." She lifted her hand toward the fields behind the barn. "Mamas will do most anything to get their kids back. It's a natural instinct." I wondered how my Mama would be if it was Christopher and me.

The day crept by on long, silent moments. We moved about like a church congregation, whispering "excuse me" when we shifted, and settled back into our places. Grandma Gabby brought out a platter of crackers and cheese, and our best glasses full of iced sweet tea. We sipped the tea, but no one cared to eat. Much to my relief, Herman had returned from the barn and was snoring, head far back and open-mouthed, in a porch chair.

Mama left early to go to work. I knew she wanted to get away from us. I watched her drive off. I rose and walked to the far edge of the lawn where I lay on my back, stretching my body full length, and, for a long time, watched high clouds scuttle past. When I closed my eyes I could hear the crows cawing from the far fields. They sounded scolding. I wondered if they knew where Twyla was.

By dusk, all the cars had left the Wendell house and driven slowly past us like a funeral procession. Herman convinced Rosalie it was time to go to Pickering where they were staying at the inn. The same place Harry always stayed when he came to town. I wondered when he would return.

Gabby made us go to school. I considered sitting beside the road with the horses all day instead of getting on the school bus, but Christopher said I was asking for trouble again. Maybe he was right. I climbed on the bus for his sake. Was I ever surprised to find I had so many friends. The news about Twyla's disappearance had already spread throughout the Pickering community. My classmates had questions, dozens of them. They also had their own opinions about what had happened to her: bitten by a rattler, ravaged by coyotes, fell and broke her leg, drowned herself in the river, and the most bizarre one, aliens took her. Even Marla tried to be friendly, but I couldn't forgive her for what she said about my mother. I suppose it was my way of still honoring Mama. I basked in the attention from the other kids, though. I couldn't help it. My fault or not, I had become a lonely girl, and their interest in me felt great.

At noon, the lunch table where I sat was packed tight with girls who wanted to talk to me. In the gym I was the first picked for a volleyball team. Classmates said they liked my hair, my shoes, my same old skirt I'd worn dozens of times. Two asked if they could spend the night with me at my house. That was when the wall came down again. My Grandma Gabby, my home, my barn, they weren't for sharing. Not with people who might turn against me at any moment.

By the end of the day I could hardly wait to get back on the bus. The adrenalin rush of self-importance was already gone. I wanted to pet the neighbor's' horses and walk home in the quiet of the countryside. I craved the quiet. I wanted to put my hand on my brother's arm and ask about his day. When I was finally able to, he said his day was strange, much like mine had been, but he was still delighted over the attention he'd received. He was one of the guys again. I didn't ruin it by warning him to be careful of false friendships.

When Gabby asked about my day, I didn't hesitate to tell all. I dunked cookies in my glass of milk and tried to explain how I felt.

"I liked it at first," I said about all the attention, "but they don't really care about me. They were being nosey. I'm not the same as them, Grandma Gabby."

"You are as good as anyone, Donna Jean, and you don't need to be the same as anybody. You are a good girl, and smart. Don't let a bunch of silly girls make you doubt your worth." I stood and hugged her so tight she groaned.

Gabby said her day had been quiet. Only a few cars had driven to the Wendell house. She had heard nothing about Twyla. We sat on the porch together until time to fix supper. I peeled potatoes and listened to Gabby hum The Yellow Rose of Texas until she called Mama and Christopher to come and eat. She and Mama were still acting distant toward each other. I wondered if they had tried to make up. I looked at Mama and silently questioned if she really wanted to give me to Grandma Gabby. She looked away as if she read my mind. At that moment I would have bet she did, but not Christopher. He was her favorite.

It was nearly dark out when I headed to my room to do my homework. I sat at the window and had hardly begun to work when I saw a car turn down the lane. It was a new model and a shade of blue. I was sure it must be someone investigating Twyla's disappearance. Who else would it be at that time of evening? The car didn't pull up in front of the house, but continued on toward the backyard. Through the dimness of evening I saw a man climb the porch steps and try the door. He turned away and walked back around the house where I lost sight of him. As I did my homework I kept an eye on the Wendell place. A light came on inside, the kitchen I was sure, and then another. By the time I closed my book and put my pencil down, darkness had fallen. The house lights glowed golden. As I watched, the upstairs windows lit up. If one didn't know better, they would think the house was a warm and welcoming place. I could only recall the filth and stench we'd found on the day we had gone to clean for Twyla. Some good it had done, I thought. Now, not only were those little kids gone, but so was their mother.

I got ready for bed and went downstairs and said goodnight to Gabby. I told her about the car over at Twyla's house. She said she was glad to know someone was still working to find her. Back upstairs I looked again and saw that the house had gone dark. Car lights shined along the lane until they swept around to follow the pavement of Gibson Road. It was there, at the turn, that I saw the scatter of sparks scurry along the blacktop. The driver had tossed a cigarette from the window.

As the sparks scattered and disappeared, I thought of all those cigarette butts I'd found. I'd shown them to Gabby and Deputy Wilkes because I was so sure they told a story about someone, but nothing had ever come of my discovery. Seeing that one fly from the car window stirred up my suspicions of Raymond.

I couldn't sleep. I tossed around, going over and over everything that had happened since the Himes had moved into the Wendell house. Once I started thinking about the kids I couldn't stop the pictures in my mind. I didn't know if being taken from their mother was harder on the two older kids who might be angry about it, or the two babies who were probably scared and had no understanding. I cried for them a long time that night. I think I cried for myself, too.

When I drug myself downstairs the next morning, I felt like I was in a fog. The night's sadness and lack of sleep left me groggy. Gabby saw it right away. She turned from the stove to say good morning and her smile disappeared.

"Good grief, Donna Jean. What's got you so blue this morning? I guess it's all the worry about Twyla," she answered herself. "Don't let it get to you. Somebody will find her." While she talked she dished up eggs and thick slices of warm, buttered toast. "Eat. You'll feel better." Christopher came and sat at the table with me. He ate like a horse. Extra eggs. Extra toast.

I told them about my night. How the worry over the kids had taken me over. I told about seeing the cigarette thrown from the car window.

"I started thinking about all the cigarettes I found at the barn and by the road," I told Gabby.

"We'll probably never know where those came from, Donna. You know that, don't you?"

When Christopher and I left the porch for our walk to the bus, I made a quick decision.

"Hold on a minute Christopher. I have to do something." I hurried along Gibson Road toward the lane, combing the pavement and roadside. I heard Christopher hollering at me to hurry up, but I kept searching. Finally I saw it. On the edge of the pavement where it met the gravel shoulder laid a tiny remnant of a cigarette. There was enough left of it that when I touched it with the toe of my shoe, I could read the letters CAM.

"What the heck are you doing? We'll miss the bus." Christopher was agitated.

"Let's run," I said. I didn't want to tell him about my curiosity over a cigarette butt.

Mama came to help Gabby fix supper that night. She wasn't exactly cheerful, but at least she joined in and talked to all three of us a bit. I swear, I could actually see my Grandma Gabby's face relax. I had to remember how much she loved her daughter. It must have hurt her terribly when they weren't getting along. I didn't want to care if Mama was there or not. My heart ached when I looked at her. How could you not love your mama?

When she asked about school, I was careful with my answers. I told about the good grades I had been given on tests in math and biology. I told her about my volleyball team. No way was I going to tell her about the phony friendships and gossip. By the time I began to help clean the table I felt exhausted from the careful choosing of the right words to use. It was later when I realized what had really taken place that evening. In my own way, no matter how tough I wanted to be, I was still begging for my mama's love. I even went so far as to let myself truly understand how Christopher had felt about her since Daddy died.

The next news we heard was that a deputy, while doing a routine check, had discovered someone had broken the backdoor lock at the Wendell house. When told about it, Gabby explained to Deputy Wilkes that I had seen a car there the evening before. He showed up to talk to me after school.

"Tell me exactly what you saw," he urged me.

I described all I could remember. He took notes in his book with his stubby pencil, pausing to touch the lead to his tongue. When I told him about the cigarette butt on the edge of the road, he peered at me, pencil hovering.

"Show me," he said.

I remembered exactly, and led him straight to it. He didn't touch it, but he bent and examined it.

"Good job, girl." I earned a pat on the shoulder. I blushed with pleasure at being praised.

He asked if I was sure the car I saw was a late model. Was I positive it was blue in color? Yes, I said. Yes it was.

"I bet it was Raymond," I said, wanting to sound like I knew something helpful.

"Well, I can't say, but it sure isn't likely Raymond has himself a new car."

Another day passed and still no word came about Twyla. She was all we could think about. Grandma Gabby walked around with tears in her eyes. Christopher, in all his innocence, asked if we could go look for her.

"But where, Christopher? Where would we go that someone hasn't looked by now?" Of course he had no answer.

I climbed to the barn loft after school and gazed across the fields through the back hay door. I thought about how many hills and valleys and trees there were between our place and Newell. How long would it take her to get there if everything went right? Two days? Three? I would have to ask Deputy Wilkes about it.

CHAPTER TWENTY-ONE

More than anything in the world, I wanted to be the one to find Twyla. I daydreamed about it until I thought of little else. The images filled my mind and were endless. Who wouldn't want to be the smart, brave person who found the missing lady? I could easily picture myself walking for miles and miles cross-country and coming upon Twyla in a gully, exhausted, hungry, and dying of thirst. I would give her water from my canteen until she was strong again. When we walked into the Wendell house yard, people would cheer, pat my back and hug me. Another daydream was about Gabby and me driving to Newell and finding Twyla in some alley, lost and crying for her kids. Gabby would drive her to her kids and they would come running to meet her. There would be pictures of us in the newspapers across Texas. I would be a kid heroine.

One night I had a bizarre dream I will never forget. I'd gone over to the Wendell house and Twyla was there. She'd swung the front door open as I was reaching for the knob, surprising me. I asked where in the world she had been.

"I don't know what all the fuss is about," she'd said. "I've been right here the whole time."

"Where, Twyla? Where were you? We all looked and looked for you. You couldn't have been in this house!" In the dream I was furious, yelling. "How could you hide like that if you knew how we were all looking for you?"

"I wasn't hiding. I was right there." She'd pointed toward the chair at the kitchen table. I awoke trembling. I threw myself out of bed and tromped to my window, where I stood for a long time and glared at the old house down the trashy lane.

Rosalie and Herman came to our house and sat out on the porch with us. Rosalie was a mess. She'd cried until her eyes were swollen to slits. Too many days had passed with nothing hopeful to hold onto. No trace of Twyla had turned up.

"What if she's dying out there?" she gazed across the fields. "Dying all alone. It's too awful to think about. What a terrible sister I've been to her." She broke down again. Herman sat close and patted her shoulder.

"We did all we could for her, Rosie. She couldn't get away from Raymond. This is all his fault."

"I agree with you, Herman," Gabby said. "We knew he was a demon. I wish we could go back again. I would pay more attention to how he treated his family, and I'd have done something. I don't know what, but something."

It grew unnervingly quiet, and as we sat in the silence, we didn't even hear the crows calling. Most likely, only for conversation's sake, Herman said, "We met Ellen's friend, Harry, at the Inn today. He was checking in. He said he would be seeing us all."

"So, Harry is back." Gabby shook her head a bit. "I suppose Ellen knows by now."

She knew. None of us was surprised when she came downstairs dressed for work long before she was due there. Without explanation she left early, getting in the car and wiggling her fingers at us. Her flitty gesture seemed out of place at such a solemn time.

So, he was back already. I'd expected him to be away for some time after our talk in the front yard that day. While everyone else began to carry on a conversation, I silently mulled over my feelings about

Harry. He and Mama had the strangest kind of relationship. If that was how people carried on a romance, I knew I wanted no part of it. I would never have a boyfriend, for darn sure. Honestly, I thought Mama was being punished for being untrue to Daddy. He was her love, and he sure wasn't anything like Harry. Daddy was dependable and levelheaded. He took care of us. Harry was the opposite. It seemed as though he lived inside a secret. He went places and did things nobody knew about. Not even Mama. Gabby would say, "Somethin's fishy in Denmark."

The next day was Saturday. I usually slept late on Saturdays, but not this one. I was wide-awake and I could hear someone moving around in the kitchen. I smelled coffee perking, so I knew it wasn't Christopher there alone. Must be Gabby. I shuffled down the stairs in my slippers, holding the railing. By the time I stepped into the living room, I could hear soft voices. Mama's . . . and Harry's. I stood quiet, practically holding my breath, and strained to listen. They were whispering. The words came in gruff breaths.

"I had to tell you, Ellen," Harry rasped.

"Well, how nice of you. Your conscience got the best of you. Admit it." Mama's whisper quavered.

"I couldn't live like this anymore without you knowing, Ellen. I love you, and I knew I owed you the truth. Please." Was he begging? "Maybe we can still go on from here. When this is all over . . ."

Mama's whisper was louder. "Go on? Are you serious?"

I turned to go back up the stairs, but it was too late. Mama had come through the kitchen door and saw me.

"What are you doing here so early, Donna? Were you eavesdropping? You seem to think everything that goes on here is your business. Go on. Get back upstairs to your room."

As I went, I heard her open the front door and tell Harry he needed to leave. I watched him tramp across the lawn and get in his car. He sat for several minutes and then backed out and sped away. I flopped on my bed and waited for Mama to come and chew me out.

She came into my room with a cup of coffee in her hand. She looked pretty, all wrapped in her pink robe and her hair fluffy, but her face was pale and showed no softness. She stood at the window and gazed out for what seemed like a long time. My heart was pounding. I felt the need to fill the time with words.

"Harry was here awful early," I ventured. She faced me and looked right into my eyes. I didn't understand the expression and I felt confused. I usually knew how to act according to her mood. This time she spoke her words with cold, sharp edges.

"You spend way too much time minding other people's business. You're only a girl, Donna, and you don't need to know what goes on in other people's lives. Just because I am your mother doesn't mean you need to know about my private life. We aren't like other families who have both mothers and fathers. I am a widow. A single woman, and I have a right to my privacy." She turned back to the window.

"Look what snooping started with those crazy people across the road. You and Mother are always thinking you have to fix somebody else. You can't fix people, Donna." Her sarcasm was mean-spirited.

"We have no control over what happens to someone else. Don't you think I would have saved your daddy if I could have? Called him home early? Met him for supper in town? Anything to change that day by only one or two minutes? We don't get to do that in life."

Tears were streaming down my face. For the first time, I felt scared of the anger in Mama. "But, why are you so mad at Christopher and me? We don't feel like we're your kids anymore. Christopher even gave up." I wiped my nose on my nightgown.

"I'm sorry. I am. Something inside me broke when Joseph died. I can't figure out how to be the same person I was. I wish I could." I didn't think I believed it.

"What about Harry? Doesn't he ever make you feel better? Happier?"

"I won't talk about Harry now, except to say he isn't who I thought he was. He has his own story, Donna. Everyone does." She moved to the door, floating in her long pink robe. "I'm going to lie down."

I took her place at the window and looked out into the morning. My insides felt heavy. I fell into my desk chair. I wanted to cry more. Harder. But the emotion had worn itself out. I leaned forward and put my head on my crossed arms. Exhaustion kept me there for what seemed like a long time. I heard a soft knock on the doorframe and pulled my head up. Grandma Gabby was there, intently looking at me.

"Hi," was all I could say.

"What's happened?" she asked softly. "Here, come sit on the bed with me." She sat so close I felt her body warm against my own. "Can you tell me what's wrong?"

It took a few minutes for me to decide what to say. Gabby waited patiently. "Do you think we mind other people's business too much?"

She hesitated, too. "Well, I think we are people with good hearts and we like to help where we can. That isn't the same as being nosey, butting into other people's lives. What has happened, Donna?"

"Mama came. She said some things about how we should mind our own business. Mostly me. I heard her and Harry whispering. She thinks I'm a snoop. I think she's mad at Harry about something. I heard them in the kitchen. I didn't mean to listen." I sobbed, finally.

"This is your home, sweetheart. You have every right to be anywhere in it. The relationship between your mama and Harry isn't a healthy one, but we can't do anything about that. They have to work it out."

"I think something has happened with Harry, but I don't know what. I heard him apologizing to Mama. She made him leave."

"It will all turn out okay, Donna. Please try real hard not to worry about them." She gave my arm a tug. "Come on. Let's go get us some oatmeal and toast."

We sat at the table dunking our thick slices of buttered toast in our oatmeal. I felt better already. I had to ask, though. "Should I tell Christopher what happened with me and Mama this morning?"

"Well, think about it this way," Gabby said. "Is it a thing he really needs to know? I mean, if it is going to make him feel sad and he can't change it, why tell him?"

"How did you get so smart, Grandma Gabby? You sure know a lot about people."

She laughed a little. "It comes with age, sweetie. We learn things whether we want to or not. Life will get easier for you. I can't tell you when, but it will."

I spent a long time in the barn. I drew for hours. I sketched a picture of Twyla sitting at her kitchen table, and I wondered a lot about the dream I'd had. I had such a strong urge to walk over to the Wendell house, I felt antsy. I hadn't been there alone since before Twyla disappeared. To be honest, I'd felt a little bit scared of the place again. Scared like I was when I was younger.

Suddenly, I knew what I really wanted to do. I wanted a chance to look at the ledger and legal book I had found in the old drawer in the shed. There might even be other interesting stuff I didn't have time to see the day Herman and I were in there. If I went, and I hadn't really decided yet, I wouldn't go into the house. I wouldn't snoop inside.

I needed a plan. As I plotted, I continued to draw. My hand sketched a view of the inside of the shed. I drew some of the things there: the boxes in the corner, the tall cupboard with the journal and ledger in the drawer, the old dusty cot. With the lightest touch I added sweeping cobwebs in the corners and draped them here and there. The longer my pencil moved, the stronger the urge to be there grew. There were other places I hadn't looked the day I was in the shed with Herman. For the first time in a while, I felt the tickle of excitement inside.

CHAPTER TWENTY-TWO

I made my plan. When Gabby left for church, I called to Christopher and told him I was going over to the barn to draw for a while. Mama was sleeping. She wouldn't have cared anyway.

I set off across the road and climbed to the loft, hurrying directly to the back hay door. I scanned the fields like a watchman and peered toward the Wendell house for several minutes, making sure there was no one around. I dropped my drawing pad and pencils on the burlap sacks and hurried back down the ladder. I left the barn by the back door and checked to be sure there was no one on our porch. I took off as fast as I could go in a bent-over gallop. I slipped behind the shed beneath the oak tree and leaned against the old wall to catch my breath. I had startled the birds into eerie silence. I'd warned myself not to snoop inside the house, but I hadn't promised anything about not looking through the windows, so I headed over there first. I climbed the porch steps to the front door but the old, tattered curtain was still there. Reminding myself again that I wouldn't go inside, even if it turned, I grasped the doorknob and gave it a twist. The lock held. I left the porch and walked around to the backyard. It was more of a mess than it had been the first time I saw it. The weeds were knee high and trash was tangled in their stems. I saw a metal barrel lying on its side, garbage spilling from it. It was no wonder Twyla's searchers couldn't find anything helpful in that mess.

Stepping carefully, I followed along the wall to the first window that looked into the kitchen. Standing on tiptoe, I could see the cupboard doors were open and cans, dishes, pots and pans were scattered about the counter and stovetop.

I moved on to the back door. What I saw startled me enough to cause me to stumble a step backward. It was plain to see, in the old, dry wood of the door and its frame, that someone had opened it again. A short pry bar and two bent nails lay on the single wooden step in front of the door. Panic ran through me like an electrical shock. What if there was someone inside? I bent low and raced back to the shed.

This time I sat on the ground in the dark shade of the oak and leaned back against the shed wall. I needed time to calm myself. When I could think clearly, it occurred to me that with no car or pickup to be seen, it was doubtful anyone was there after all. I tried to make sense of the door being broken open again. Maybe kids from town came out and snuck into the house. Everyone knew about Twyla being missing and that the house would be sitting empty. And who else would make such a mess in the kitchen?

I don't know how long I hid there, but I realized I was staying too long. I would have to get back home before someone, namely Gabby, came looking for me. There had not been a single sound to be heard. I rose and peeked around the front of the shed. If I could get inside, I would take a quick look around and hurry home.

My hand trembled when I turned the knob to the unlocked door and slipped inside. I had to leave it ajar to have enough light to see much of anything. I tiptoed and crept around as if someone might hear me. The old dresser had been moved from its place and one of the corner boxes had been pried open. I could see it held clothing that looked to be men's things: denim pants, a bundle of shirts, and a wad of ties like Daddy had worn. Dust had been disturbed and there were hand and fingerprints everywhere. I moved to the tall corner cupboard and looked into the open drawer. There lay the blue leather legal book and the journal. I pulled them both out and, without another thought, headed out of the door. I closed it quietly behind me and rounded the shed. From there I ran as if I were being chased by a demon all the way back to the barn.

I was a mess by then. Shaking and gasping for breath, I ran inside and clumsily climbed into the loft. The leather books had grown heavy and cumbersome by the time I dropped onto my gunnysacks. While I rested, I began to face up to exactly what I had done. I had stolen those personal items that had been important to someone, even if it had been a long time ago. I knew I should be ashamed. I wasn't, though. I was excited.

Deputy Wilkes was at our house when we came from the school bus the following day. Because of my guilty conscience, I was sure it was because I had stolen those books from the shed. But he was there to tell us there was still no sign of Twyla and they were losing hope that she would be found alive. Too many days had passed since she'd gone missing. His words didn't seem real to me. I couldn't believe Twyla was gone. Even with all the sadness and worry over the past days, I was so sure she would be found.

"What will happen to the kids?" I was near tears.

"Well, they will be in foster care and eventually will be put up for adoption. I can't believe they would be given back to Raymond even if he shows up." Deputy Wilkes shook his head sadly. "Terrible thing. Just terrible. Twyla has . . . had her issues, but I know she loved those kids. "

I could hardly wait for him to leave so I could hurry to the loft. With a promise to Gabby that I wouldn't stay too long, I loped across the road and scurried up the ladder. I dug the books out and plopped down on the sacks. The blue leather-bound book felt weighty in my hands. I opened it to the first page, having decided to start from the actual beginning instead of flicking through the pages. The first page listed addresses for people whose names I had never heard of. At first

I was disappointed and bored with what I saw. All I could make sense of was short descriptions of places that spoke of acres and land plots, and amounts of money listed in the columns on the far right side of the page. The writing was fancy and had lots of curlicues and flourishes forming the letters. It was slow reading. The ink was blue but had faded some. There were dates, some going back to the 1890s. As I turned the fragile pages, I began to see the names of the Gibson brothers along with other property addresses. It was such a disappointment to realize I didn't know what any of it meant. I knew it was all about money and property, but that was all.

The other book was a wonderful surprise. It was a diary. It was written in very neat and precise handwriting and started right out on the first page telling someone's thoughts about their life through a period of days or weeks. Inside the front cover, the name Wendell Gibson was inscribed in the same fine writing. I decided right then to sneak the diary home so I could read it at bedtime. I tucked it securely into my belt and buttoned my coat over it.

Wendell had written a lot about his brother, Franklin, and the business of mining. He had concerned himself with the cost of things, and hinted that Franklin was being careless about his spending. "He insists on buying the property near the Young River. I feel it is a waste, as it is not particularly fertile ground and is far from the nearest town." I knew he was writing about our place. "Perhaps he would be glad to have a dwelling there, but it is not a place for me."

He had skipped time periods from days to weeks long, and then picked up in the middle of some other undertaking. They purchased other properties, whose place names I recalled seeing in the blue leather book. Sometimes he expressed his pleasure in owning a property with Franklin, but often he was critical. By the time I closed the book, and my eyes, I had decided I didn't like Wendell much. I was wishing Franklin had a diary, too.

CHAPTER TWENTY-THREE

It was Mama who told us she saw Raymond. She admitted she wasn't positive, but a man who looked familiar was walking away from the gas station out on the edge of town when she was driving home from work. She said he was bent as if against the cold and was carrying a red gas can. She didn't actually see his face clearly, the lights from the gas station were behind him casting him in shadow, but there was something about the man that made her think instantly of Raymond.

"Raymond would be hard to mistake," Gabby said. "With his bushy beard and his long hair, he looks like a bum."

Mama said the man she saw didn't have a beard. Or, at least, she didn't think so. He wore a dark colored cap and coat. "I don't know, Mother. Maybe it was his posture, or the way he wore that cap. There was something about him."

"If you really think it was him, we have to tell Deputy Wilkes," Grandma Gabby said.

Mama hesitated. "Well, I could be wrong. Besides, what would he be doing there at that time of night?" She shrugged her shoulders as if it wasn't a big deal anyway.

"Good question. But the sheriffs still need to know. You better call before you go to work." Gabby wasn't letting Mama off the hook. "Or, I will if you like."

"No, I'll call, or stop by the office."

I didn't think Mama had seen Raymond. In fact, I believed by that time Raymond was long gone. Maybe he went back to his hometown to hide out. Maybe he was in some other state. Who knew? It was anybody's guess. I still had hopes for Twyla. Visualizing her dead body lying out in the hills somewhere made my stomach turn over. Again I thought of her kids, and tears welled in my eyes. My heart physically ached.

It was that afternoon when Grandma Gabby sat Christopher and me at the kitchen table for a talk. I thought for sure we were going to discuss Mama and Harry. I knew something had happened between them from their whispers in the kitchen. But that wasn't what Gabby wanted to say. She didn't waste any time and didn't try to sugarcoat what her thoughts were.

"You kids are big enough to have your own ideas about Twyla and her family, about all the things that have happened since we've come to know them. It has been a terrible time for so many people. Twyla, the kids, and even us. I think someday you will see the lessons learned from enduring the hardships that have taken place here." She looked directly at me. "I see the strain in your pretty face, Donna Jean. You run off to your barn or stay in your room. It's okay to want to be alone, but it isn't always the best thing for you."

"And you, Christopher, I see you pretending like nothing out of the ordinary is going on around you. I hear you let off a little steam once in a while, and then you ignore your own emotions. Ever since your daddy died, you have been loyal to your mother. You always had a strong love in your heart. These days I am not so sure. I feel you separating yourself from us." With her hand, she indicated both herself and me.

"Wait," she stopped my words from coming. "I'm not finished. If I am to be honest with you, and myself, I have to say I don't think Twyla is ever coming back. Oh, I could be wrong, but I don't think so. No mother who loves her children disappears on her own. If she had one ounce of life, she would be trying to get to those kids."

"Now, one more thing. I blame myself for letting things go as far as they have for you two." Christopher and I both tried to protest. "Let me say this. I knew Raymond was trouble and I allowed us all to become involved in spite of that. We . . . I should have minded my own business. Donna, I should not have let you get involved with those kids. Your innocent heart made you want to help them, and I encouraged it. Shame on me for that."

Gabby turned toward Christopher and put her aged hand on his smooth arm. "Your worry might be deeper and stronger than either of ours, but you don't express it the same. I am afraid you are holding your emotions inside and that isn't healthy. You can come to me and spit those thoughts out anytime. You used to know that. I am reminding you. Don't hold the hard stuff inside."

"Now, one last thing. About your mama . . . I remember I promised you a long time ago that she would come back around to loving you same as she ever did. I can see that you likely won't believe me, but I still hold to it. There will come a day when she will let both of you know her love for you. Meanwhile, I hope you can be good, and kind, and prepare to forgive her." She took a long breath. "There, I've said enough." She stood from the table. "Who wants hot chocolate?"

Because I believed every single word Gabby spoke to me, her talk with Christopher and me made me feel calmer. It also made me feel guilty. I really wasn't a very good kid. After all, right upstairs in my room there was one of books I had stolen from someone else's property. One of them was private, or had been, to someone. I had never written in a diary, but I felt my drawings were my way of describing my thoughts and feelings. They felt personal to me. I didn't show them to anyone. I hadn't since before Daddy died. I knew the blue leather journal in my room was none of my business.

I'd drawn pictures of the people in my life in so many different ways. The same person could look sad or angry depending on what I saw at the time. I had the one where Mama looked like a crazed woman. I had one of Gabby crying and one of her laughing. I had those pictures of

Raymond, leering and ogling and nasty looking. I even had pictures of Twyla's babies. Drawing pads were my journal.

I decided I had to return the journal to its place in the drawer where I found it. It was the right thing to do. I promised myself I would put it back as soon as I could. I would do it right after school. I would go to the barn and sneak across the field again. It would be the last time I would go to the Wendell house. I wanted to be the good kid Gabby said I was.

I could hardly wait to get in our house. I ran all the way from the bus, leaving Christopher behind. I changed my clothes in record time, grabbed the diary from beneath my dresser, and tore down the stairs, hollering to Gabby that I was going to the barn to get my drawing pad, which was partly true. In the loft I picked up the ledger and carefully managed the ladder rungs with the books tucked under my arm. I checked all directions to be sure no one was around and high-tailed it to the shed. I stopped there, like before, to catch my breath. I peeked around the corner of the shed, but didn't see or hear anything unusual. I opened the shed door and stepped inside, pulling it partially closed behind me. I went directly to the open drawer and bent to lay the books there.

I heard shuffling noises to my right and whirled around, coming face-to-face with Raymond. I stared. I heard Mama's words again. This was who she had seen. Raymond. He was different. Short hair and only a bit of stubble on his face. He didn't have a cap on and I think it was the first time I had seen all of his hair. It was dark and slicked back. It looked oily. I could smell him.

"Well, well. Look who's here." He chuckled a soft, easy laugh. "What brings you to this lovely place, dear Donna? Still nosin' around in other people's bizness, are ya?"

"I came to return something. I shouldn't have taken it. I'm sorry." I was terrified. So much so that my voice wavered.

"So yer not just nosey, but a thief, too. What ya got there?" He pointed to the books folded in my arms.

"Books. Old ones. I'm putting them back, then I have to get home. My Grandma Gabby is waiting for me."

He laughed again and I could see his dark teeth and the spaces left by the missing ones. Even the gap of his mouth looked disgusting. His eyes were little and dark, but there was a spark of light in both of them. He was having fun. He stepped closer, too close, and when he spoke I felt his spit on my forehead. I automatically brought my hand up to wipe it away. Raymond grabbed my wrist. I dropped the books and they thumped to the wooden floor. His bony fingers squeezed hard. I tried to yank my arm back from him, but he held it tighter. He pulled my hand to his face and kissed the back of it. I could feel the wetness of his mouth.

"Don't fight me, Donna. I been waitin' to get my hands on you for a long time. It was gonna be your pretty mama, but I never got the chance to get at her."

I was so afraid of him, there came a roaring sound in my ears and I could feel my pulse pounding there.

"Why . . .?" I barely whispered the word.

"Why, indeed." He laughed. "All my life I been puttin' up with people who think they're better than me. Always tellin' me how I oughta be and what I oughta do. I finally get out here to this place where I can do whatever I want, and you people come nosin' around."

"Only for the kids," I whispered.

"They ain't your kids. See, you people don't get it. We ain't your bizness."

"But, Twyla? Don't you care about Twyla? And getting the kids back?"

This time, he laughed loud and long. "You don't know nothin'," he finally said.

Raymond went to the back wall, pulling me along by my wrist. While he took down a strap of old leather, I tried to turn away but he yanked my shoulder and spun me back around to face him. I closed my eyes so I wouldn't have to look at him. He held my arms wrist-to-wrist with one hand and knotted and wound the strap tighter and tighter until my fingers felt numb. With his hand on my head, he shoved me onto a rickety chair. When he turned to get another strand of leather, I threw my body forward and ran for the door. I only made three or four strides when a powerful thud landed between my shoulder blades. Down I went, and because my hands were tied, I fell on my elbows and my face hit the wooden floor. My nose and my cheekbone burned with pain. My elbows were scraped bloody. Raymond yanked me up from the floor and shoved me into the corner nearby. I leaned hard into the walls so I wouldn't fall to the floor.

I watched as he went to the old canvas cot and dragged it from the wall. He pushed an oak desk aside a few inches. He moved around it and bent low. I couldn't see what he did, but in a moment a trap door opened upward. Raymond disappeared like a rodent down a hole. He was gone for some minutes but I was too scared and hurt to run again. My mind was madly trying to think of something I could do. Nothing made sense to me. "Please come and get me, Grandma Gabby," I whispered. I began to sob uncontrollably.

Next I knew, Raymond pulled me to the cot by my arm. He pushed me down and held my head back with a grip on my hair. With his other hand he reached down for his zipper. I began flailing and twisting my body as hard as I could. I raised my bound feet and kicked out at him. He grunted hard and bent over. He lifted me by my neck. I felt his fingers poking my throat and the pressure made me choke. He shoved me to the other side of the cot. He pointed to a dark hole where the floorboards had been opened up. "See there. You get on in there and be quiet about it. Sit yerself on yer butt and slide on them stairs."

I shook my head "No" as hard as I could, and put a foot forward so he couldn't force me to take a step. I felt like I was having a nightmare and couldn't wake up. I kept repeating, "Please, please, please."

I can't say how long it was before I became aware of my surroundings after Raymond had finally pushed me into the hole. It could have been a minute or an hour. I had not opened my eyes yet when I became aware of the sour stench. I felt nausea churn my stomach again. An image of baby Leland flashed in my mind. That was it. The smell. It was the same as Leland's dirty diaper that first day I saw the kids out on Gibson Road.

When I did open my eyes, all I saw was black-dark. I blinked and strained to find an image. Finally, above my head, two long, thread-thin cracks of dim light materialized between the floorboards. I was afraid to move my bound hands, or even my feet, for fear of what they might touch. I began to scoot one foot to the side, shifting it an inch at a time. When the toe of my shoe came in contact with something solid, I remained still for a long time. Ages went by before I allowed myself to move again. When I reached out, my shaking hands found a rough wall, and by running my stubby nails across it, I knew it was dirt. A dirt wall. I pushed my sore face toward the wall and smelled earth. I leaned a shoulder there and tried to think.

Eventually I began to scoot lower, one shallow step at a time. I counted them: one, two, three, four, all the way to seven. In the silence, I thought I heard the sounds of hissing or whispering. Snakes? I pictured them coiling at my feet. I put my head on my knees and listened as hard as I could. Breathing! It was breathing I heard.

"Hello," I said, but my voice was so weak it barely came. "Hello." I tried again. A groaning sound came back. At first I was terrified of it. But then I was so glad because it sounded like another human.

"Hello, is somebody there?" I sobbed louder.

"Hello." A whisper came back, raspy, throaty.

My body trembled again. Hard. My teeth chattered. "Who's there?" I breathed.

"My name is Twyla," the voice said. "Are you here to help me?"

"Twyla? Oh! Twyla! It's me, Donna Jean. Where are you? I can't see anything."

"Here. I'm here." She was sobbing.

"Where are we? Is this a cellar?"

"Yeah. This is the part under the shed. It goes t'ward the oak, but the roots have took it over. There's a cellar door above this wall, here, but it don't open. Probably ain't opened for years." She paused and I tried to picture what she'd told me. "Do you have any food? Did he send me any?" She wasn't asking, she was begging.

"No. How long have you been here? Everybody's been looking for you."

Twyla groaned and cried some more. "I don't know. Seems so long. I'm starving to death. I can't move, hardly. Too weak."

"Raymond doesn't bring you any food? What about water? Do you get water?"

"I think beside you . . . there is a bucket of water. It's foul but I been drinkin' it some anyway. Over here by me, this is a toilet bucket."

That was the stink that had nearly gagged me. I'd had a flicker of hope I might wake up from the nightmare, but it faded fast.

"Am I dreaming, Twyla? Is this a bad dream and I'll wake up?" I whispered.

"No. I'm afraid not. I wish it was true. Raymond's gone out of his mind. He brought me here sayin' he'd come get me out pretty quick, but he ain't. I think he forgets I'm here. Maybe he'll bring some food now you're here."

"My Grandma Gabby will come and get us," I said through sobs. "She'll come."

"She's got to find us first. She ain't goin' to know where we are."

164

I couldn't stand the reality of that. Suddenly I couldn't breathe and I felt like I was fainting, fading away to nothing into the darkness. My heart pounded so hard my chest ached inside. I put my face into my bound hands. I knew for sure if I moved one inch, only one, I would plummet into a deep black hole. Terror made my scalp prickle. I recoiled when I felt a touch on top of my head.

"It's me, child. Try to get you a little breath. You're havin' one of them spells." Twyla had moved closer to me in the pitch-black space.

"I want my Grandma Gabby." I said it over and over.

"I know." She petted my head. "Sshhh . . . now. You have to calm down so you don't get sick."

The air around me felt cool but my forehead was clammy with sweat.

Raymond

It was late and he was hungry again when he pulled around behind the house. He banged on the back door. Nobody came so he pounded again and hollered Twyla's name. Still nothin'. Where the hell was she? He went back to the nice car and opened up Leon's little red toolbox. Found him a little pryin' tool.

Took nothin' to pop those nails outta the old spongy wood. Raymond stomped into the kitchen and hollered again. This time he heard somebody ploddin' down the stairs.

"That you, Raymond?" Twyla called.

Who'd she think it was? The president? She looked like hell. All wrinkled up and kinda yeller-lookin'. She looked sick. She pulled out a kitchen chair and flopped down. Rubbed her face. She asked what he was doin' here. "It's my house," Raymond told her. Told her he could come back anytime he wanted. He was hungry. She needed to fix him somethin' to eat.

Twyla stood up slow-like and stared at Raymond. Right in the eyes. She shuffled to him, meetin' face-to-face. She saw the smirk on his wet, fleshy mouth. Her cheeks and tongue moved around and she worked up a big gob o' spit. She let go right square in his face. The foamy gob landed on the right side of his nose and went in his eye. She smiled.

Reflex. Raymond popped her a hard one across the face, his hand bunched into a fist, and Twyla staggered back. She tried to hunch forward to stop herself but she fell right down, whomp, on the floor. He wiped his face with his shirttail.

"I hate you," she said, and then said it again.

Raymond laughed. "Well, while yer hatin' me, get me somethin' to eat."

Raymond pulled what there was out of the cupboards and the Frigidaire.

Twyla used the chair to help herself off the floor. "Where you been all this time?"

Raymond said it was none'a her bizness. She went to the stove and fixed food out of a box. Raymond ate it outta the pan.

He tossed it in the sink with a racket and looked at Twyla. She could see he looked wild. Crazy-like. Glassy-eyed and he was breathin' hard. Pantin' almost. He told her, come on. Grabbed her wrist with his filthy hand, pinchin' the thin skin there and hurtin' her bad. She followed him out the back door and over to the shed, stumblin' to keep up. Down she went, so he dragged her up by her hair and one arm. He yanked the shed door open and pushed her in ahead of him. He tied her hands together with a bristly piece of rope, burning her skin when he yanked it tight. He kicked the cot away from the wall and with one hand lifted a door in the wood floor. "Get in," he told her.

"No sir, no way," Twyla said, but her voice whined, weak and scared. So he gave her a shove and she fell into the hole. She yelped like a pup when her ankle turned on a step down.

"There!" he hollered. "See how you like this."

The door slammed shut. Twyla lay sideways on the steps. "So, this is where I die," she whispered to nobody.

CHAPTER TWENTY-FOUR

He came. I don't know how long it was, but he came back. Twyla and I had both tried talking some to comfort ourselves and each other, but mostly I cried, and Twyla didn't have much to say, or didn't have the strength.

"Weren't for me you wouldn't be here in this hell place."

I didn't understand. She was there and I was there because Raymond was crazy. It had nothing to do with either one of us.

"Has Raymond always been crazy?"

"I reckon in a way. He was a daredevil and cocky when he was a boy, and he had an ornery streak, but I honestly didn't know he was mean-crazy like this. Maybe he wasn't quite so much back then."

"Why did you let him treat you so bad? You and your kids? You should have made him go away and leave you alone."

"Ha, you got no idea what you're sayin'. I was weak. A weak human bein'. He could tell me it was nighttime at noon, and I'd believe him. He fed me, well, us, when the kids came, and kept us alive. Barely, but he did. I thought we couldn't make it without him."

"Couldn't you get a job?" The idea seemed so simple to me.

"I tried. Wasn't much I could do for pay, and who was gonna take care of my kids?" There was a long, dark pause. "I don't expect you get that. You're too young and you got people who love and care for you."

I thought of Gabby, and Christopher, and Mama, and I cried again. I pictured Gabby in our kitchen, hollering at Christopher to get me from the barn, and Christopher, poor Christopher, running back in and telling her I wasn't there. Not in the loft. Not anywhere.

We fell silent again and maybe I slept leaning against the dirt wall.

There was a loud thump, above us light washed over the steps. I had to blink a few times to adjust.

"Mornin' ladies," Raymond hollered. "Here's some grub. Better save 'em. Don't know when I'm comin' back." A sack rolled and flipped down the dirt steps and landed by my feet. For the first time I saw Twyla in the light as she bent toward me to reach for the sack with her bound hands. Even in the dimness I was stunned by her appearance. Her skin was drawn and gray and she looked older than Grandma Gabby. Her hands were filthy and her skirt was ripped to shreds. Her hair was shaggy and matted. Something hit my back but not hard enough to hurt me. Raymond, above us, laughed.

"Don't worry, I'll come back. I ain't through with you, little Donna. I'll drag ya back up here ta this ol' cot and we'll have us a good time. Yes, ma'am. We'll have us a good time." He was laughing again when the wooden door slammed shut. I heard the sound of something scooting across the wooden floor above. We were absorbed into the dark again as if we didn't exist to each other.

"Did he rape you, girl?"

"Almost," I whispered. "I kicked him. Hard. And he quit."

"Thank the Lord for that. Thank the Lord."

Every time I dozed off, I would dream of killing him. It made me feel better for a minute. I would do it if I could. Maybe I would stab him. I squeezed my eyes closed against the image but it returned again and again.

We both foraged around, feeling for the sack and whatever else might be there. I heard the crackle of paper when Twyla opened the sack. I smelled the stink of old food. She pulled something out. I knew because I heard the chewing sounds.

"Bread." She said the word and gagged. Still she chewed. The two of us scrambled around on the dirt floor until we found two apples and one orange. They had soft, rotten spots in them and our fingers poked into their middles. I pulled an orange apart and nibbled at it like a rat. The tang of its rot lay on the back of my tongue. I tried to spit the bitterness out.

"You better eat that, hon. Don't know when there will be anything else comin'. Here," she said, "have this here piece of bread." She handed me a hard lump. I wouldn't realize until much later how generous the offer was. She was starving.

We both dozed off and on. There seemed so little to say and talking took so much effort. All I could think about was my family, and I'm sure Twyla must have thought of her kids. There was no measure of time. I thought about my pretty watch that Harry had given me for Christopher. I stood slowly, hunched and aching, and guided myself around the perimeter of the cellar. I came to the place where I supposed steps had led up to the other cellar door. Tree roots grabbed at my pant legs. When my foot kicked against the waste bucket the stink of it made me gag again. Our area was a rectangle, big enough to take a few strides from end to end. I tried to take a sip of water from the water bucket, but I couldn't lower my face to the surface of it.

"Twyla, can you tilt the bucket so I can sip some water?" She felt her way to help me. She grunted with the small effort. I put my lips to the surface and took in a tiny sip. It was so awful, I couldn't swallow it. I turned my head and spit it out.

"You better drink. Can't live without water."

"Come sit in front of me, Twyla. See if you can untie my hands."

"He comes sees you with them hands untied he'll prob'ly kill you. I wouldn't put it past him."

"Just try, Twyla. Please."

She did. I felt her tugging at the knots in the leather strap. Her fingers trembled. After a while she gave up. "I can't budge 'em," she said.

"Okay, let me try yours." Reluctantly, she put her hands out to me. The hard, rough rope poked at my hands, the bristles prickled beneath my broken nails like needles. I kept trying anyway. Horsehair rope, knotted so tight I couldn't pry up one single strand of it. I finally gave up.

I found the steps again and sat. In my mind I talked, first with Gabby and then Mama. I told Gabby I knew she would never stop looking for me. I told her I would be waiting for her. For a time, I didn't know what I wanted to say to Mama. When, finally, I did, I began telling her that no matter what, I loved her and she would always be my mama. My head pounded with pain.

By accident, pure accident, when I rested my head on my knees, the strap that bound my hands touched my lips. I let the loop of leather slide between my teeth and when I bit down I tasted the slightest trace of salt and the bitterness of the old hide. I nipped at the edge with my front teeth. As the leather became moist I bit harder. I bit my tongue, causing horrible pain and I tasted blood. I would have to be more careful. I bit again and again.

"What are you eating?" Twyla asked.

"Nothing. I am chewing the strap around my wrists."

"What in the world good is that gonna do?"

"I don't know, but at least I won't be tied anymore if I can bite through it." It was true. It wasn't that I had a plan. I continued to gnaw until I bit my lower lip so hard it brought tears. I think I slept for a while. When I tried chewing the leather again, my tongue felt blistered and my bottom lip was swollen. When, at last, I tried one more time, the two ends divided in my mouth. I held my breath and tried to tug my hands apart. Nothing happened. Raymond had knotted the strap as he'd wrapped it. I would have to try all over again.

Eventually I had to give in and use the filthy waste bucket. Twyla handed over a piece of cloth for me to use, and I realized why her skirt was in shreds. She had been tearing it away to use for the awkward job of cleaning herself. Every single move I made was difficult, either because my hands were tied or because of the pitch dark.

Time. Eventually, I quit giving any thought to time. I had quit thinking about how badly I wished I had my Christopher watch on. There was a vague sense of hours passed. Two hours since I chewed the leather strap. Six hours since Raymond threw the food down the steps. Maybe. Or was that a day ago?

Twyla moaned almost constantly. Sometimes she sounded like an animal. Sometimes like the wind bringing on a storm. When I didn't hear anything from her I began to worry that she might really die. I would call her name until she answered with a grunt. That was how I knew she was still alive.

I sucked on the rotten apple core and used my bound hands to scoop water from the bucket. The wet leather was easier to chew. I gnawed through two more wraps of the binding. I only had one more to go. I slept more and more often. My mouth was a mess; swollen lips and bloody tongue.

At last the leather fell away. I was elated and laughed aloud. Twyla moaned.

"What?" she rasped.

"The leather. I did it, Twyla! The leather is off." I felt the ache when I flexed my wrists. I rubbed them gently against my thighs. I had a strange sensation of weightlessness in my hands as if they wanted to flutter on their own.

I tried to reason what it really meant to have the use of my hands back. What if Twyla was right and Raymond would kill me if he saw them untied? I decided to keep the leather in my pocket in case I needed to use it or wrap it in a way to make my hands look bound. The normalcy of coiling the leather and stuffing it deep into my pocket felt wonderful.

"Twyla, help me think of something to do next time Raymond comes. I don't want to die, Twyla." I wasn't crying as much, but I was weak and sick. "We have to at least try."

"I don't know." I had to strain to hear her.

"Don't die, Twyla. Please don't die. Keep trying to live, okay?"

"Okay. I will."

And so, I sat in the dark listening to our breathing. I matched my breath to hers, willing her to live. I slept and woke, slept and woke. At some time, I crawled one slow step at a time up to the trap door. I put my hands in the air and pushed against the wood. Nothing moved, didn't even make a creak. Exactly what I expected, but it made me cry again anyway. A picture began to form in my mind. What if Raymond came and I pushed through the opening before he could grab me? What if I could hit him or hurt him somehow?

"Help me, Gabby," I whispered. "Help me think of something I can do."

CHAPTER TWENTY-FIVE

I was having a hard time concentrating on one thought for long. Images passed through my mind, one having nothing to do with another. I could see Raymond scooting the dresser away from the trap door, and then I would remember something about Gabby, or Mama, or Christopher. I saw Daddy in my mind's eye, smiling and gentle. When he came, I talked to him. Twyla would hear me and say, "What? What are you sayin'?" But I would keep trying to talk to Daddy. Please come and help me, I asked him.

When, finally, I heard noises above us, I perked up with more energy than I thought I had in me. I was alert and the noises were loud in my ears. Twyla spoke my name and I hushed her.

"Shhh, be quiet," I whispered. "I want to hear what he's doing."

I scooted up one step at a time. I could see the lighted slits between the boards of the trap door again. I pictured myself bursting up through the door like Superman would. I had brought my legs underneath me and squatted there on the second step so I wouldn't bump my head. I braced against the dirt wall with one hand, and balanced with the other. I heard the cot being moved and the scraping of the heavy dresser. Shadow moved across the light beams of the cracks between boards.

I heard a grunt of effort from above, and a muffled word or two I didn't understand. I heard the crackle of paper, probably another sac of rotten food.

"Hello there, ladies. Yer savior is back," Raymond called, and the next thing happened without any thought I can recall. In the blinding light of the gaping hole above me, I saw no one. Nothing. I pushed myself up as fast as I could with all the strength I had in my arms and legs. The first image I made sense of was the shed door where the brightest light shone. In my first stride, I fell over the cot, crashed to the floor and scrambled back up.

"Hey! You little witch! Where you think yer goin'?" I heard scraping on the floorboards and a loud clatter. At the door, I looked back to see Raymond sprawled on the floor, legs tangled in the blankets of the overturned cot.

"Sombitch!"

I made it outside into the glaring light. My eyes burned and watered, and I kept wiping them with the back of my hand and squinting to make out objects around me. My mind couldn't make sense of what I was seeing at first, and my sense of direction was hopeless. I began to run on my rubbery legs, and realized I was going the wrong way. I was running toward the Wendell house! I was finally able to focus my weak vision on the shapes of tall elms along the lane, and ran that way. I fell, got up, and fell again. I could hear a high-pitched squealing, and realized it was coming from me. I gaped my mouth and let it out. Loud as I could.

I wasn't yelling for Mama or Grandma Gabby. I was screaming for Daddy, over and over. Half way along the lane I looked over my shoulder, and saw Raymond disappear around the house. He was going to come after me. I ran, stopped, and vomited up foamy, yellow liquid, and ran again. At the end of the lane, I crossed Gibson Road and crawled through the barbed wire fence into the field. I caught my shirt on the barbs and frantically ripped it to get loose.

I could see my own house. My eyes still watered from the bright morning light. As I stumbled over the rough ground I began to notice how everything looked so vibrant: the emerald green grasses, the stones below my feet, and the high white wall of my house. Beautiful as crayon colors! It had been many days since I'd seen color.

The hum of an engine penetrated my senses and terror overtook me. I heard the squeal of tires on the pavement. He was coming to get me. When I finally dared to look, I couldn't believe my eyes as Raymond drove right past me on Gibson Road. Fast! He was going so fast.

I couldn't run anymore. I wanted so much to lie on the ground and rest. I had one more fence to get through and then I could make it to our yard. My yard. I separated the bottom wires and tried to roll through the fencing. I became caught up in the barbs again. I had to stop and rest to find the strength to pull away from the snags. My shirt ripped away, but my jeans were tough and the barbs held onto the denim. I lay on my side and pulled my legs away as hard as I could.

The next I remember was Christopher's hysterical voice. The only word I recognized in his shouting was "Grandma Gabby." I felt the coolness of the grass I lay upon and I began to shiver. I gagged to vomit again, but only heaved bile. I pushed myself up on my knees. Looking around, I saw I was on the edge of our lawn, facing the old barn. The familiarity of the sight brought on a wondrous feeling, like a beautiful, soothing dream. I lay back down.

"Oh Lord, oh Lord," I heard her shouting. "Christopher, get your mother." Gabby called my name over and over. I tried to answer, but I couldn't hear myself. Mama's face appeared and I reached up to touch it, to see if it was real. That was when I looked at my hands for the first time. My wrists had deep, raw sores encircling them and my nails were black and broken. My palms were peeled and bloody.

"Call the sheriff, and tell him we need a doctor, too!" The voices all around me were high and overwrought. I felt the soft warmth of a quilt weigh on my body and tugged it to my chin. Someone, Mama I think, patted it close around me and told me to be still.

"Twyla," I heard myself say.

"Shhh. Don't talk now."

"Twyla's in the cellar," I whispered.

I faded, and returned, over and over. I heard new and different voices. I thought I was speaking, but maybe I was only dreaming. Finally, I was safe. I began to relax and drifted into a deep sleep of exhaustion. The ride in the ambulance seemed to last only a matter of minutes. I awoke in a bright, white room.

"The lights," I said.

"What about them, hon?" a gentle voice said.

"Too bright."

I felt something cover my face and the room went black. I howled with fear, and grabbed at the covering, yanking it away and throwing it to the floor.

"Oh, hon! I thought it would help!" said the gentle voice.

I felt the sting in my arm when the needle went in.

CHAPTER TWENTY-SIX

I woke slowly to see the face of a pretty, dark-haired lady. She wore the reddest lipstick I had ever seen. She had her cool fingers on my painful wrist, feeling my pulse.

"Hi there," she smiled big white teeth. "How are you feeling?"

"Okay."

"You have lots of visitors waiting to see you. Soon as I'm done here. How old are you sweetie?"

"Fourteen."

"That's a good age to be. We're going to take real good care of you here, so you try to rest, okay?"

Gabby, Christopher, Mama and Deputy Wilkes filed into the room and stood around the bed. Both of my hands were gently held by someone's. They spoke in hushed voices. How was I feeling? Did I sleep? Was I up to eating something? I continued to nod.

Deputy Wilkes said, "Donna, I have to ask you a couple things now, okay?" I nodded more.

"Who put you in the cellar, Donna? Do you know?"

"Raymond." My voice was raspy. Somebody held a glass with a straw in it to my mouth. I sucked great gulps of ice water.

"Did he put you and Twyla down there together?" His question confused me.

"Yes. Not at the same time."

"She was already there first? Or were you there first?"

"She."

"Do you know how long Twyla had been there before you?"

I shook my head no.

"Do you know where Raymond might have went? After you got away, I mean?"

It began to occur to me that no one could know what took place while we were in the cellar. They wouldn't know we had no light at all. They couldn't begin to understand that there was no way to measure time. Gabby could not know how I counted on her to find me. They didn't know how terrified I had been that Twyla would die, and no one would ever come.

"He never talked to us," I answered. "Is Twyla alive?"

"She is. In fact, she is here at the hospital. Maybe you can see her later, okay?"

After that, someone was always there beside me when I woke. The pretty nurse bustled in and out. A clear bag hung above my head from a metal stand. I watched the drops trickle down its plastic tube and into my bandaged arm.

"We're going to plump you up with some good fluids, sweetie. You came in dry as a peanut. We'll get that little mouth of yours healed up and you are going to feel so much better." She helped me into a shower. I was weak but the warm water felt soothing.

That day, or maybe the next, I was helped along the wide hallway to see Twyla in her room. I wasn't prepared for what I saw. Her face, neck and arms were the color of plums. Her hands lay like claws beside her. Someone had stretched a paper bonnet over her hair, but I could still smell the sourness from it. She opened her eyes when I said her name.

"Hi, Twyla. Are you okay? We're safe." That was all I could think of to say. I sobbed in great gulping breaths. "We're safe."

I stayed in the hospital for five days. Going home, riding in the backseat of Gabby's car, was the most glorious thing. The countryside seemed to glide by. I felt a sensation of floating. Once inside our house, I sat for a long time on the couch and gazed around me. Our things looked fresh and new to me. The furniture, the television, everything. I went to the kitchen and slid into my usual chair and watched Gabby make tea. She hummed, and it was beautiful. Christopher, Mama, Gabby, they all kept smiling at me.

I had been excused from school for an indefinite period of time. I would have to make up my classes in summer school. I knew I wouldn't want to go in the summer and I pouted about the thought. Medical doctors, and a child psychologist, Dr. Brewer, who I had to see once a week, said I would need time to regain my concentration. He said flashbacks would keep me restless and I would, no doubt, have times of exhaustion. Being locked away in the dark would affect me psychologically. I didn't know what that even meant, but I was awfully tired.

After tea, Christopher and Gabby helped me upstairs to my room. It smelled like home there. I went to the window and looked toward the old house down the lane. I stared at the outline of the back corner of the shed. I had the oddest feeling I was able to watch all that had happened inside there, as if to someone else.

I saw my drawing pad was there on my desk. I picked it up, held it to my chest and sank against the pillows propped on my bed. I began to draw with healing hands, filling page after page with memories from the cellar. Even though I had been in the deepest darkness, I drew pictures of the things I'd touched and smelled and heard. Rotten apples, the waste bucket, moldy bread, and earthen steps. I drew Twyla, but I drew her as she was before her time in the cellar. I drew Raymond. I shaded until he looked dark and evil and smirking.

Herman and Rosalie came to see me often in the days that followed. They sat at the hospital with Twyla most days and they assured me she was getting better. The best news was they were going to move Twyla into Grandma Gabby Gabby's little rental house in town when she was well enough to leave the hospital. She wouldn't have to go back to that awful place down the lane. Rosalie would stay with her for the time being.

———

Mama. She still went to work each day, but when she wasn't sleeping, she came to me. She was quiet and pale. She had a look I had not seen before, big-eyed, worried. I knew it was because no one had found Raymond. She was afraid he would come back. Deputy Wilkes or one of the other deputies drove out Gibson Road several times a night but the days passed with no word about Raymond.

"I honestly don't believe he'll come back here," Wilkes said. "He knows how bad we want him."

His words didn't seem to help Mama much.

One morning I woke late and heard a man's quiet voice downstairs, and then Mama's. Though he spoke nearly in a whisper he sounded familiar, someone I knew. It was Harry! I hadn't thought we would see him again. My first thought was how happy Christopher would be. I still remembered when Mama made Harry leave. He had told her something that had upset her so much she'd sent him away. But here he was, and he and Mama were coming through my bedroom door.

"Hi, kiddo," Harry said in a kindly voice. "I hear you've had a real bad time. Are you feeling better?"

"I am."

"Is it okay if I sit here a minute?" He gestured to the foot of my bed and I nodded and pulled myself up against the headboard.

"Your mama and Grandma Gabby told me about what happened. I know it must have been so awful for you and poor Twyla. I'm sorry, honey."

I looked to Mama, wondering why Harry was here and what was going on. She gave me a small smile.

"I think Harry will be visiting us pretty often," she said. "It will be real nice to have a man around here to keep an eye on us. What do you think about that?"

"Good. I think that's good." I did. The idea was comforting. I quickly became used to hearing Harry's smooth, deep voice mingled with Mama's and Gabby's. Christopher wasn't as thrilled as I thought he would be. He came in my room after school and plopped on the bed.

"What's going on?" he said.

"About what?"

"With Harry? He leaves out of here like we will never see anything of him again, and now he's back like nothing ever happened. All of a sudden Mama isn't mad anymore? Now she likes him again?" His tone rose with exasperation.

"I know. I wondered too. All I know is it feels safer here with a man in the house. I'm not as scared now." It was true. I was fearful a lot. I slept with the light on and couldn't walk the short distance to the bathroom at night without the hall light. Sometimes I had to be completely exhausted before I would let my eyes slide closed for sleep. It was too dark.

Christopher took a deep breath and puffed it out. "I guess so. I'm still mad at him. I really liked the guy, but he left us when he left Mama. Don't know if I'll trust him again."

"Let's wait and see, Christopher. Maybe they're going to be friends now. We don't even know why Mama made him leave in the first place."

"You should ask Grandma Gabby. She tells you things," he said.

I had to smile. It was true. "Maybe I will," I said.

CHAPTER TWENTY-SEVEN

Twyla was being released from the hospital, but she was still frail, both mentally and physically. Gabby said Twyla's main distress had been that she would die without getting to see her kids. It had already been so long since she had seen them. Rosalie was more concerned about Twyla's mental state than anything else. She went to Deputy Wilkes and asked him to try to find out what he could so she could help Twyla know about the kids' welfare.

Meanwhile, Herman and Rosalie, with Harry's help, went back to the Wendell house to collect some of Twyla's things. There wasn't much. Her clothes were mostly rags and she didn't have many keepsakes. No pictures of her children. No cute knick-knacks. They had survived like vagabonds for too long. There were some blankets and bedding that could be laundered and used in the little house in town. Kitchen utensils were boxed to take. The rest could be taken away at another time.

Later, we learned from Rosalie that Herman had asked Harry if he wanted to go to the shed with him to have a look. Harry said he guessed so, and they left Rosalie to finish up in the big house.

"It was pretty damn awful in there," I'd heard Harry say as he sat in Gabby's kitchen. "Filthy dirty and that big gaping hole in the floor. Man." He shook his head.

"Oh, Lord! You didn't go down there, did you?"

"No ma'am, I sure didn't. I couldn't bear to see what poor Donna endured all that time."

Tears sprang to my eyes when I heard him say that. How did I? How did I survive such a terrible thing? Grandma Gabby would say it was God's will, so I guessed I would have to believe that.

Upon my next trip downstairs, I reached the bottom step to see books and papers scattered on the coffee table. I was confused when I saw the ledger and journal from the old cupboard in the shed lying there. Why in the world would they be back here in our house again? Hadn't I put them back?

"Gabby!" I called. "Grandma Gabby, why is this here?"

Gabby rushed into the living room looking concerned. "What in the world are you hollering about?"

"The journal, and the ledger." I pointed. "Where did they come from?"

"The men brought them back when they went to Twyla's. They wanted to take a look. See what they were about. Harry has been reading over them. He says they sure say a lot about the Gibson brothers and the history of all this land around here. He's interested, that's for sure."

I sat on the sofa and looked at some of the notes Harry had made. His writing was small and smooth. He had written Irvin William Davis, and below, a list of names. I. W. Davis was one of the names on the front of the ledger book. I wondered what it meant to Harry. I knew both books were especially old. Mr. Davis and G. B. Ewing must have been gone a long time.

We were all sitting around the living room while Harry told us a bit about what he was looking for in the journal and the ledger. As he spoke, I looked from Gabby to Mama. I could hardly believe what he was saying. When he was a boy, Harry had become aware that his family owned some property in our county. At that time, he lived with his parents in a faraway part of Texas. He told us his father had looked into property ownership, but couldn't find anything specific about what or where it was. It was said the land had belonged to an uncle, Harry's great-uncle, who was a Davis, but there were no records to be found. Long before he passed away, Harry's father gave up his search. Had the name, I. W. Davis, not been printed on the front of the blue leather ledger, Harry probably would not have taken any notice.

Harry tried several times to find more information and only got as far as finding some transactions made by the Gibsons on several other properties. Most of them were mining related. After all, that was how they made their money. Unfortunately, there were many gaps in the information Harry had discovered.

"I feel like something is off kilter," Harry said. "It's almost as if parts of the story of Mr. Davis and the Gibson brothers has been left out or kept secret. Davis and Ewing were obviously attorneys for some of the brothers' land deals as it shows right here." He held up the books. "So far, I have found no reference to any land deeds for the Gibson Road properties."

"How can you ever find out?" I was curious.

"I'm not sure. I'll keep digging around. Something might come up."

"Maybe there are more papers about the property in the drawer where I found these books."

"Let's go look!" Christopher was getting into the conversation.

A strange feeling washed over my entire body. "I'll never go in that shed again. Never."

Gabby squeezed me against her. "You will never have to sweetheart. Don't you worry."

"I meant Harry and me," Christopher said.

Mama, who had sat quietly, suddenly stood. "Wait a minute! I have the deed to this property. I'll be right back!" We all watched as she practically ran up the staircase.

Harry stood, and paced. It was easy to see he was anxious. Gabby went to make some coffee and Christopher and I watched the stairs for Mama's return.

"Got it!" She carried a thick manila envelope in both hands. She sat on the edge of her chair and pulled the papers from their packet. Harry stood over her. "Being a lawyer, it was important to Joseph to keep everything. This is a copy of the property deed. The real one is in a safe at the bank."

I could picture Daddy carefully sliding the papers into the envelope. His look of satisfaction when he was pleased about something had always made the corners of his mouth turn up the tiniest bit. I remembered his big, smooth hands, and his gold wristwatch on his wrist, and his broad, shining wedding band. An old familiar lump stuck in my throat. I blinked fast to stop the tears.

"Can I hold them?" I wanted to touch something Daddy had held in his hands. Mama knew. I could tell by the way she looked at me.

"Let's let Harry take a look first, then you can," she said.

Harry sat with the papers on his lap and thumbed through them. I waited, drumming my fingers on the arm of the chair. It was my turn to stand and pace the room. I let my mind wander back to the time we all first came to see our house. I had been excited and ran around from room to room until Mama made me settle down. I know it was love at first sight for my family. Christopher and I had clambered noisily up the stairs and explored each room. We chose the ones we wanted before the house was ours.

"Aha!" Harry's voice brought me back to the present. "This is what I wanted!"

"What is it?" Gabby stood from the sofa.

Harry explained that it did indeed look like a legitimate deed for the property our house stood on. It was simply written, stating the land descriptions and, most importantly, the seller. Joseph had bought the house through an agent who sold it for a man named Ralph Danner.

The name meant nothing to any of us. Harry seemed more determined than ever.

"I'll keep digging," he said.

———

Most days, Gabby drove us to the bus stop when it was time for Christopher to come home from school. We usually left a bit early so I could spend some time with the horses. They never failed to come trotting to the fence for a good scratch. There was something about them that was comforting to me. With their warm, grassy breath and big, friendly eyes, they calmed the anxiety that hounded me daily. I'd decided right there at their fence that my future would somehow include horses. When I told Gabby, she said I'd better get to thinking about what I wanted to do after I graduated from high school so I could afford to have my own horses. My Grandma Gabby was my best friend. She didn't discourage my dreams.

One afternoon, on the way to the horses, we met Harry driving toward our house. Seeing him got me thinking again, and I finally blurted out that question. The one Christopher wanted me to ask.

"What is going on with Mama and Harry?"

"Maybe you should ask one of them, Donna Jean. I'm not sure it's my place to say."

"But do you know? I'm mostly asking for Christopher."

Gabby grinned at me. "Yeah, right. And you don't even want to know, right?"

"I don't know why it has to be this big secret. Are they friends now?"

"In a way, I'd say that's true. I think they have decided to be friends and see where it goes. Everybody has a story, remember, and Harry has his own." She became quiet for several minutes. "Harry had been in some very serious trouble for some time. He even had to spend some time in jail." Gabby looked at me out of the corner of her eye.

"That's awful! Is that why Mama kicked him out of the house?" My anger was instant.

"Yes, it was. He was able to be released while he waited for a trial. The Mining Tool Company he worked for laid him off, so he had no job. Do you know what embezzlement means?"

"Is it stealing?"

"Yes, it is. He was accused of stealing a large amount of money from the tool company. It is a business that manufactures and sells all kinds of equipment used in the mines. He worked there for many years and was a top salesman. An investigation traced missing money back to Harry. Apparently it had been going on for some time. Harry had to hire lawyers to defend him and do their own investigation."

"That's why he came and went all the time?" I was remembering how, at times he was quiet and seemed worried about something.

"Yes. He was very scared. He would have gone to prison for a long time if he was found guilty. He had to meet with his lawyers over and over again."

"He didn't do it? Take the money?"

"No. It was another salesman. The last time he left here and was away for so long, it all came to a head. He has his job back again."

"So, he came back to tell Mama so she would be with him again?"

"Yes, I would say so. There had been times when he stayed away because he thought it would be best for your mother, then when the truth all came out, he came to win her back. But all that terrible stuff happened to you, and they could hardly think about themselves. Maybe they will now." Grandma Gabby was quiet as she drove. "It could be a good thing, you know. For all of us."

By the time we pulled over by the horses, I had let it go. I felt better. More comfortable about Mama and Harry's relationship. I was sure Christopher would feel better, too.

Raymond

Raymond couldn't let go of his anger at Donna. The damn brat had ruined everything. Gettin' away from him like that shouldn't have ever happened. He should've been more careful. And besides her runnin' off, he'd hurt his knee something awful from when he fell over the cot in the shed. Felt like somebody had took a hammer to his kneecap. Damn brat.

He was sick of livin' in his old piece a crap car. Should've kept that nice Chevy and left the country. As usual, he had no money. He had spent his last couple of bucks on gas and Camels, and shoplifted some crappy food from the gas station store. He moved from one weedy back lot to another. One pitiable town to another. Sneaking. Forever sneaking. He knew they would be huntin' him down.

All he could think about was goin' back to see Twyla one more time. Just once more. That's all he needed. He'd love to get his hands on that girl, Donna, one more time, too, but he knew he'd never get so lucky. They'd be guardin' her like she was the Queen or somethin'.

He thought about all those nights he'd hung out at the old barn where he could watch that pretty mama. Ellen. Prettiest woman he'd ever set eyes on. When her ol' man was still livin', she spent her time out in the yard gettin' a suntan and readin' some shiny magazine. She was hot and she made him hot. It was so easy then. He could hang out over at the barn and wait for her to come out of her house with her little towel she laid out on. He'd thought for sure he'd hit the jackpot the very first time he drove out Gibson Road to see the old house somebody told him might be comin' up for rent. He drove by the big purty house by the road, and there was the lady and her kids out there. After that day, he went a bunch of times, hopin' to get a look. Got a little carried away about the whole thing. What a deal. If they moved in that old house, he'd have him a bonus right there across the road.

And then get to come out and live right there across the road!

After Ellen was widowed, he figured his chances might even be better. Just as he was figurin' a way to get close to 'er, Ellen was gettin' out and around again. He watched her leave Goldie's some nights. Even went in a couple of times. In all those nights he waited for her over by the barn, he never got the nerve to trot across the road and say . . . what? He should a grabbed her when he had the chance. Hell, she never even knew he was there. She was a widow. Maybe she woulda liked some time with him. But he had the pleasure of watchin' the daughter with them filly legs and long hair. Young thing like that could drive a man crazy. Now, here he was, dumber than dumb, sleepin' in the backseat of an old junk car.

Naw, it was Twyla he wanted now.

Once in a while he'd think about his kids, but he didn't like doin' it. One night he damn near cried. Cried! Raymond hadn't cried since he was a baby. Cryin' was for babies. But if he could get Twyla and the kids back with him, they could go to a different state, collect money on the government there until he got another job and could start over.

Maybe he was losin' his mind. Goin' crazy. If he let himself think about his Oklahoma home when he was a kid, he'd remember how important he was in that town. How he could scare people. How he always got what he wanted one way or another. Now, now he was just a loser.

He had to make him a plan. How and when could he sneak back out to the old house out on Gibson Road? Surprise the hell out of Twyla. There had to be a way. Had to be. Maybe he could roll by about midnight, go on toward the river and walk across the field.

What if they caught him, saw him? By now, they'd probably shoot him. Oh well, better dead than livin' in the car with no money. Maybe he'd lay down on the seat here and starve to death. Someday somebody would find his bones and tell Twyla. Then she'd be damn sorry.

CHAPTER TWENTY-EIGHT

Harry still had to go to work, but he kept his business as close to Pickering as he could. He was gone overnight once or twice a week. We became so used to having him around, we missed him when he was away. He and Mama were much nicer to each other. More considerate. Sometimes he drove her to Goldie's and picked her up after work. I began to see a change in her after he had been around for a couple of weeks. A sweetness I had not seen for so long crept back into her personality. I loved hearing her laugh at some silly thing one of us said or did. And Grandma Gabby glowed with happiness. The twinkle in her eye was shiny bright.

Harry pursued his interest in the property across the road, and spoke often his long-time dreams of having a country place. He made phone calls to county seat courthouses, lawyer's offices and real estate companies. He kept lists of notes and people's names who he had spoken with. He asked questions and more questions. He was forever thumbing through that journal. I watched him become more and more frustrated with all the dead-ends. Finally, he asked Christopher to go over to the old shed with him on a Saturday.

———

Rosalie called. She talked so loud I could hear her from where I sat at the kitchen table. Gabby held the phone away from her ear.

"I just had to tell y'all! Children's Services are coming to see Twyla. We all have to pray as hard as we can that they give those babies back to her. I don't think she can survive if they say no. Oh my Lord, Gabby. I'm so excited I can hardly breathe! She'll be looking for a job soon as the doctor says it's okay."

I still got choked up when I thought about those kids. I wondered if they would still be the same. Would Melly still be the bossy one and Wade the sweet one? And the little ones, would they still love their mama?

<hr />

When Harry and Christopher came back from the shed, Christopher was pale and quiet. Harry carried several sheets of yellowed papers in one hand and rested the other hand on Christopher's shoulder. They came into the kitchen where Gabby and I were, pulled out chairs and sat.

"What's the matter, Christopher?" I thought he might have been crying. He looked at me with big, soulful eyes, but didn't answer.

"He's still a little upset over seeing the cellar where Raymond kept you and Twyla. It's a hard thing for us to see, Donna. It's so awful." He looked at Christopher. "He made the mistake of going to the bottom of the cellar steps."

"It was so horrible down there. I couldn't stay for two minutes, much less days," Christopher said softly.

"It was terrible, Christopher," I said with tears in my eyes. "But, we have to let it go now, okay. It's over and I'm alright, and so is Twyla." For his sake, I spoke much braver than I felt. Christopher nodded his head.

"So, what did you boys find over there?" Gabby asked.

"Cobwebs, mouse droppings, junk and lots of dust," Harry said. "And these!" He held up the papers. He spread the out across the table. We could see some were personal letters and some carried a letterhead from a real estate company. Harry began reading each one, setting it aside for us to look over. It soon became clear that they were correspondence between Wendell Gibson and the Plains Real Estate Company. Wendell was asking, in several different ways, why a land transaction had not yet been recorded. It seemed he was trying to update some information, and found that the property was still in the name of I. W. Davis, and now Harry was discovering nothing had changed in all the time passed.

"My guess is no one wanted to pay the back taxes to claim ownership and get a transaction recorded. It was probably sold down the line privately and never got straightened out."

"So, whose property is it?" I asked.

"Good question." Harry rubbed his eyes with his palms and shook his head. "By now the back taxes are probably more than the property is worth. To think some of my own relatives were such shysters."

Twyla called and I answered the phone. "Donna, honey. Is that you? Is your Grandma Gabby home? Y'all got to come see my kids! You won't believe your eyes."

I could hardly get a breath. "Twyla!" I heard myself shriek. "Okay. Okay. We'll be right there!"

I ran upstairs yelling for Gabby, completely forgetting Mama was trying to sleep. She and Gabby opened their bedroom doors at the same time.

"What in the world, Donna?" Mama said.

"What's happened?" Grandma Gabby said at the same time.

"We have to go to town. The kids are back! Can you believe it? Come on, let's go."

In less than five minutes, Gabby, Christopher and I were backing out of our driveway. All the way to town we speculated on the circumstances. We had so many questions. Were they back for good? Were they the same as they were when they left? Bigger?

"It hasn't been that long, you guys," Christopher said. "You act like it's been a year."

Gabby parked on the street in front of the little house. We all jumped out of the car and hurried to the front step. Christopher rang the doorbell, but I turned the doorknob and went right in. Twyla sat on the sofa in the small living room. Rosalie stood in the kitchen doorway. And there were the kids! All of them looking at us with big eyes. Startled by us, I supposed.

My eyes saw baby Leland first. He stood next to the coffee table. He grinned big when our eyes met and gurgled something I couldn't understand. His hair had been cut like a boy's, but it was still as curly as could be. Melly walked right up to me as brave as ever. She was pretty with her hair pulled back and tied with ribbon. She looked so clean and healthy. Her crystal-blue eyes looked right into mine.

"Hi, Donna," she said. "Did you know we get to be with our mom now?" I could only nod, too emotional to speak. I nearly took a step back, but Wade had quietly come up behind me. He seemed so shy. I reached to put my arm along his shoulder and he stepped away.

"Hi, Wade." I said. "It is so good to see you. I sure have missed you." That got one gentle smile, but no words.

"He isn't ready to talk much, yet," Twyla said. "It'll take some time."

And there was Jeffy. Cute as ever with his blonde curls lying close to his head and eyes that matched sister Melly's. He grinned and so did I. "Hi," he said. "I'm three." And this time he held up three fingers.

Gabby had sat next to Twyla on the sofa and by that time she was crying huge tears and wiping them away with a soggy Kleenex. "They're all so beautiful," she kept saying. So, of course Twyla started to cry, too. We were all a mess.

"Isn't this the most wonderful thing? They are back for good. God answered my prayers. I have my babies."

I hadn't seen Twyla since she left the hospital. She looked great. In fact, I had never seen her look so good. Her hair was cut shorter and she had gained weight. Her face had changed. Her eyes seemed bigger in her smooth face. She looked awfully pretty.

Jeffy took Christopher's hand and led him away into a bedroom. "I'll show you somethin'," he said. Christopher wasn't used to being around little kids and he looked back over his shoulder at me. I knew he was unsure about going. I smiled and nodded to him. Wade, Melly, and little Leland piled in one chair. We all found a place to sit. The kids never took their eyes off Gabby and me.

"We were at your house," Melly said.

"Yes, you were," I answered.

"You have a big television." We all smiled at that. Of all things to remember.

"We do. Maybe you can come out and watch with us."

Quiet as a mouse, Wade had moved around the end of the coffee table and wedged his bottom between the sofa arm and myself. I felt him lean his thin body into my side. It was the sweetest gesture I had ever known. I would have sat there all day.

Rosalie came back from the kitchen and said it was time for the kids to come and have something to eat. They all went quickly. Even Jeffy came in a hurry, still leading Christopher by the hand. We all laughed as they went through the living room.

"They probably had to hurry in to get their share of food at those places they were in," Twyla said.

"But, they look wonderful," Gabby said. "Someone has taken care of them."

Twyla looked hurt. Gabby's words had stung her. "I wasn't a good mother for a while. I know it. I couldn't cope with Raymond and our terrible life. I was awful weak."

Gabby quickly apologized, said she didn't mean it like that. She said she was glad they were okay. We didn't stay much longer. They needed time to get settled in. Rosalie said they had two cots for extra beds. Herman was coming the next day and they would be staying at the inn. Twyla needed some time alone with her kids.

On the drive home, Gabby told us things would all work out eventually. It would take some time for them to have a family routine and to get to know each other again. We talked about how great they looked and how healthy they seemed. Soon Melly and Wade would be going to school there in Pickering. Another big adjustment for them. They'd been through so much.

No one had mentioned Raymond all day.

Raymond

He'd driven by twice. He'd had to beg money like some bum for a little gasoline so he could plan his night. He waited until after midnight, drove slow and turned his lights off. He worried because his crappy ol' car was so noisy, but wasn't nothin' he could do about it. Maybe someday he'd have him a new car. He wouldn't let the trash pile up in it like this one. This ol' beater stunk for sure. Couldn't help it. He had to live in it.

So, he'd been drivin' right on past the lane, on t'ward the river. Practice runs, he called 'em.

He'd park out there and watch Gibson Road and the ol' house. Sure enough, once, he saw a sheriff's car bump along the lane and turn around in front of the house. He figured they'd be checkin'. Raymond got a kick outta close calls. Made him feel like a big shot, like he got away with somethin'.

Next time he came, he'd park back off the road somewhere and wait 'til the cop car drove away from the ol' house, then he'd drive down the lane and go see ol' Twyla. Man, was he ready. Was he ever.

He'd have to take her away with him. Who knew where? Just away. He sure couldn't stay around here no more. And the kids? Naw. They'd be better off somewhere else.

CHAPTER TWENTY-NINE

I still spent time at my window. Grandma Gabby had hung pretty new curtains that closed with the pull of a cord. She said I might feel better if I could block the view of the Wendell house and the shed. I didn't tell her, but it didn't work at all. I couldn't stand feeling closed up, even in my own room. Besides, I had always loved the outdoors and I liked seeing my barn. I couldn't go there much and I was still angry that Raymond had taken from me something I so dearly loved. I was constantly in fear of his return. He knew I went to the barn and he could easily wait there for me.

Harry was kind enough to walk over to the barn with me a few times. We had nice talks about the old place and how beautiful it was in its old age. He told me stories about the barns he'd cared about in his life. His family had horse barns and dairy barns. He missed that life, he said.

"Why don't you have them anymore?" I asked.

"Well, I couldn't make a decent living out of that life anymore. Wish I could have. I've been fortunate to work the job I have, though. Living off the land can't always be counted on. Be a dream coming to life if I had a piece of property to fix up. Have some horses again." With that he looked all around the barn with a sad expression. I felt sorry for him.

So, I would pull my new curtains aside and sit at my desk with my drawing pad and sketch away. My newest pad had plenty of pictures of happy things. I drew Twyla and her kids, loving the curls in their hair. I drew Mama looking beautiful and happy. I drew more pictures of the horses down the road, and even gave some of the better ones to their owners. But, at times, something dark would take over my mind and I would draw something shadowy and ugly. Once I drew a hanging dummy like the one I saw in the backyard of the Wendell house, but this one had Raymond's face. My hate for him was not leaving me.

I still woke often in the night. The slightest noise would startle me awake. Sometimes I would hear the sound of a car out on Gibson Road, only to fly to the window and discover I had been dreaming. There was no car. No car lights.

An extraordinary thing happened to Harry. He wouldn't, couldn't, give up on the property matter. He plugged away at finding anything he could about ownerships. For Harry the search had also become about learning of his family. There had been cousins he never knew. His great uncles were hardest to trace, but they had all passed and left no information to do with any land. One day, after talking on the phone for what seemed like hours, he'd hung up and literally danced into the living room.

"You will never believe this!" He pulled Mama from her chair by her hand and spun her around. "It looks like I might own some property near here!"

"Where?" Christopher bit first.

"Right over there!" Harry pointed in the direction of the Wendell house.

We gawked at him, not understanding what he was saying. Gabby looked suspicious. Mama squinted at him.

"It isn't absolute," he said, "but, because there have been so many transfers of the property and so many relatives are deceased, it appears the property has belonged to a second cousin of mine and me for a number of years. The problem now will be figuring the property tax that is due. I will eventually need to be in touch with this long-lost cousin." He stood silent for a moment. "Can you believe it? After all these years, I might own the property right across the road from the gal I love?"

Mama giggled like a young girl. Christopher and I looked at each other and he rolled his eyes and threw his hands over his face, which made me laugh. We were almost like a normal family. Almost.

The next two days were the best since my time in the horrid cellar. I felt more at ease, to the point that I went for hours at a time without the memory of being there in the dark coming to haunt me. The doctor had called them flashbacks. Once again, we were all able to talk to each other about everyday things: what to put on a grocery list, what was on TV, and plenty of town gossip.

I slept two nights in a row without waking. I felt more rested than I had in a long time. I asked Gabby and Mama if I could walk to the bus stop to meet Christopher. I wanted to leave early and take my drawing pad to sketch the horses. First, they both said no. I begged. They clucked around me, considering what I should be allowed to do. They finally relented, but made me promise not to speak to anyone, and if a car came by, any car, I had to turn and run home. I promised. They stood on the porch while I walked away and were still there every time I looked back.

The walk was amazing. I felt wonderfully free and light as air. I gazed far across the fields where the land was familiar, and pretty, and colorful. I watched a huge chicken hawk sail above me and alight in a grove of trees. It screeched, and another answered. As young as I was,

I believe I had a new sense of appreciation for life. Lives. Not only my own, but for all living things.

The horses perked up their ears and headed for me across their pasture, and one nickered a greeting. They shuffled around each other, trying to get the best scratch. I had come to love their warm breaths and gentleness. There was something about our mutual friendliness that made me feel special. Worthy of their attention.

I sat in the grass and opened my pad. I drew from that viewpoint, concentrating on the horse's big eye looking down at me. Maybe, at last, life was going to be kinder to us. To me and Gabby, Mama and Christopher. How good it would feel to be at ease! It would only take one thing for that to happen: Raymond needed to be captured and jailed for all the terrible things he had done.

Christopher hopped from the school bus, looking surprised to see me there by myself.

"Hey. What's up? Where's Grandma Gabby?" He looked toward home as if he expected to see her car coming.

"You are a spoiled boy," I teased him. "You have to walk all the way home today."

We walked slowly and talked about his school day. He liked school and since our lives had calmed down, he was doing well. He told me he and Harry were going to the river on Saturday to look for special rocks. Christopher was so happy-go-lucky. His mood made me feel good.

We were strolling along the pavement when I saw something to my right that made me stop short. I walked to the edge where the pavement met the dirt, and there lay a cigarette butt, unfiltered, that said Camel on the paper. My heart fluttered in my chest. Raymond. Harry wouldn't throw his cigarettes out of the window. I knew that for sure.

"Watch for more, Christopher. Look real careful over on your side."

We searched and searched. Me on one side of the road and Christopher on the other. We were close to home when I found another one. My heart was racing by then. I called to Christopher and we ran the rest of the way home. Harry and Gabby were in the kitchen when we burst in the house.

"Whoa," Harry said. "What's up with you guys?"

"We found Raymond's cigarettes!" Christopher said. "On the road . . ."

"Calm down," Gabby said. "What do you mean his cigarettes?"

I took a breath. "We found his cigarette butts along the road. Two of them. Unless you threw yours out, Harry." I hoped he had.

"Oh no, I never do that."

"I know. I know they're Raymond's."

"Well, wait a minute, now. Lots of folks smoke that brand. It could have been someone else."

"It wasn't," I said. "It was Raymond. He's back." I began to cry. Gabby put her arms around me and started to agree with Harry.

"No. It was him." I didn't understand why I felt so sure, but I did.

⌒

Deputy Wilkes came out soon after Gabby called him. Christopher and I got to ride in his squad car to show him where we found the cigarettes. Christopher rode in the back seat behind the wire cage.

I pointed out the place where the first cigarette was, then we went on to where the other lay beside the road. Deputy Wilkes picked it up and wrapped it in a slip of paper from his notebook.

"We've no way to know if it's his, but we'll assume it could be and act accordingly. We'll check the road more often when we're able to." He put his hand on my shoulder. "Try not to worry too much, Donna Jean. Gabby is right. They could very well be someone else's cigarettes." He gazed back toward the Wendell house for what seemed a long time. "No doubt he's a crazy man. I can't believe he'd chance coming back here again."

Back at our house, we sat on the porch and once again talked about Raymond. The deputy talked about what a big county of open land

200

we lived in, and how Raymond would be hard to find if he holed up somewhere. There wasn't enough law enforcement to cover every nook and cranny. He would send out the new information and deputies would keep their eyes and ears open.

Just like that, the sleepless nights were back. I tossed and turned and when I slept from exhaustion, the dreams haunted me again. I sprang up at every noise. I lost my appetite, couldn't eat much of anything without feeling sick. I felt depression weighing on me. But most of all, I was angry. So angry deep inside.

CHAPTER THIRTY

When Harry spent the nights at our house, he slept on the rollaway in the little office off the living room. He kept a room at the inn in town and the company he worked for paid a stipend for room and board. Sometimes we wouldn't see him for a few days at a time, and when that happened we all missed his presence. After one of those absences, he came back in a different mood. He was quiet, hardly bothering to make conversation. I found myself avoiding him. The lack of openness made me uncomfortable. Christopher came to me one night and asked me if I knew what was wrong.

"I don't," I had to tell him. "Maybe it's his work."

One mid-morning I saw him drive right by and go straight on to the Wendell house. I headed upstairs to my window and watched as he left his car, walked to the house and up the shabby steps. The door must have still been locked because I saw him walk around toward the back. I waited a long time for him to show again. When he did, he leaned on a fender, looking around. Finally he got in and drove back to our house. I was so curious about his peculiar actions I could hardly bear it.

I waited all day for him to say something about why he had gone there, but he was still in that same odd mood and spoke little. When Mama woke and came down for supper, he cheered up some, but he never said a word about going to the Wendell house.

I couldn't stand it. "How come you had to go to the old house today?" I asked it as innocently as I could. Mama, Gabby and Christopher stopped eating and looked at Harry.

"Oh, I thought I'd take a look around since it might be my property one day. Just curious, you know."

"How does the old place look?" Gabby asked. "The mice and rats will be taking it over if nobody cleans it up."

"Yeah, I was thinking that, too," Harry said. He became quiet again. He left when Mama had to go to work. We didn't see him again for a couple more days.

Gabby and I visited Twyla and the kids every few days. Gabby always had something to take to them. She made them pies and cakes and fried chicken. The kids would be excited to see us, and the little ones would squeal with happiness. I swear, Twyla was like a different lady. She looked great, but mostly I noticed a gentleness about her I'd not seen before. Even her voice was kinder. She spoke so lovingly to her kids and her eyes were soft when she looked at them. The best part was they all laughed a lot. Strange, I had never heard Twyla laugh before.

Another wonderful thing came about in the small town of Pickering. As the news spread of Twyla and her children's predicament, people began to help them out in so many ways. Food and clothes for the kids came flooding to them in bags and boxes. A group of ladies volunteered their time to sit with her kids while Twyla looked for a job. She applied everywhere she thought she might be able to do the work.

"I hardly know how to act when them ladies come by," she told Gabby. "Besides y'all, I haven't had a real friend in a long time."

"You'll do fine," Gabby told her. "Just be yourself. You're a good woman."

I saw tears flood into Twyla's blue eyes.

When Harry came back, he still acted moody. He didn't speak of the property. I would think about him dancing Mama around the living room and wonder what had happened to that happiness.

"Somethin's up with Harry," I told Grandma Gabby. We were doing the dishes together.

"I will say, I think you're right. Your mama hasn't said a word, and I won't ask."

"He sure changed his tune fast," I said. "He acts like he's mad at somebody. Maybe it's about the property deal."

"Maybe. He's been spending time here so he would be around to keep us gals safe. I don't know how long that's going to last."

We grew silent for a time, Grandma Gabby washing, and me drying. Suddenly, visions of Raymond began flashing through my mind. Him and his cigarette butts. His face was crystal clear, and I tried to blink him away. I felt my heart speed up, and I couldn't breathe in enough air. I heard myself gasp, and Gabby turned toward me. My knees grew weak, and I reached a hand out to her. She was quick to grab my arm and steer me to a chair. I heard her say to put my head down but it was too late. I slumped forward in the chair and my head bumped to the tabletop.

I came to with a wet towel on my forehead. I still felt as if I couldn't breathe deep enough. I was trembling and crying. "Am I going to die?" I'd said to Gabby." I feel like I'm going to die."

"Oh no, honey. You're going to be fine. I'm calling your doctor right now. You just be still right here." I could hear her talking on the phone but her voice sounded far away. Next I knew, Mama was there beside me. She held my hand and brushed my hair back. I finally began to calm a bit, but Grandma Gabby said we had to get to Doctor Brewer's office right away. By the time we met him at his office, I was exhausted and sweating through my clothes. I told him about the image of Raymond that came to me just before I began to feel sick.

"I believe she's had a bout of anxiousness because of her recent experiences," he said after examining me and asking me questions about what had happened. "They can be frightening, and they can come on suddenly. Donna Jean has endured so much stress for a young girl. I fear it will take some time for her to recover." I had to stay in the small room for a while so they could monitor my pulse and blood pressure. When I could finally go home, Mama made an appointment for me to return the following week.

After that, I was seldom alone for any length of time. My family, and even Harry when he was there, watched me like a hawk. After a few days passed by and I was feeling fine, we all began to relax and not live with the constant worry of another attack.

CHAPTER THIRTY-ONE

Harry finally told us what was wrong. The property across the road would never be his. There was no way he could pay all the past-due property and inheritance taxes, and the only other person responsible was that long-lost cousin. Harry had found him, only to learn he was elderly and poor as a church mouse. He had no interest in the property.

Harry had spent hours and hours delving into old records and making phone calls. The day I had watched him go to the old house, he had been searching again, desperate for anything that could be helpful. He told us he had gone into the shed and shuffled through every scrap hoping for more papers or records to show someone had made at least some of the payment.

"I'm sorry," he said to us. "I know I've been moody. I had such high hopes. There were so many ideas in my head. I dreamed of building a brand new home over there. I could farm the land and have horses and dogs. And . . ." he shrugged his shoulders. "Oh, well."

I remembered what he had told me at the barn the day he talked about how he had grown up with those things. I knew then it really had been a vision for him.

"Maybe you could do some of those things here, Harry," Mama said.

"Why, Ellen, are you asking me to marry you?" Harry found a smile.

Mama turned red as a beet. She stammered and finally said, "Well, I was thinking maybe you could use this land around our house to do those things. It isn't much, but enough for some of your dream."

Harry stood and went to Mama and gave her a sweet kiss on her cheek. "Thank you for the kind offer," he said. "I might take you up on that."

I was sitting on the porch with my drawing pad, working on yet another picture of my beloved barn. The evening was warm and the light was soft. Christopher came out to join me.

"Hi, buddy. Whatcha doin'?" I was sketching and didn't look up as I spoke.

"Do you ever think about killing Raymond?" His voice was strong. It was an honest question. I couldn't lie about the answer.

"Yes. At times I do. When I remember particular things he said or did. I don't like thinking it, though." I would never tell him all the ways I had imagined killing Raymond. How I'd had visions of stabbing him. How I had thought of burning the Wendell house down while he slept there. How many times I had wished he'd died in a terrible accident like our father had.

"I could do it. If he came back, I could do it." I saw his jaw was set, tight and square, like a grown man's.

"No. No you couldn't, Christopher. I think killing another human would be hard for a good person like you. Besides, it would make you a murderer and you would go to prison."

"Not if nobody knew I did it."

"Stop now. Enough of that talk."

"If you were going to kill him, how would you do it?" He didn't look at me, just gazed across the field toward the Wendell house.

"Christopher! Stop. Quit thinking about Raymond." His demeanor disturbed me as much as his words. He was too intense for a boy his age.

He sat for another minute or two, stood suddenly and went back inside. I sat there, dumbfounded. I began to think about how Raymond had affected my entire family. It wasn't only me he'd damaged. None of us would ever be the same. I wondered how many nights Christopher had lain awake thinking about how to get back at Raymond for what he'd done to me. He was still a boy, but he was maturing and his emotions were heartfelt. My anger was building again. Yes. Yes, I could easily imagine killing Raymond. I tried doing what Doctor B had advised. "Allow yourself the thought, then conger something good and happy, breathe deeply and let the bad thought go." The barn. I concentrated on the light and evening shadow, and began to draw again.

Mama was sleeping, Christopher was in school and Gabby had gone shopping. The morning was cool. I pulled on my clothes, padded down the stairs, and headed out the door, closing it quietly so as not to wake Mama. I had thought nearly all night about what I wanted to do, and this was my chance. I trotted across the road, past the barn and out into the field. I was going over to the Wendell house. I needed to go once more. I even felt a strange excitement about it. Maybe, I kept thinking, maybe I was going crazy. I could have waited. Asked Harry to go with me. But there I was, traipsing across the rough, familiar ground, headed straight for the oak tree.

I stood in the rutted lane between the house and the shed. I saw the shed door was slightly open, the hasp swung back. I turned slowly looking at every single thing surrounding me. I recalled trying to run from Raymond, my eyes squinting against the light and tears running from them. I remembered finding the familiar shape of the elm row, and running toward those gnarly trees as fast as I could. I had been so weak. I recalled falling, scraping my hands along the rough, hard ground, and scrambling to my feet, and, Oh Lord . . . looking back.

Waiting for a hand to grab me and yank me down. With devastating humiliation, I remembered the feeling of urine running down the inside of my legs.

I put my hands to my head, willed myself back to the present, and turned to the big house's front steps. I sat on the top one and gazed around the yard. Someone had rolled the big stones back into place around the fire pit. The same ones Grandma Gabby had backed over that day. The grate and a lighter fluid can were nearby, both bent and rusty. My thoughts slipped back again and I recalled the first days Twyla and Raymond lived there. I could smell the cooking odors, and could hear the noises and voices we listened to from our own porch. It all seemed so long before that day.

I stood and walked slowly to the shed door, lifted my leg and pulled the door open with my foot. I couldn't bear to touch it. It creaked open and I stepped forward and peered inside. I was not surprised at what a mess it was. Mice and spiders had taken it back again. The trap door was closed. The sagging cot was in the middle of the room. The two filthy blankets were draped across it and a grimy pillow lay at one end. Someone, maybe the deputies, or whoever came to the shed after my escape, must have set it back on its legs. The last time I had seen it, it was upturned atop Raymond.

I backed away and walked behind the house. I wondered what would happen to everything if no one could own it. Would it collapse someday and be a pile of boards? I had seen places looking like that and would wonder whatever happened to the people who had lived in them. A sadness hung about those old places. But, not at the Wendell house. All I felt there was an evilness.

I made my way back home, pausing for a few minutes in the barn. I breathed in the odor of dust and old wood that I had come to find comforting. I found my "'good'" thought the doctor had spoken of. How wonderful it would be if Harry really could use our property to build his dream. Maybe we could fix up the old barn. Save it.

Raymond

He figured he was maybe dying. Maybe he'd got the cancer or somethin'. Could be the gas he'd swallowed when he had to suck on that damn hose. He'd been to about every ranch in the county lookin' for trucks or cars he could syphon gas from. He went back to the ones where the people parked out away from the house, and the ones that didn't have a damn pack of mean dogs.

He hardly got hungry anymore. He could live on a package of saltines and a candy bar for a day or two. His clothes were too big on him so he knew he was gettin' skinny. The worst thing was the stomach aches. They bent him right over sometimes. Felt like somebody put a knife in his belly.

It was time to go to the house before he died in this damn car. He'd never give much thought to the Lord or Heaven or any of that religious stuff. His ma had tried to teach him and the other kids about it, but he didn't remember much of what she read to 'em outta the Bible. He'd thought it was just a way to get 'em to behave. If they didn't do things the Lord's way, they'd go straight to the devil in Hell when they died. Well maybe he would, but first he was going to see Twyla and his kids. He wished if he was gonna die, he didn't have to do it all alone.

He'd park his car in a tree grove by the river and walk to the house from there. He'd wait for the cop to leave the old house, then he'd head there. He wanted to lie down on a bed, and eat at the kitchen table. Watch ol' Twyla move around. And them kids. He found hisself wonderin' about them, too. That little Melly, she was a firecracker.

If he could rest for a couple days they could pack some stuff in the car, whatever would fit, and leave the country. Maybe go back to Oklahoma for a little while.

Maybe he could be a better man so he wouldn't go down to Hell and burn up.

CHAPTER THIRTY-TWO

"She needs closure. She keeps suffering the story over and over again because there is no ending. If it happens that Raymond is never found and arrested, she will have to find another way to live around the emotions of what happened to her." Dr. Brewer explained my behavior to Grandma Gabby and Mama.

We all, including myself, had thought for a time I was doing better. Dr. B called it recovery. I had slept better for several nights and felt calmer throughout the days. It didn't last long. One night of nightmares, and it all came flooding back. I was restless. I wandered the house aimlessly, trying to find something I wanted to do. Poor Gabby. She tried her best to help me. We cooked together and cleaned together. We started going for morning walks after Christopher left for school. Getting out and walking helped me more than anything. Breathing the cool morning air cleared my mind. Grandma Gabby was so funny sometimes I could really get a laugh. She could make me feel safe.

By afternoon I would feel myself shrinking into the changed person I had become, someone I didn't know and could hardly cope with. The very worst thing that happened was that gradually I didn't want to draw anymore. I would sit with my pad and pencils and stare into my inner thoughts. My love of the art, and my imagination, seemed to have disappeared. And I cried. I cried until I was sick of myself.

Sometimes I didn't even know what brought the crying on. I would spend an entire day on the verge of tears.

Dr. B wanted to see me twice a week, and when we met, he'd had suggestions for me. "More exercise, girl. You are young," he'd said. "Go out and do some running. Do jumping jacks. Climb a hill."

He also wanted me to start doing school assignments again. "Don't wait for summer school. Get your books and do the work. Even if it isn't done perfectly, I want you to use your mind for structure."

Harry helped me with my school assignments. I was amazed at what a good teacher he could be. He was able to help me with all my subjects and especially math. Harry was a smart man.

"You should have been a school teacher," I said.

He'd laughed. "No way could I put up with a classroom full of teenagers unless they were as smart and well behaved as you and Christopher." That was said with a wink. He helped me feel better about myself.

———

Deputy Wilkes came by every few days and each time I saw him drive in I would pray he had good news. This time, I would pray, this time let him have news about Raymond's capture. Finally, one afternoon, he had something to tell us. He had us come out to the porch where we sat in a stiff row and waited for the news.

"I don't want to get your hopes up," he said kindly. "We have heard what we have to consider as a rumor because there are no facts to support it yet. Someone over in Newell was overheard to say he had seen Raymond in a Quick-Mart on the edge of town. An off-duty city policeman was within hearing distance and struck up a conversation with the guy. When he asked him when it was he had seen Raymond, the guy was so vague the officer thought maybe he was just talking."

"But why would he even say it if it wasn't the truth?" asked Christopher.

"Raymond is still a hot subject around this county. Maybe you all don't realize how badly folks want him caught and made to pay for what he did to Twyla and Donna here." He touched my shoulder. "He's a hated man, and people are still talking about him. They're also a little fearful. He's been dubbed a crazy man, and folks tend to be scared of crazy people. Anyway, that fella could have been trying to make himself sound important. Like he knew something nobody else did."

"Does Twyla know about this?" Gabby asked him.

"Yeah, she does. I just left her before I came here. Best she keep the kids close for now. If, and that's a big if, Raymond really is around, we don't know what he knows. He could possibly think Twyla and the kids are still living out here." He indicated the Wendell house with a wave of his arm.

After he climbed into his car and drove away with a wave, we all sat and watched him go. I don't know how to explain what I felt, but I was almost glad to hear the news. It might have been better that someone had actually seen Raymond than to be wondering a hundred times a day if he was still nearby or not.

I decided right then I would be ready for him if he came around us. I'd had some thoughts about it from time to time, but I had begun to feel a strong urge to take it seriously. I made my plans the same night and by the next day, I knew what I would do.

I'd seen it a dozen times while looking for some tool or another. It was in a rusty bucket in the old implement shed behind our house. The handle was wooden and had a split along one side. The blade was long and slightly curved and had probably been used to cut corn stalks many years before I came across it. It was dull and rusty, but the tip was sharp. I took it to the side of the house and stashed it behind the ivy vines. I would have to decide if I should leave it there or take it up to my room and hide it, taking a chance on Gabby finding it.

It was not that I could recall any noise, or even that I'd had a nightmare, but I awoke with a start. I sat up in bed straining to see, and held my breath to hear better. It wasn't unusual to often hear the creaks and pops of our old house as it warmed or cooled, but I couldn't hear a thing. I lay back, closed my eyes and tried to go to sleep. I recalled Dr. B's suggestions for relaxing my body to encourage sleep. I tried to take some nice deep breaths and think pleasant thoughts. It was no use.

I tossed back my covers, left my bed, and moved over to the window. With only a slice of moonlight, it was especially dark. The elms barely made a silhouette. I flopped onto the chair at my desk and put my head on my arms. A disturbing thought came to mind and I felt the tears coming. What if I had to live the rest of my life being afraid? Being on guard? How could my life ever be normal? Hunched there, I began to worry over one thing and then another. How could I ever go to school? Would I always be afraid of the dark? Would I ever be able to live in my own home when I grew up?

I sat up and wiped my tears on my pajama sleeve. At that moment, I did not know what I was supposed to do. The helplessness I felt overwhelmed me. I finally pushed myself up, and turned to go back to my bed. That's when I saw the tiny light. Through the blur of a tear, it seemed the size of a firefly. It didn't appear to be moving, it was just there, far out across the field beyond the Wendell house.

The minutes had ticked by while I tried to reason out what I was seeing. The light was moving. That meant someone had to be out there. I sat again and watched for a long time. The light brightened as it came nearer. I'd knew then who it was. Who else would be coming from the river in the middle of the night? Suddenly I could see him as if it was mid-day. The image of Raymond, trudging along, stumbling on the rough ground. I saw him in my mind, filthy clothes, and greasy hair. I could even smell him, the same stench he'd brought with him when he came to the cellar.

I stared until the light disappeared behind the oaks at the Wendell house. I dressed quickly and carried my shoes down the stairs without making a sound. I took some wooden matches from the box Gabby kept by the stove, and left by the back door. I snatched the harvest knife from the ivy leaves, and headed toward the barn. I had a vague feeling I was dreaming. I could have been watching myself play a role in a scary movie.

The light in the sky had not brightened yet so I moved slowly toward the Wendell place, bent nearly to the ground. When I reached the back of the shed, I stopped and kneeled to catch my breath and listen for any noise. I didn't hear anything at first, but then there came a hollow knocking sound from behind the house. I held the knife handle in a tight grip.

"Twyla," he called. "Twyla, let me in. It's me, Raymond."

After all that time, he still didn't know Twyla didn't live there anymore. He rapped harder and called out louder. I could hear him crunching through the weeds and oak leaves as he came around to the front porch. He climbed the steps, knocked, and called again. I heard him rattle the old doorknob. I saw the flash of his light and knew he'd shined it toward the shed. That was when I began to hear my heart thumping in my ears.

He went inside the shed and I heard him drop something to the floor. He stepped back out and relieved himself against the shed wall. He groaned and went back inside. After some shuffling of heavy shoes and scraping sounds, all grew quiet. I leaned my head back against the wall, breathed deeply and willed myself to be brave. Be brave, Donna Jean. This is your chance. It seemed I sat there on the ground for an hour. There had been no more sounds, until I heard the rumble of a deep snore. I stood and stretched the ache from my knees. I laid the knife at the corner of the building so I would know exactly where to reach if I needed it.

When I silently reached the shed door, it was ajar. I saw the hasp had been nailed firmly in place again. At that very minute I knew what I was going to do.

CHAPTER THIRTY-THREE

I do not recall having one second of doubt or hesitancy. I went down on my hands and knees and felt for a thick, sturdy twig or stick. I slowly pushed the door closed and moved the hasp over the ring. I slid the stick I'd found downward through the ring, forcing it, being sure it fit tight. Perfect! I bent again and felt for the driest leaves and small bits of stems and bark. I gently piled them against the shed wall. I could hear Raymond inside, still snoring and occasionally mumbling, or calling out something unintelligible.

I took a wooden match from my pocket and looked around for a place to strike it. Feeling for a stone, I kept widening my search. I'd lit matches a hundred times for our stove at home when the pilot light wasn't working, but I'd always used the strip on the matchbox. I finally found a stone but it was huge and too far from the shed. I tried to unearth it. Finally, out of frustration, I struck the match against it. It lit easily and I turned back to the shed. The match went out almost immediately. I tried again, this time cupping my hand closer around the flame. Again it flared and died. I tugged at the rock again and when it finally unearthed, I lugged it to the shed wall. As I bent to place it, the stone rolled awkwardly from my hands and bumped against the bottom edge of the shed wall.

"Who is that?" Raymond called out. "Who's out there? Open this damn door!"

I froze briefly, and then scrambled to light another match. There were only three left. It flared and I held it against the pile of leaves. A wisp of smoke curled upward but the tiny blaze died out. My hands shook, and I reached again for another match. Every ounce of calmness and confidence had left me. I felt frantic. It came to me I should run. Run back home. By the time Raymond could escape the shed, I could be back home safe and sound. No one need know what I had tried to do.

"Twyla, is that you? What the hell you doin'?" The shed door banged and rattled. "Let me outta here. Twyla!"

I stumbled my way across the rutted driveway toward where the old fire pit was. The lighter fluid! If there was any left in that old can . . . ! I tripped and fell, got up and hurried to where I thought the container should be. Making out the shape in the dimness, I got my hands on the can and shook it. I could barely hear the splash of liquid inside.

Raymond had gone crazy inside the shed. He was kicking at the door and hammering the wall. I knew that if he came through that door he would kill me for sure. I began to shake so violently, I had a hard time squirting the fluid in the right place and striking the match. A voice in my head kept saying, "Run. Run away!" But the voice of that girl who had been locked away in a cellar and had been abused by the crazy man in the shed said, "Do this! You can do this!"

The leaves caught quickly and a flame flared up from the pile. It began to sink so I blew as much breath as I could muster. Up it went, and this time it climbed higher. Little waves of fire began to crawl into surrounding leaves and they flared, too.

"Twyla, what the hell are you doin'? Is that smoke? Open this damn door!"

I stood back and watched the fire grow. The dry wood of the shed wall caught easily. Caught, and crept upward. I threw the lighter fluid can toward the fire pit and ran. My legs pumped with energy I didn't know I had.

It was when I reached the barn that I remembered I'd left the knife behind. Too late. I couldn't go back. I quieted my step as I circled behind our house. I opened the back door and slipped inside, relocking it behind me. I silently tiptoed up the stairs and into my room. There, I went straight to the window. I couldn't see the glow of flames. I was certain the fire had died out. I stared for several minutes, not knowing if I wanted to see fire . . . or if I didn't.

I changed back to my pajamas and hurried in a tiptoe down the hall to use the bathroom. I was a mess. My hair was a tangled mass and my face was red and splotchy. I brushed my hair and splashed cool water over my face, then returned to my room. I gasped at what I saw, and moved closer to my window. The glow was eerie. I saw it spread skyward, into the darkness.

For the first time it struck me that if Raymond went to the cellar, he might live through the fire.

I hurried along the hallway, tapping on each door. "There's a fire!" I called loudly. "At the Wendell house! There's a fire burning! Come on!"

They came, disoriented from their sound sleep, barefoot and wearing questioning looks on their faces. We all leaned into my bedroom window.

"Oh, my Lord." Gabby rushed off to call the fire department and sheriff's office. I heard her shout for Harry. The rest of us followed her down and went out on the front porch. So many questions were passed around. What in the world? How could it have started? Could there have been someone there? Kids from town, maybe?

Harry was pulling on his shirt and shoes and said he was going over there. Mama begged him not to. "Please, Harry! It will be so dangerous there."

"I bet it was Raymond! I bet he did it on purpose to be mean," Christopher raged.

I couldn't join in. What would I have said? I did it. Raymond is burning to death over there. I stood back against the wall and brought my hands up to my face. As I stood with the people who loved me most in the world, the horror of what I had done washed over me. I slid down and gripped my knees against my body. I closed my eyes, but it did no good. I could still see the burning shed and hear Raymond's voice.

The sirens whined from far away on Gibson Road. We all looked in their direction, silent and waiting. The trucks started braking to make the turn into the lane and I could see the men inside the cabs. One of them would discover a person had been inside the shed. Somehow they would know what happened. They always knew.

There was to be no control of the flames. The firemen tried hard, their hoses shooting streams of water. Hissing sounds and the stench of wet smoke reached us where we stood. The shed was disappearing. The oak tree had caught, and fire had rushed along the great limbs to the roof of the house. The Wendell house would burn to the ground, leaving nothing whole.

It all seemed to go on forever. People came and left from the lane. All of us, except Harry, went inside our house and as usual, Gabby tried to be helpful. She made tea and cocoa for us and anyone who might stop and come in. Christopher sat at the end of the couch and pulled an afghan across his chest. Mama went up to her room and put a warmer robe on. I sat at the kitchen table watching Grandma Gabby bustle around. She'd glanced at me several times as if she wanted to say something. Harry came in and poured himself a cup of coffee and sat next to me. I could feel him looking at me.

"Are you okay, Donna Jean?" he asked quietly.

"Yeah. Yes, I'm okay. Just, you know. . ." What in the world could I say?

"I know. Such a terrible thing. And so many questions."

We were all exhausted as the sky lightened with the tinge of dawn. I left the others and went up to my room. I was not prepared for what I saw through my window. The oddity, the emptiness of the landscape, was unbelievable. The view, the horizon I had gazed out upon every day for the last few years, was gone. The oaks still stood, but their lower limbs were badly burned and barren. Most of the elms along the lane were gone, leaving only the few charred trunks closest to Gibson Road.

I lay across my bed and waited.

CHAPTER THIRTY-FOUR

He came early, before any of us slept. I went back downstairs when I heard his voice. He sat at the table and Gabby served him coffee. His uniform shirt was stained and he smelled of smoke. They'd found Raymond, he said. His remains were recognizable, though barely. There would be more ID-confirming done by the coroner, but they were sure. Maybe suicide, but fire was an unlikely way to kill oneself. Accidental death was possible. If someone was drunk and passed out . . . maybe a cigarette. They weren't ruling out murder. Intentional. Deputy Wilkes kept shaking his head. They'd figure it out.

I listened in silence. All I could think was they had not been able to tell the hasp lock had been jammed from the outside. The wooden stick had burned away.

Someone asked about Twyla. The deputy said she seemed to be doing okay. Her sister was on her way. Gabby talked about how, someday, she would have to explain to those children what had happened to their father. Deputy Wilkes agreed it was a terrible thing to happen to anybody. They spoke of how sad it was that Raymond couldn't ever pull himself together and be a better husband and father. Be a better man. I didn't like hearing them speak of him as someone to be pitied. He was a monster.

The next few days passed slowly. Moods were sluggish, partly from being tired but more from the ordeal of the fire. I found I could hide behind pretending to be myself. Like an actress. I began to get good at it. I saw Dr. B two days after the fire.

"Yes," I said, "I feel better knowing he can never harm me or anyone else again."

"Yes, it was awful how he had to die. Better had he been caught and put in jail."

Yes, I was sure I would be fine, given time.

I'd played the part like an Oscar winner.

Grandma Gabby did laundry on Tuesday. It would take more than a fire to keep her from doing laundry on Tuesdays. I was helping her sort the clothes.

"Check those pockets. If there's money, the laundry lady gets it."

It was her habit to stick her hand in all the pants pockets and pull them inside-out. I laughed at her little joke, and looked up to see her doing just that. She rolled something between her thumb and fingers and opened her hand. She brought the pants, my jeans, up to her face and sniffed. She looked at the object in her hand again, and went completely still. When she finally held her palm out to me, she stared into my eyes. Hers had turned a darker shade of blue, and her mouth was set in a straight line. There, in her palm, lay a wooden match.

"Why in the world do you have this in your pocket, Donna Jean?"

"I . . . don't remember. Oh, yeah." I snatched a reason out of the air. "I picked it up from the kitchen floor. Meant to put it back in the box." It sounded like a bad lie while I was saying it.

She knew. I couldn't look at her anymore. I waited for the questions but they never came. Never.

"Well," was all she said.

EPILOGUE

In spite of what a clock or a calendar indicated, time was not constant for me. Days and weeks crawled by after the fire. Nights were erratic, some used up in the blink of an eye, some lasting while I thrashed and dreamed and willed myself, even in mid-sleep, to wake from a nightmare.

They all asked over and over if I was alright. The only answer I had was, yes. I stood on the edge of my life, looking in, observing, waiting for someone to come out and say what I was. Murderer. I went to summer school and loathed it. I pretended to be the smart girl I had been and was given good grades for my performance. I got through my junior year of high school. They all quit asking if I was okay.

I can almost put my finger on the moment the change happened. I had stepped off the bus alone. Christopher had stayed for football practice. The bus doors slid closed behind me with their thunk. The horses, still the same, stood at the fence, waiting. I talked to them, scratched ears and necks, and turned to walk home.

Something . . . I don't know what or how, but something unlocked inside me. It felt physical. I could feel an opening, a gap somewhere below my heart, above my stomach. The next breath I took was deep and pure. I felt inflated. The self I had become accustomed to, the one shriveled and turned into herself, suddenly felt buoyant and free. My shoes hardly touched the ground as I walked home.

When I entered our house, I felt welcoming warmth I had nearly forgotten. I climbed the stairs and sobbed with relief.

I have had therapists try to explain to me what happened that day. They spoke of how our minds released us from trauma when they grew exhausted. Their words sounded mechanical and meaningless compared to the wondrous emotion I'd felt.

I'm doing well these days. I live, go to school, and work part-time at a veterinary clinic in Newell. Someday I will be a veterinarian and take care of horses like the ones on Gibson Road. Christopher visits me here when he can. Life is good for him. Harry is our stepfather. He attends Christopher's football games and he and Mama come to see me when I can't get home.

Grandma Gabby is still my guiding star. She lives in town again. Back in her sweet little house. I will forever owe her my life.

And Twyla. Twyla and her beautiful children are doing well. She makes her money cleaning houses. She gets assistance, and is able to pay her rent and feed her children. She says she has never in her life been as happy.

I know what I am and so does Gabby. Once in a while I say a prayer for forgiveness, but not often.

~ THE END ~

"The characters in Janice Gilbertson's *The Canyon House* become a part of our lives. And the canyon walls, the oaks along the creek bed, the dust and then the rain—we can see, hear and smell them. This story will hook you early on, the tension like a taut strand of barbed wire. And then, the quintessential Gilbertson surprise."
~ KEN RODGERS, AWARD-WINNING AUTHOR, TEACHER, AND FILMMAKER

"Gilbertson's artful writing almost reaches out from the page and grabs her readers' attention like a dust-devil twisting across a sun-baked New Mexico plain. In her first novel, *Summer of '58*, the author loads her readers into a beat up Oldsmobile, and off they go, riding along on a rambling journey down the rodeo trail of the 1950s with pre-teen Angela and Lanny Ray, her 'much too young to feel this damned old' bronc-ridin' father. . ."

"She is my favorite contemporary author and I can't wait for whatever comes next from her pensive heart."
~ VIRGINIA BENNETT, AUTHOR OF IN THE COMPANY OF HORSES AND COWGIRL POETRY: 100 YEARS OF RIDIN' AND RHYMIN'

READ A **FREE** CHAPTER OR GET YOUR PRINT OR EBOOK COPY TODAY!
AT WWW.PEN-L.COM/THECANYONHOUSE.HTML

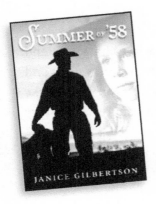

The Summer of '58

How long can you keep a secret to protect someone you love? Forever? That's what Angela Garrett promised the man in the dark.

Estranged from his daughter, bronc rider Lanny Ray decides he'd better try to mend their relationship before it's too late. It is a dream come true for Angela when they roll out of Jewel, New Mexico, to travel the summer rodeo circuit. In spite of her reluctance to make new friends, Angela finally meets someone whose loyalty becomes a comfort to her. But she also encounters people who frighten her.

Her idyllic summer is shattered when Angela witnesses a brutal act while waiting in the car for her father. The event catapults her out of childhood and changes her forever.

Can family love hold her world together through the worst of times?

PRAISE FOR *SUMMER OF '58*

"Janice Gilbertson has long demonstrated her mastery of language as a poet. With *Summer of '58* she establishes her command of storytelling and an absorbing ability to capture the thoughts and feelings of a coming-of-age girl who finds more adventure on the rodeo road than she bargained for."
~ ROD MILLER, SPUR AWARD-WINNING AUTHOR AND POET

"Pack your suitcase and hit the rodeo road in Summer of '58. Janice Gilbertson guides a convincing cast of characters on a summer-long adventure as expertly as the bronc riding protagonist cruises between contests. Told by the cowboy's daughter, the storyline speeds along two-lane highways in the American West. Warning: Detour ahead."
~ JERI L. DOBROWSKI, WRITER, EDITOR AND REVIEWER AT COWBOY JAM SESSION

READ A FREE CHAPTER OR GET YOUR PRINT OR EBOOK COPY TODAY! AT WWW.PEN-L.COM/SUMMEROF58.HTML

EPILOGUE

Janice lives in the foothills of the Santa Lucia mountain range overlooking the Salinas Valley. She and her husband, Ron, live only a couple of miles from her childhood home. She grew up with a fierce love for animals and was riding her own horse when she was four years old. Her idea of fun was helping her father with his cattle, gathering and herding. She rode Mickey and then Ginger endless miles in the hills. Since she usually rode alone, she developed an imagination that she says now aids her in her fiction writing.

Before she wrote her first novel, *Summer of '58*, Janice wrote cowboy and western poetry and has been invited three times to perform at the National Cowboy Poetry Gathering held in Elko, Nevada. Her poetry books, Sometimes, in the Lucias and *Riding In*, were published in 2004 and 2006 and are available from her at PO Box 350, King City, CA, 93930

Janice box's second novel, *The Canyon House*, was voted 2017 Willa Literary Award finalist by Women Writing the West.

Janice says, "I am thankful every day for my home in the hills. I can't imagine being a city dweller. My spirit is here in this canyon that is filled with history of the Lucias, old trails, routes of the conquistadores and Salinan tribe, and with all the native animals."

MORE ABOUT JANICE AT KIGER@ONEMAIN.COM

Dear Reader,
If you enjoyed this book enough to review it for Goodreads, B&N, or Amazon.com, I'd appreciate it!

Thanks, Janice

Find more great reads at
Pen-L.com

Made in the USA
Monee, IL
30 July 2020